# DON'T H... THE PLAYER
## ...hate the game! ♡

Katie Ashley

Copyright 2013 Katie Ashley Productions

Cover Image: Shutterstock

Cover Design: Letitia Hasser of RBA Designs

Formatting: Indie Pixel Studios

*Natalie,*

*Thanks for loving a Player!*

*Happy reading*

*Katie Ashley*

# Dedication

I would have never written this book without the loss of one of my students. Cooper Newsome—you were taken far too soon, and while you were far from the character who became Jake Nelson, your tragic loss planted the seed for this novel. And for Lindsey Norrell—whose sweet smile could light up a room and is sure to be lighting up heaven now. This book is in loving memory of you both.

And special gratitude to all the students of Liberty, Creekland, and Adairsville Middle Schools along with Creekview, LaFayette, and Cass High Schools who touched my life in so many ways. Although writing was my dream since childhood, I know being a teacher was what God called me to do for eleven and a half years. The lessons you taught me, the laughter you brought me, and the tears we shed together will live bright in my memory for all my life. I thank you from the bottom of my heart and hope God richly blesses you all the days of your life.

And finally to the memories of Travis Appling and David Wheeler—the Cherokee High Class of 97' was never the same without you guys. All these years later, we still desperately feel your loss and like the Kenny Chesney song, we wonder who you'd be today.

# Chapter One

As I slowly drifted back into consciousness, my knee jerked upward, banging against the desk. "*SHIT!*" flashed like neon in my mind, and I had to bite my lip to keep it from escaping out my mouth. Instead, I peered around the room, trying to gage whether the noise alerted anybody to my nap.

Nope. The coast was clear. Everyone else in the classroom looked stoned or spaced out. Mr. Jones, a man who was a cross between Clay Aiken and Pee Wee Herman, was perched on his stool in the front of the room, droning on and on about the evils of Big Brother in *1984*.

I rolled my eyes towards the ceiling. Jesus, the man must have a screw loose. I mean, it was the first day back after Spring Break and what was he doing? Lecturing.

What a dumbass.

I could have assured Mr. Jones that no one gave a flying shit about George Orwell. Half the class was still hung over from the previous week's antics. Even the usual goody two shoes wore expressions of pure boredom as their pens hung in midair over their notebooks.

I ran a hand through my dark hair, hoping to smooth down some of the places that looked like 'desk hair' where I'd been napping. My mouth felt the way I imagined a moldy gym sock would taste, so I rifled through my pockets to find a piece of gum. I chewed on it as I glanced down at my cell phone. No new messages.

*Where the hell is Jake?* I couldn't help wondering. Jake Nelson was the biggest douchebag I've ever known. He was the prankster who always gave freshman swirlies in the toilets or shanked them, leaving them bare-assed and humiliated in front of the entire school. He was the illiterate jock who always wanted to copy off your homework or cheat off your test. He was the idiot who could never hold his alcohol and always ended up puking in the back seat of your car before slurring an "I looove you, man!" Yeah, he was all those things and more.

Most of all he was my best friend.

Our friendship was cemented in kindergarten. That's when Jake decided to duct tape me to my chair before recess. There's a saying in the South that 'Duct tape'll fix anything'. Yeah, I'm a living testament to that. It will certainly render a five year old captive to a plastic chair until hostage negotiators—or your teacher—comes to the rescue. Once the tape was removed, along with the first layer of my epidermis, I had a new friend.

Years later, the story of how we met was one of Jake's favorite stories to tell. Usually it was right after some hot as hell girl asked about that distorted patch of skin on my right arm where hair refused to grow because the follicles had been damaged by duct-tape.

"What happened?" she'd ask, eyes wide with compassion as she traced the area playfully with a finger. They always hoped for a good story—I'd been burned in a fire trying to save the neighbor's newborn baby, or it was from the time I skidded out on my motorcycle trying to outrun the Georgia State Troopers. But like the true douchebag he was, Jake always shot that fantasy down within seconds.

"Dude," he'd say, sloshing his beer out of the cheap plastic cup that seemed permanently attached to his hand from Friday night til Sunday morning.

"Jake…" I'd begin, my eyes pleading with him to drop it and not go there for the hundredth time.

"Get this. I duct taped him to his chair when we were five."

"Jake, shut the fuck up!"

Ignoring me, Jake would snicker. "He like, practically pissed himself he was so scared when Mrs. Cook ripped that shit off."

I rolled my eyes thinking about him. He was supposed to get home from his grandparent's farm late last night, but instead, he'd sent me a text around ten saying he was blowing off the first day back and would be home around three if I wanted to hang out after school. It was ironic that Jake, the unofficial King of Partying, spent his Spring Break off chillin' in the mountains among rolling pastures filled with steaming cow patties rather than hitting the sandy white beaches and orgies of Panama City or Daytona. Of course, he always managed to raise some hell while he was away or take advantage of some hillbilly girl high off moonshine.

The last time I'd heard from him was around eight this morning when he'd sent me a cryptic text during first period that read *I fucked up. She's gonna be pissed!* I took it to mean he'd done something stupid to piss his mom off. But after my last few *Dude, WTF?* texts had gone unanswered, I was seriously beginning to think he was in major trouble—like blue lights and handcuffs trouble.

Suddenly, a voice came over the intercom.

"Mr. Jones?"

"Yes," Mr. Jones answered impatiently, clearly pissed that the powers that be had dared to interrupt his literary ramblings.

"We need Noah Sullivan to Administrative Services, please."

At the sound of my name, I shot upright in my chair, straightening my slouching posture. Administrative Services? Once again, SHIT! flashed in my mind as I frantically tried to figure out what I'd done wrong.

"I'll send him up," Mr. Jones replied, giving me a disapproving look.

Without a word, I gathered up my books and left the room. Part of me was thrilled to be spared one more minute of British Lit, but at the same time, I was a little concerned that I'd been summoned to administration.

Out in the hallway, I ran into my cousin, Alex. He raised his dark eyebrows at me. "You got called up too?"

I nodded. "What do you think is up?"

Alex shrugged while his dark eyes twinkled. "Beats the shit outta me. I'm just stoked to be getting outta AP Government right now!"

I laughed. "Tell me about it. Jones is on one of his freakin' tirades again."

"Damn, I gotta sit through that shit next period," Alex moaned, and then he shuddered. "Having Brit Lit with Jones the last period of the day blows."

Before we could get to the administrators' suite, Mr. Elliot, one of the assistant principals, rerouted us to the auditorium. When Alex and I strolled through the double doors, there were twenty or so kids scattered throughout the first three rows. I noticed immediately that they were some of Creekview's A-crowd of popularity—football and basketball players, cheerleaders. It was most of the "crew", so to speak, that Jake and I hung out with on a daily basis.

Dr. Blake, the principal, and three counselors stood solemnly at the edge of the stage.

"Damn. Must be something pretty serious," Alex murmured.

"I'm so whipping Jake's ass if this has anything to do with us skipping out on Friday," I hissed.

Since most of the "the crew" had different plans for our week off, Jake had thrown what he called a Pre-Break Binge on the Friday we got out of school. When it was just us, he'd called it his "Going Out of Partying Party" since he claimed to be turning over a new leaf. I didn't believe him for one minute, but I let him think I did. Jake always had a way of coming up with these bat-shit crazy ideas that seemed cool to him in the moment, but in the end, he'd always abandon them. He struggled with the follow through.

So, we'd basically all skipped school right after lunch and went over to his house. By three, the party was completely out of hand with drunken beer pong, half-naked people, and one fist fight. Luckily, everyone spilt before Jake's parents got home at six.

Alex and I slid into a seat on the front row. The Homecoming Queen and reigning Ice Princess, Avery Moore, glanced up at me and smiled. "Hey," she whispered.

"Hi."

"Where's Jake?"

I shrugged. "On his way home from the mountains I guess."

Dr. Blake interrupted our conversation by clearing her

throat. She then took a tentative step forward. "I've just been informed of some very distressing news," she began.

I cringed. I didn't know how in the hell she'd gotten wind of the Pre Spring Break Binge, but by the look on her face, she had the goods on all of us. Great, I was going to be in deep shit at school but even worse at home when my mom found out.

Dr. Blake stared down at the auditorium tile for a few minutes, trying to gain her composure. Finally, she glanced back up at us. "In this age of technology, it's hard to keep news of this kind a secret for long. Since we were only notified thirty minutes ago, the counselors and I have tried to find the easiest and least detrimental way to tell you all. Sadly, there's not a strategic plan in place that we can follow when something like this happens." Dr. Blake drew in a ragged breath. "More than anything, I wish that there was an easier way for you to find out—that there had been time to call your parents and families to have them here to temper the tragic news by comforting you all."

Hmm, okay, maybe this wasn't about the Spring Break Binge. Furrowing my brows, I turned to Alex who shrugged his broad shoulders.

"What happened Dr. Blake?" Avery demanded from my other side.

Chewing her bottom lip, Dr. Blake's gaze flickered to one of the counselors who bobbed their head. "I regret to inform you that Jake Nelson was killed this afternoon."

A collective gasp of pure horror rang throughout the auditorium. I jolted back in my seat like I'd been shot with a taser gun. An icy feeling pricked and stung its way over my body like I'd never experienced before in my life, causing me to shudder. Jake was…dead. No, no, no! Someone had to be fucking with us. Guys like Jake didn't die.

Like in some freaky outta body experience, I heard my voice croak, "What the fuck?"

Dr. Blake glanced over at me. Instead of riding my ass for cussing, she just gave me a sad look. Slowly, I found my voice again. "Are you positive it was Jake? I mean, he's not even in town, so it might not have been him. I mean, when did it happen? *Where* did it happen?" The questions seemed to continuously fumble out, and I began to wonder if I should clap my hand over my mouth to stop them.

"I'm so very sorry, Noah, but I was notified by Jake's father." She drew in a deep breath before she continued. "It seems that Jake and some of his friends were hanging out, shooting at cans when a bullet ricocheted—"

"Jake was shot?" I demanded. In my mind, I pictured a group of hillbilly vigilantes or the Dixie Mafia taking him out.

Dr. Blake's expression became pained. "No—it seems he was sitting on his grandfather's tractor when the bullet ricocheted off a tree, hitting the fuel tank."

11

At the realization of Jake's fiery end, I fought the bile rising in my throat. I pinched my eyes shut and willed myself not to blow chunks on the auditorium floor. Jake had been blown up. Jesus, that was too horrible to even imagine. A car accident was one thing, but to be blown up...fuck, that was gruesome. The girls around me gasped, and some began crying. Avery reached out and grabbed my hand in hers. She started doing this horrible hiccupping, hyperventilating cry. Her frantic eyes met mine. Momentarily my own grief and potential freak-out were forgotten as I focused on the fact Avery was seriously about to lose her shit.

Without a word between us, I got up and led her out of the auditorium. Alex followed close on my heels. We stood out into the hallway. Mr. Elliot saw the state Avery was in. He motioned us inside the counseling suite across the hall.

Presley Patterson was already inside with several of her friends. Presley was Avery's rival in everything from popularity to, most importantly, Jake. But it wasn't her personality that necessarily made her popular or notorious at Creekview. It was the fact she slept around.

Through her tears, Avery shot Presley one of her icy stares. In retaliation, Presley jerked her chin up and wiped the tears from her blue eyes.

I steered Avery over to one of the chairs. The minute she sat down she buried her head on the table and began sobbing uncontrollably. Her tiny frame shook so hard I was afraid she might break under the strain. It wasn't long before an eerie and unnerving chorus of wailing echoed off the walls of the room. As the lone guys in the room, Alex and I glanced at each other. Neither one of us really knew what to do.

We stared helplessly at Mr. Santos, the head counselor, but he was useless. He'd spent years immersed in the business side of high school counseling. Where Little Johnny was going to college and what Little Susie needed on her SAT to get into Brown. I think the man was dried up of any shred of psychobabble spin. He did manage to pat Avery on the back and say, "There, there, honey."

Geez, what an asshat!

At that moment, the most random memory I could fathom wormed its way into my mind, cloaking me with its intensity. When I was ten, I'd gone on a camping trip with Jake and his family. We'd picnicked by some waterfalls, and after lunch, we started messing around in the water. Somehow I managed to step in a mammoth hole in the rocks. Within seconds, I got tangled up in some willowy weeds, and I couldn't break free of their viselike grip.

When I realized I was trapped and would likely drown, panic crept from my chest up through my throat. I wanted to scream, but I couldn't. I could see sunlight breaking through the surface of the water as I flailed and jerked around.

Suddenly, an arm grabbed hold of my t-shirt and pulled me forward. Coughing and sputtering, I tried clearing my eyes to see my savior while expecting nothing short of miraculous like Jesus himself standing there with arms outstretched.

But it was just Jake.

He was ashen and trembling worse than me. As I sputtered and vomited up water, he did something so unexpected I almost fell back in the water.

He hugged me. Not just a quick, "Hey, man, you okay?" kinda hug. It was a full on bear hug that took my breath. "Jake," I'd wheezed. "Can't breathe!"

When he'd released me, there were tears in his eyes. "I-I thought you were dead." He shook his head wildly back and forth. "Don't you EVER do that to me again!"

I was so taken back by his emotion that I could only nod my head. At the sound of voices behind us, he quickly wiped his eyes with the backs of his hands. "If you tell anyone I was crying, I'll beat the shit outta you!" he'd warned.

Since I knew Jake would do it, I'd kept silent all these years. I'd never told anyone.

But now closed in that tiny room with the girls all sobbing around me, I felt the same panic of impending death. I was under the surface of the water again, and I couldn't breathe. Even when I tried sucking in air, my chest constricted, and I felt like I was slowly suffocating. My eyes honed in on the

14

door—my one escape from the churning sea of grief and loss enveloping me.

Without another thought, I bolted from my seat. I ignored my name being called over and over as I sprinted out the office and then burst through the double doors leading out of the school. I didn't stop until I ran around the side of the building. I gulped in the air the same way as if I were breaking the surface of water. I bent double, trying to calm myself of the emotions coursing through me. My hands on my knees trembled against my jeans, and I realized then my entire body was jerking all over. *Jesus, Noah would you get a grip?* I could almost hear Jake's voice echoing through my head. *"Dude, quit acting like a total pussy!"*

As I stood there trying desperately to steady myself, a realization washed over me. This time I didn't bother fighting the bile rising in my throat. Instead, I heaved the entire contents of the cafeteria's shitty lunch onto the emerald grass. Over and over again, I threw up as if I were trying to purge myself of the dark feelings overtaking me.

Jake is dead.

My best friend is dead.

I was never going to drink beers with him around a bonfire down by the lake or scope out chicks at the mall. We weren't going to share a dorm room together at Georgia Tech like we'd planned or rush the fraternity that his brother and some of my uncles had been in.

Not only was he dead, but he'd been blown up on his grandfather's tractor. I mean, what the hell? Car accidents, accidental shootings, illness—I could get that, but to be blown up on a fucking tractor? My mind just couldn't comprehend that. I shook my head as I thought of what Jake would've said about the situation. *"Hey man, you know I always meant to go out in a blaze of glory! And damn if I really didn't!"*

No, no, no. This couldn't be real. It all had to be just a bad dream. Pinching my arm, I willed myself to wake up and to start the day all over again. But it didn't work. In another act of desperation, I grabbed my cell phone out of my pocket and began furiously texting.

*Jake?*

*Come on, Jake! Answer me you sorry fucker!*

*Tell me you being dead is just a joke you're pulling to keep from getting in trouble for skipping out today.*

*Please Jake...*

When no reply came, I sank to my knees on the grass. Oh God, it was really true. Jake was dead. He was gone and never, ever coming back again. Before I realized it, I was crying. Not just silent tears streaking down my cheek, but sobbing hysterically. Gut wrenching cries that caused my body to spasm. The harder I tried to stop, the harder the sobs came. It was a crazy, manic feeling not to be able to control my emotions. I hadn't cried in years—at least not when I was sober. When I was drunk, I usually cried about old girlfriends. The last time I'd cried like this was when I was fifteen and my grandfather, who had been a father to me, died.

*Suck it up, dickweed*! A voice repeated over and over in my head. In a snot-filled finish, I wiped my nose on the back of my hand and shook my head. Quickly, I threw a panicked glance over my shoulder, hoping I was safe where no one could see me.

I was wrong.

Cold fear washed over me as Avery came striding out the double doors. Dammit, I couldn't let her see me like this—a blubbering pansy with tear streaked cheeks down on his knees in the grass. Men were supposed to control their emotions—be strong and comfort chicks when they were upset.

In a fluid movement, I pulled myself to my feet and sprinted around the side of the building. I could hear Avery calling my voice, but once again, I ignored her. My phone buzzed in my pocket. I knew it was Alex or one of the other guys asking where the fuck I was. But I didn't care. I had to get away. I was no good to myself or anyone else at that moment.

Unless I was with Jake, I usually played by all the rules. But now that he was gone, I just didn't give a shit, so I bypassed the front office and headed straight for the parking lot. When I slid across the scorching seats of my Jeep, I tried stilling my erratic breaths.

*Jake is dead. Jake is dead. Jake is dead. Jake is dead....*

As that thought played over and over in my mind, I brought a shaky hand to the ignition and cranked up. Squealing out of my parking spot, all I could think of was getting away. Where I was going, I didn't know or where I could go to let go of the suffocating pain, I didn't know.

I just knew I had to try.

# Chapter Two

I spent the rest of the afternoon walking in the thicket of woods behind my house. I didn't want anyone seeing me in my manic state. I cried, I screamed, I kicked down a dead tree, and I laughed as old random memories flickered through my mind. I don't know why I thought I could escape to the woods and leave my grief behind as easily as stripping off my clothes of something like that. Suffocating and somber, it hung around me—a silent specter taunting and goading me. It draped over me like a heavy coat, weighing me down. The usually easy trek up the small hills felt like trudging through thick mud. My chest constricted so tightly every breath was agonizing. While over and over in my mind, the words echoed *Jake is dead. Jake is dead. Jake is dead.*

When I finally swept through the back door shortly before six, I found my mom pacing around in the kitchen. She was out of her usual blue or green scrubs along with her pristine white doctor's coat. Instead, she wore one of her dark and somber "funeral dresses". With her long, dark hair swept back in a twist, it made her blue eyes, which were sparkling with tears, stand out. I'd barely made it two more steps before she leapt at me, wrapping her arms around me. Her wet cheeks dampened my shirt, and I knew then she had been crying for a long time. "Oh Noah, when I heard, all I could think about was what if it had been you. Just the thought of losing you…" Her voice choked off with her sobs.

"I know," I croaked, although I wasn't sure I did. Patting her back absentmindedly, I tried in my own fumbling way to comfort her.

"Thank God, you're all right." She then began rubbing comforting circles over my back just like she had done my entire life when I was hurt physically or emotionally. "I'm so sorry, sweetie," she murmured over and over in my ear.

I pushed myself away from her, giving her skeptical look. "Oh, come on, Mom. You know you hated Jake."

"That's not true!" she protested.

I cocked one eyebrow at her. "Really?"

"Okay, maybe I disliked what he became later in life, but I never hated him," she admitted.

I knew that was probably closer to the truth. She hated that Jake was a manwhoring player because it hit too close to home with her when it came to my father.

Mom exhaled a sad, defeated sigh. "I like to think of Jake when he was younger—that mischievous little boy with the crooked grin." A hesitant smile played on the corners of her lips. "Remember when you guys were little how he always acted like Eddie Haskell from those old *Leave it to Beaver* reruns whenever he was around me?"

I couldn't help laughing. Before he hit puberty, Jake was forever helping her carry in groceries, straightening up the kitchen, or telling her she looked pretty or smelled nice. Basically, he hung on to her every word like a lovesick puppy.

But then the way my mother felt about Jake began to change when we got to high school. It was then that that Jake informed me my mom was a MILF. I was well acquainted with the term from the movie *American Pie*. The moment the words left his lips I almost punched his face in. So what if it's a well-known fact my mother is beautiful? She's a dead ringer for the late Elizabeth Taylor. So much so, that all her friends nicknamed her Liz, which wasn't too far off since her middle name was Elizabeth. Growing up, I never got the analogy since my only frame of reference was the old chick in the really airbrushed White Diamonds perfume commercials. My mom's mom, or Grammy as I call her, swears when I was three, I saw one of Elizabeth's earliest movies, *National Velvet,* on TV and cried, "Mommy!"

It wouldn't have mattered to me if she looked just like Angelina Jolie cause no self-respecting male wants to acknowledge the fact their mom is hot. It's freakin' sick and warped.

Mom snapped me out of my thoughts. "Did you hear me, Noah?"

"Huh?"

"I spoke with Jake's mom earlier while you were gone to the woods. She wanted you to come over tonight."

Shit. That explained Mom's mourning attire. Damn, the last thing on earth I wanted to do was go over to Jake's house and face his parents.

Mom noticed my hesitation. She ran her hand over my cheek. "It would mean a lot to Mrs. Nelson, Noah."

I nodded. "I'll go change."

"When you get done, come help me load the car, okay?" She motioned towards the table that was loaded down with food for the Nelsons.

"Whatever," I replied, and then pounded up the stairs.

I knew that deep down my mom hated Jake because he reminded her too much of my father. Though I guess sperm donor would be a better way of describing my dear old dad. You see, my mom got pregnant with me when she was seventeen. It was a major shock to everyone considering my mom was the angel of the family. As the only girl with five brothers what the hell could you possibly get away with anyway?

My uncles were legendary at Creekview High School. They were known as the Mighty M Sullivan's because of their athletic ability. There wasn't a sport there they didn't dominate, and surprisingly, they each had one that was their specialty. Mark was a Golden Glove in baseball, Mike was the quarterback of the football team, Matt was an all-state guard in basketball, Mitch was a wrestler, and Mason was lighting in track.

By the time my mom entered high school, their reputation was enough to steer every horny asshole away from her. Once any panty chaser found out she was Maggie *Sullivan*, they ran the other way with their tail between their legs. But it really didn't matter to my mom because she was the ultimate goody girl, Straight A's, National Honors Society, Academic Team— any brainiac thing, she did it because she had her eyes set on medical school and becoming a doctor.

Like Jake, Joe Preston was a major player. A real smooth operator who weaseled himself into the good graces of all my uncles and my grandparents and made the entire family believe he walked on water. He was my Uncle Mark's best friend all through high school, and then they both ended up at the University of Georgia with a full ride in baseball.

By senior year, Joe and my uncle, Mike, were both being scouted by major league teams. Because his family wasn't the lovey dovey type that my mom's was, Joe spent occasional holidays at the house—a Thanksgiving, an Easter, an odd weekend here or there. But this time, he spent the entire month of August at my grandparents' cabin in the mountains.

Now my mother's never told me any of this. All my information has come from my uncles or older cousins over the years. The way they told the story read like some NC-17 rated fairy tale: oversexed wolf charms innocent lamb resulting in an unexpected pregnancy.

I guess it goes without saying that at twenty-one with a major league career ahead of him filled with money, fast cars, parties and women, my dad wasn't ready to settle down. He bolted, and basically he's never looked back.

Sometimes I personally think it's easier for some kids to have a dead-beat dad. Yeah, the pain is there, but you can push it to the backburner cause you don't see the asshole much. For me, my douchebag dad was shoved in my face constantly. The worst was April through October—the months of the major league baseball season. I had to see and hear my father's stats constantly. Even now at thirty-eight, he's still one of the most sought after pitchers in the National League. He's currently playing for the San Diego Padres, but he's been with some of the biggies all over the country.

So for a while my mom was the black sheep of the family. A kind of conspicuous black sheep who had been the salutatorian of her graduating class and was slated to start medical school. But she didn't remain that way for long for two reasons. One was that my Uncle Matt went on a mission trip to

Brazil, met a girl, and got married all within eight weeks. To my very Southern, old-school family, marrying a foreigner was some pretty heavy shit. But just like my mom, they got over it. That's where my cousin, Alex, comes in, or I guess I should say Alejandro Matthew Sullivan. Seriously, there's nothing like a Brazilian Irishman! Of course, Alex has always been more of a brother to me than just a cousin. We didn't go to the same elementary or middle schools, but luckily by the time high school rolled around, we were back together. Jake took an instant liking to Alex, and during the summers, we were a lot like the Three Musketeers hanging out together.

The other reason was my mom worked her ass off to make her dream of becoming a doctor a reality. Fortunately for her, one of the best medical schools in the country, Emory University, was practically in her backyard. Because of her love of babies, she became an OB/GYN, and she was now part of one of the biggest practices in town.

My eyes rolled towards the ceiling as I thought about how Jake always found Mom's profession fascinating. Whenever I would shrug my shoulders and be like, "So?"

"Dude," he'd say. "Don't you get the beauty of it? She looks at tits and ass all day long!"

Yeah, that was Jake.

At the thought of him, the burning ache I was growing accustomed to seared its way through my chest like bad heartburn after an all-night beer and pizza binge. He wouldn't be making any more pervy comments about my mom being a MILF or that she specialized in looking at vaginas.

Because he was dead.

I shook my head wildly back and forth so fast I thought I might get whiplash. No, I couldn't start with the bullshit emotions again. I had to keep it together, especially now that Mom was dragging me over to Jake's house. Just the thought of being over there without Jake sent a shiver down my spine. There hadn't been a single time in my life that I'd been there without him.

With a heavy sigh, I dragged myself over to the closet. Swinging open the door, I stepped inside and scanned the racks. I knew Mom wanted me looking nice and respectable, so I grabbed a pair of khaki pants and a nice blue button down shirt. After I slicked my usually out-of-control dark hair back, I hurried back downstairs and met my mom in the kitchen.

Rolling a silver tube of lipstick across her lips, she nodded in approval at the sight of me. "You always look so handsome in blue," she mused. "It brings out those beautiful blue eyes."

"Whatever, Mom," I grumbled as I eyed the feast on the table. "So, when did you do all this?"

She smiled shyly. "I didn't. Grammy did."

I picked up the pot roast and nodded. I hadn't seriously considered Mom had done the cooking. Besides the fact she had some crazy, batshit hours, she'd also never quite learned to cook like her mom, the fabulous Southern diva who could put Paula Deen to shame.

By the time we finished loading, the back of my mom's SUV was packed with food. Mom closed the hatch and threw me a glance. "Ready?"

I wanted to say, *"Ready? Are you freakin' crazy? There's nothing on earth I want to do less than go to Jake's house!"*

But instead, I gave Mom a weak smile. "Yeah, let's go."

# Chapter Three

I drew in a deep breath as I rang the doorbell. Jake's older brother, Jonathan, answered it. With a nod of his blonde head, he then gave me a slight smile. "Hey Noah. Ms. Sullivan," he said politely. He then swung open the door for us.

We exchanged a sort of awkward hug—the kind guys give who are afraid of showing too much emotion. He was just two years older than Jake and me, so most of the memories I had with Jake were connected to Jonathan too. I guess I connected with him more than Jason, their oldest brother. Like a true middle child, Jonathan did the sports thing, but he also played the drums in a band. He and I used to have some awesome jam sessions until Mr. Nelson would run us out of the basement for being too loud.

He was a sophomore at Georgia Tech where Jake and I had been accepted. I guess he'd made it home as soon as he'd heard the news. Jason, on the other hand, was a senior at Duke, and I knew it would take him awhile to catch a plane.

Mom and I didn't wait for Jonathan to lead us. We headed through the foyer, past the living room, towards the kitchen. I knew the layout by heart. Jake had lived in the same house the entire time we'd been friends, so I probably could have made it blindfolded. Until we'd moved out of my grandparent's house two years ago, Jake and I had lived two streets over from each other—just a short walk or bike ride away. The hours, minutes, and seconds I'd spent in this house were too innumerable to count. Every room, every floorboard and practically every wall held a memory connected to Jake.

Mom and I were just putting the food down on the table when a voice behind us caused me to jump. "Noah," Mrs. Nelson said in a somewhat strangled voice. I whirled around to see her standing at the edge of the living room. She suddenly appeared a lot older than I remembered. Her blonde bob looked grayer, and there were blackened circles under her usually warm, hazel eyes.

She didn't have to beckon me to go to her. Instead, I crossed the rest of the kitchen in two long strides. As she pulled me into her arms, I whispered the only thing I could think of into her ear. "I'm so sorry."

She hugged me tight against her—as if she was afraid I might disappear or get away from her. And then she lost it. Her body shuddered so hard that it shook the both of us. I bit down on my lip, willing myself not to cry. I couldn't do that to her. I had be strong for her because men are supposed to be strong, right? They're not supposed to collapse in hysterics like flamers.

Towering over her petite form, Mrs. Nelson's breath hovered over my chest. "You were such a good friend to him, Noah. You can't possibly know how much he admired you and appreciated your friendship. He really...loved you."

I tensed in her arms as the metallic taste of blood rushed into my mouth. I'd bit down so hard on my lip that I'd drawn blood. *Please God, make her shut up!* Then I realized more than I wanted her to stop talking, I wanted her to let me go. I wanted to get the hell out of there and never look back. But I couldn't. My feet were rooted to the floor.

Finally after what seemed like a painfully, agonizing eternity, she let her arms drop from my waist. Her body went limp like a deflated balloon. I steadied her and helped her over to a chair by the table. Mom sat down beside her and took Mrs. Nelson's hands in hers.

Jonathan hung back in the doorway. When our eyes met, I knew he could see right through me. Past the bullshit tough guy exterior to the candy ass who didn't know how to handle his emotions. But then again, he was the same way. He didn't bother going to comfort his mother. He hovered as if one false step could be his drop off into emotional chaos.

I wanted to laugh—manically—at the pure stupidity of it all. I mean, my best friend and Jonathan's brother had just died, but neither one of us were willing to give ourselves over to the grief. Neither one of us were willing to shed one ounce of our assumed masculinity to show emotion. What did that say about our feelings for Jake? Could we not afford him a tear? Maybe a little sob? I thought back to earlier that day when I'd actually let my guard down. But I realized it was a sham. I'd only shed tears for Jake when I was sure no one was around to see me crying. Then I'd been scared to death that Avery would see me, so I'd even gone to the extreme of running away.

Yeah, I was a bastard.

Mrs. Nelson's voice brought me out of my self-deprecating tirade. "Noah, Mr. Nelson, Jonathan, and I have been discussing the funeral plans. We want you to sing *Free Bird*. It was Jake's favorite, and we think—well I know—that's what he'd want."

I didn't know what to say. Sure, I'd sung *Free Bird* millions of times. I'd even sung it around Jake dozens of times—usually when he was highly inebriated. Course, he never failed to find a cigarette lighter and hold it up throughout the song while slurring through the lyrics with me. It became a competition between him and my old hound dog, Boo Radley, to see who could howl the loudest—Jake usually won.

But Jake wouldn't be howling this time. I'd be singing it in front of a packed crowd of mourners at his funeral. Damn, it was such intense thought that for a few seconds I couldn't find my voice. Finally, I replied, "Um, yeah, sure Mrs. Nelson."

She smiled. "Thank you, sweetie." She turned to my mom. "I've got to get some of Jake's things together to take down to the funeral home. They said they'd set them up for me before the wake tomorrow. It's just…"

Mom and I exchanged a glance when Mrs. Nelson trailed off. Mom squeezed her hand reassuringly. Mrs. Nelson wiped the tears from her eyes. "It's just I can't bear to make myself go into his room," she replied in a pained whisper.

"You don't need to do that, Evelyn. I'm sure Martin or one of the boys will do it," Mom said.

Mrs. Nelson jerked her head up like a light bulb had gone off in her mind. "Noah, would you mind getting some of Jake's things together? Jonathan is supposed to go to the airport in a little while to pick up Jason."

I glanced over at Jonathan. He momentarily wore an expression of pure relief. When he met my gaze, he quickly wiped it away.

What was I supposed to say? "*No thank you, Mrs. Nelson. I'd prefer to be a self-centered prick today cause, you know, I'm not really feeling the whole 'going up and rummaging through my dead best friends stuff' vibe*".

I didn't say that. Instead, I tried clearing my throat of the continuous massive lump of emotion that seemed clogged there . "Yeah, I can do that. What exactly do you want?"

"Just some things to set out around the urn. Things that

Jake was interested in," she replied.

I fought the urge to reply, *"Why don't we just decorate the table with condoms, lube, and thongs since that was what Jake was mainly interested in?"*

"Like some of his trophies and stuff?" I asked.

"Yes, that would be wonderful. Anything you think Jake would want. You knew him so much better than I did."

I almost choked over the last line. I wasn't sure if I really ever knew Jake. Have you ever had friends like that? Friends you spent every waking minute with, but when it came down to it if the police asked you deeply personal questions, you might not be able to answer them? Jake and I were guys—we didn't let a lot people in. When I wracked my brain, there were maybe five or ten times throughout our friendship that I could remember really seeing his guard down. But who knows, maybe that was enough. Maybe that's all that anybody had with their friends. And maybe Dr. Phil had screwed a whole generation into thinking we had to "think and feel" too much and "say what we meant". Ugh.

It was then that Mr. Nelson breezed through the garage door and into the kitchen. He shot an aggravated look at Jonathan. "I thought you would have already left by now. Don't tell me you've managed to forget about picking up Jason?"

Jonathan rolled his eyes. "No, Dad, I haven't."

Mr. Nelson clenched his jaw back and forth before speaking

again. "Hartsfield-Jackson is gonna be a madhouse this time of day. I would hope in a situation like this, you wouldn't make your brother wait!"

Jonathan held up his hands in surrender. "Fine, I'm on my way!" He grabbed his keys off the table and swept past his dad with a scowl on his face. After the garage door slammed, Mr. Nelson merely nodded his head at Mom and me. Finally his face softened a little when he glanced at his wife.

"Martin, Noah's going to help you get together some of Jake's things to take the funeral home," Mrs. Nelson said.

"Whatever. I just want to get it over with," he grumbled. Without another word to me, he stalked out of the kitchen. I practically had to jog to catch up with him at the staircase.

I gotta say I've never been a big fan of Jake's dad. The main reason being he's a major asshole. Seriously, he's a chauvinistic jerk-off. He's one of those macho douchebags who believes his boys came out the womb playing sports, and he expected perfection on the field and court. As I followed him up the stairs, pictures lined the walls of Jake and his brothers playing baseball, football, and basketball from when they were practically in diapers.

Back in the day, Mr. Nelson had been an uber-jock, too. He'd gone all the way in basketball until his senior year when he'd busted his knee, and his hopes of the NBA and his scholarship went down the toilet.

I've never thought Mr. Nelson had much use for me since I wasn't an athlete. He probably considered me a failure to the male species, and I'm sure he harbored questions about my sexuality. To him, I was some artsy-fartsy guitar playing fairy. Like I said, the man was an asshole.

While Mr. Nelson blew through the door of Jake's room and started snatching and grabbing, I hesitated. Something just didn't seem right about going in there without Jake. Mr. Nelson glanced back at me. "Coming?" he asked sarcastically.

I nodded and stepped through the threshold. I might as well be a pansy and admit that the memories hit me like a ton of bricks. It was like a harsh kick to the gut—or groin for that matter. I'd never been in this room without Jake. It was like his presence was everywhere.

My stroll down memory lane was interrupted by Mr. Nelson's gasp. "What the hell?" he demanded.

*Oh, shit!* I thought. My mind was flooded with possibilities. He'd stumbled onto Jake's porn collection. Worse, he'd found Jake's stash of pot. Jake and I had once joked that if something happened to one of us, the other was supposed to go get rid of anything incriminating in our rooms. Great, I'd let him down.

I turned around. "What's wrong?"

The world slowed to a crawl as Mr. Nelson extended his hand. I drew in a deep breath as he opened his fingers.

I stared at a small, black box. I exhaled slowly since it

wasn't pot, porn, or anything else shock-worthy. But the look on Mr. Nelson's face caused my breath to hitch. "What is it?"

"You don't know what this is?"

*Duh, would I have asked you if I did, asswipe?* I wanted to say, but I managed just to shake my head.

Mr. Nelson sighed and stalked across the room to me. He thrust the velvet box into my hands. When I cracked it open, the sound echoed throughout the room. A glittering diamond winked back at me. But it wasn't just any diamond. It was a carat of commitment in a platinum setting.

Wow, even I could tell the man-whore had taste. I didn't know much about diamonds, but I did know it glittered like it cost a fortune. That made me wonder where in the hell Jake had gotten the coins for such a ring. He was probably dealing drugs for all I knew. Mr. Nelson jolted me out of my thoughts.

"Did Jake have a steady girlfriend?" he asked.

I gave him a dumbfounded look. The words "Jake" and "relationship" just didn't mix unless it was combined with multiple *sexual* relationships.

I staggered backwards. The mere fact I was standing in the middle of Jake's bedroom with an engagement ring in my hand made me dizzy.

"Noah?" Mr. Nelson questioned.

"I'm fine," I murmured. He continued staring at me, so I cleared my throat. "No, Jake didn't have a steady girlfriend. I mean, he and Avery were off and on again, and he and Presley…" I glanced up at Mr. Nelson, and he nodded.

"What about this? Do you know what it means?"

He handed me a piece of paper. It was the song lyrics to *You Were Always On My Mind*. As I read over the lyrics, I remembered a couple of months ago when I'd gotten into Jake's truck after one of the basketball games.

When Jake cranked the car, music came blasting out of the speakers.

"Dude, what the hell is this shit?" I'd asked.

"It's Willie Nelson man," he replied, turning the heater on.

"That's freakin' fabulous, but *why* are we listening to it?"

"Cause I like it."

"Don't you think it's a little hokey?"

Jake grinned. "I like hokey. Besides, it's my song."

I snorted. "I thought your song was more 50 Cent's *Pimp* or JT's *Sexy Back*!"

"Yeah, I am kinda a pimp, aren't I?" Jake mused. Then he laughed. "No man, you're wrong. This is a song to warm a girl up."

I raised my eyebrows skeptically. "Warm one up? I thought all you had to do was look in their direction, and they'd fling their clothes off and fall over."

Jake laughed. "Usually…but not this girl. She needs a little

37

work, and trust me, it's sexy as hell."

I had scoffed at the thought and dropped the subject. Funny, how the most ridiculous conversations could have some deep seeded meaning. Now that I looked back, it was a private moment between two friends—one I wasn't willing to share.

So, I looked at Mr. Nelson and shook my head.

He opened his mouth to say something, but the doorbell rang. Mr. Nelson rolled his eyes. "That would be Pastor Dan," he grumbled.

Dan Parker was the pastor of the church Mrs. Nelson attended, and the one Jake had been court-appointed to attend after one of his sophomore year stunts. Well, the judge hadn't actually mandated he attend church—just the rehabilitation program that Pastor Dan ran for wayward teens who did dumbass things like get drunk and drive a lawnmower naked down to the school and mow grass into the shape of a penis on the football field.

I handed the velvet box back to Mr. Nelson. He glanced at it and then back up at me. "Don't say a word about the ring to my wife, Noah. Not until we get through all this funeral bullshit."

*Asshole.* "Whatever," I mumbled.

As I went out the doorway, I glanced back at Jake's room one last time, and then I followed Mr. Nelson downstairs.

Standing in the foyer alongside Pastor Dan was a girl who looked just like an angel. No shit, she was decked in a flowing white summer dress. Only her dark brown hair contrasted against her pale skin and attire.

I skidded to a stop on the bottom step and stared. It was then I realized she wasn't really an angel. I'd seen her around school many times before. I may have even had a class or two with her. She'd transferred to Creekview when I was junior. That was the year her family moved to town, and Pastor Dan became the pastor of one of the local churches.

Mrs. Nelson smiled. "Noah, I'd like to introduce you to Pastor Dan Parker."

"Nice to meet you," I said, as I shook his hand.

"Nice meeting you too, Noah." Pastor Dan turned to the angel. "This is my daughter, Maddie."

At the sound of her name, Maddie dutifully raised her head.

I reached out and took her hand in mine. "Yeah, I think we know each other from school," I said.

She nodded. "Yes, we do."

Mrs. Nelson put her arm around Maddie's waist. "I don't know what Jake would've done without Maddie. She's been such a help to him this year. Why I doubt he'd earned enough credits to graduate without her."

I noticed tears glistened in Maddie's eyes. She leaned over and hugged Mrs. Nelson, and they both wept. I shuffled back and forth on my feet and glanced over at my mom. She had tears in her eyes, too.

If there was anyone more uncomfortable with people showing emotion, it was Mr. Nelson. His face darkened. He interrupted his wife and Maddie by thrusting the duffel bag of Jake's things into Mrs. Nelson's arms. "Noah and I got the things you asked for."

She wiped her eyes. "Thanks, dear," she replied, pressing the bag against her chest.

Mom cleared her throat. "Noah, I told Mrs. Nelson you'd be happy to take those items down to the funeral home for her."

I shot my mom a look. The last thing on earth I wanted to do was go down to the funeral home. I didn't like to admit it, but I kinda had this thing about funeral homes.

"Sure, that'd be fine."

Mrs. Nelson smiled and then reached over to hug me. "You're such a good boy, Noah."

Pastor Dan peered out the window. "Uh-oh, if that's your SUV, we're blocking you in. Maddie, why don't you give Noah a lift down to the funeral home real quick?

Maddie and I both stared at him in disbelief. "W-What?" Maddie stammered.

Pastor Dan nodded. "Sure. I was going to have to drop off

40

Mr. St. Clare's eulogy for tomorrow anyway." He glanced at Mrs. Nelson and smiled. "You know, they've got to translate it into French for all those Cajun relatives coming into town."

"Oh that's right," Mrs. Nelson replied.

He reached in his briefcase and pulled out a large envelope.

Maddie reluctantly took it from his hand and started for the door. I followed close on her heels.

I slid into the silver Camry still clutching the bag. Without a word, Maddie cranked the car. Christian Worship music blared out of the radio. She flushed a little and quickly turned it off. We started down the road as an uncomfortable silence hung in the air.

Out of the corner of my eye, I checked her out. I was a guy—I couldn't help it. I started thinking about why I'd never really noticed her—you know the way a guy was supposed to notice a girl, especially one as beautiful she was. Then it hit me. Maddie didn't wear low cut shirts and tank tops with her jacked up cleavage winking at the free world, and she didn't have her ass cheeks hanging out of her shorts and skirts. She kept herself covered.

But it took just one glance at her long legs wrapped underneath the steering wheel to make me imagine them in short skirts. With my eyes roving upward, I realized she was also hiding a fabulous rack underneath her dress. Damn, what a waste.

My below-the-belt thoughts along with being in close quarters made me blurt out the first thing that came to my mind—after her amazing legs and Double D's. "You smell nice." The moment the words left my lips, I cringed. *Way to be an utter lameass, Noah!*

"It's Noa," she murmured.

"What about me?" I asked.

A smile tugged at her lips. "No, the perfume's name is Noa."

"Oh, I get it," I laughed.

Maddie's smiled widened. "Jake really liked it, too. He used to joke about it being a biblical experience or something silly like that."

"Yeah, I'd forgotten you were Jake's tutor," I said.

She glanced over at me. A dark look flashed in her eyes. "I was his friend."

"Yeah, I know." The truth was Jake had mentioned her to me before, but I'd never really paid attention. Not to mention he and I were both going in such crazy directions senior year. I had just taken it as one of those random "Jake" comments—the kind I'd blow off and then wait until he moved on to something else. But the more I thought about it, he never moved on to anything else. I remembered him stopping to say hey to her in the hallway or at lunch. Hell, when we were with him, we all said hello to her because everyone in the group knew better than to say something bad about her or tease her. If we did, Jake would have kicked our ass.

Maddie brought me out of my ramblings with the tone of her next question. "Are you sure?"

"Sure of what?"

"That you knew Jake and I were friends," she replied, an edginess creeping into her voice.

"What's that supposed to mean?" I asked.

"You know."

I raised my eyebrows. "Um, no I don't, so why don't you give me a hint or something."

She sighed. "I know I'm not part of the in-crowd or one of Jake's usual conquests. And I'm sure you don't know how it's possible for someone like Jake to have given someone like me the time of day, but he did. He was always a sweet and perfect gentleman to me."

I thought about the way she'd been crying at Jake's house. She'd really cared about him. "I'm sorry. I really don't think that, I promise. Jake was...complicated. Even our friendship was complicated sometimes," I said.

Maddie looked at me in surprise. "Yeah, I guess he was a little complicated," she agreed, softly.

She didn't say anything else, and thankfully, we pulled into the parking lot of Whitfield Funeral Home.

When we got to the door, I balked. The last time I'd been there was when my grandfather had died. Suddenly, my mind tripped out, and I was flooded with memories. I was afraid the moment I opened that door, I would smell the sickening, sweet aroma of funeral flowers. Worst of all, I would see my grandfather's chalky dead face the way it had looked the last time I'd seen him in the casket.

Maddie turned back to me in confusion. "Are you okay?" she asked.

"Yeah, I'm fine," I muttered.

Her face flooded with concern. She reached out and touched my arm. "Oh, I'm sorry. If I'd known you had some sorta phobia about funeral homes, you could've waited in the car."

Okay, I didn't the like the way she was able to see through me so well. There were only two women in the world who could do that, my mom and my Grammy. I quickly got a hold of myself. "I don't have a phobia, Dr. Phil."

Maddie raised her eyebrows. "Well, by the look on your face and your tone, one could only assume you have some sort of fear. If you do, it's perfectly fine because—"

"Don't you know what they say about making assumptions?"

"Um no."

"It makes an ass out of you and me!" I snapped.

By the look on her face, I knew I'd gone too far. I sighed. "Look, I'm sorry. I shouldn't have said that—"

She interrupted me by holding out her hand. "Pay up."

"Excuse me?"

"I have this thing about people cussing in my presence. It's disrespectful, and I think it reflects on one's lack of vocabulary. So I've started this thing called a 'Cuss Can'. You cuss around me, and you have to put a quarter in the can. All the proceeds go to the mission work at my dad's church."

My jaw dropped. "You're shitting me, right?"

"Now you owe me fifty cents."

I stared at her in disbelief. I didn't know who the hell she thought she was standing before me demanding money simply for cussing. What planet was she on?

"Listen Miss Priss, I'm not paying you a damn thing."

Maddie didn't miss a beat. "Seventy-five."

When I still stood there gaping at her, she simply cocked her head. "Not man enough to pay up?"

For reasons unknown to me, I reached in my back pocket and pulled out a dollar bill. "Now let's just get something straight. Nobody tells me what I can or can't do, you got that?"

She eyed the one dollar bill and then looked back at me. "Need change?" she asked, clearly fighting back her laughter.

"Keep it," I grumbled.

We were interrupted by Mr. Whitfield opening the door. "Can I help you?"

Maddie smiled. "Yes Mr. Whitfield, my father wanted me to drop off his sermon for tomorrow, and we also need to drop off some personal effects of Jake Nelson's."

Mr. Whitfield returned Maddie's smile and opened the door for us. "Please come right on in."

The funeral home was silent. Dead silent in fact. The last few times I'd been there I guess they'd been at capacity with relatives and friends hanging all over the place. The hallways were dark and empty. "Where's the other family?" I whispered to Maddie.

Before she could answer, Mr. Whitfield answered for her. "Mr. St. Clare's family isn't doing visitation. Just simply a funeral tomorrow, which I think will be better in the long run. I imagine we will be at full capacity at the visitation tomorrow evening with all of Jake's friends and family."

I nodded. He ushered us into his office. "Please have a seat."

Maddie and I sat down in the leather studded chairs in front of his desk. "Now let me see. Why don't I take care of Mr. St. Clare's eulogy first?" He held out his hand, and Maddie handed him the envelope.

As he was shuffling through some paperwork, one of his workers strolled into the office with a white box in his hands.

"Hey Bill, I got a call to head over to Memorial Hospital. Some tractor trailer jackknifed—looks like we're getting two from the accident," he said.

Mr. Whitfield glanced up from his paperwork. "All right, Ed. I'll expect you back later then."

"Oh, by the way, Paul just got back from the crematorium. Here's the Nelson kid." Ed plopped the box down on the edge of the desk and then headed out of the room.

"You gotta be fucking kidding me," I hissed as a strangled cry erupted from Maddie's throat. We both stared in horror at the sight of what was left of Jake sitting on the edge of the desk not a foot in front of me. Nausea overcame me that the larger than life sports god and manwhore was compressed into one tiny box. It didn't seem possible.

Mr. Whitfield grimaced. "Do let me apologize for Ed's callousness. He should have never brought these cremains in here. We usually keep them in the back until the urn is picked out."

Maddie's breaths came in harsh pants, and I swiveled my head to meet her frantic gaze. By the looks of it, she was about to start hyperventilating. Before I knew it, she reached over and fumbled for my hand. Part of me wanted to smirk and say, *"Yeah, who's freaked out by funeral homes now, huh?"* But I would have been a total prick if I'd done that. Instead, I did the compassionate thing for once, and I squeezed her hand before I

47

cleared my throat and stood up.

"Mr. Whitfield, we're really in a rush, so if you don't mind, I'd like to just give you Jake's things."

Mr. Whitfield nodded. "Once again, I do apologize. We'll see you two back tomorrow evening then."

I nodded. I cast one final look at what was left of Jake before I tugged on Maddie's hand, leading her out of the room. Her sniffling echoed through the empty hallway. When we got outside, I inhaled sharply of the fresh air as I leaned against the mahogany door. With her back to me, I could see Maddie's shoulders rising and falling with her cries.

"Um-are you okay?" I asked.

She nodded.

"I'm sorry about having to—to see Jake like that. Uh—he would want us to—you know—remember him the way he was—when he was alive," I stammered. I realized I sounded like an uber dickhead, but comforting grieving females was so out of my realm of expertise.

When she turned around, her dark eyes glistened with tears, and my heart thudded in my chest. I don't think I'd ever seen anyone more beautiful than Maddie was in that moment. Jesus, what was happening to me? I may have never seen anyone more beautiful before, but I'd also never felt more like a creep and a weirdo either.

"You're right," she murmured. She smiled weakly. "Thanks

Noah."

I was too dumbfounded to do anything else but nod. I tried to shake off the weird feelings that were crawling over my body. I was going to be eighteen in two months, and I'd never, ever experienced the emotions I was feeling right now. I didn't know what was more frightening: the fact I was entertaining attraction for the "goody" preacher's daughter, or the fact that I was experiencing these feelings in the parking lot of the funeral home not ten feet away from the ashes of my dead best friend. Either way, I felt like checking into the psych ward of the hospital immediately.

I led Maddie over to the car and opened the driver's side door for her. She gave me an appreciate smile before I headed around the side of the car. As we started down the road, a thought popped into my mind. "So did you do the 'cuss can' thing to Jake, too?"

She giggled. "Yes."

My eyebrows shot up in surprise. "He actually did it?"

"Sure, he did." A wide grin stretched across her face. "He liked to joke that his foul mouth probably paid for the spring mission trip!"

I laughed. "I wouldn't be surprised. I mean, Jake was known to have a pretty serious potty mouth."

"He did for a while. Then he got to where he never even made a slip-up."

I shook my head. "Wow, that doesn't sound like Jake," I murmured.

Maddie appeared lost in thought for a few seconds. Finally, she drew in a deep breath. "Noah," she began. "You're probably going to be hearing some things in the next few days about Jake that will—you know, surprise you."

"Oh?"

She nodded. "I just want to prepare you."

"What kind of things?"

"Well, things that you wouldn't have expected from him. Things he didn't want everybody to know or to see about him…yet."

I thought about the ring and the song lyrics. I knew Maddie was on to something. Plus, there had been all that craziness in the last few weeks about him making a change and giving up drinking and partying. Frankly, as an extreme Michael Jackson fan, I thought Jake had listened to *Man in the Mirror* a few too many times.

We pulled into Jake's driveway and got out of the car. I walked around and met Maddie on the driver's side.

"Thanks for going with me, Noah."

"Thanks for taking me," I replied.

She gave me her beaming smile—the one that spread across her face, causing her dimples to pop out—and then she reached over and hugged me. As she pressed against me, I tried not to think of the way her fabulous rack felt. Instead, I tried thinking about how comforting it felt being hugged by her. Once again, I wasn't sure which one was the worse of the two evils.

# Chapter Four

That night when I climbed into bed, sleep evaded me. Instead, every memory I could conjure of Jake barreled its way through my mind. All I could do was think about him. A fire raged in my chest. Small flames licked at my heart until it grew into a billowing inferno. I knew what I needed to do, but I was too stubborn to give in to it. It was simple enough…I just needed to weep and to mourn. If I cried, I could release the pain…I could put the fire out. But I wouldn't do it. Instead, I lay in bed, choking and suffocating in my own hard heartedness.

At two, I heard Mom's footsteps out in the hallway. After tip-toeing out of bed, I cracked open the door. "What's going on?"

Outfitted in her scrubs, she was pulling her hair into a ponytail. "Oh sweetie, I'm sorry to have woken you. Most of all, I'm even sorrier that I have to leave you, but Dr. Cooper's had an emergency, so I've been called in to cover for her."

"Don't worry. You didn't wake me."

Mom stopped rushing around and looked at me. Her face

then filled with worry. She came over to me and put her arms around me. "I'm sorry to have to leave you tonight, Noah. I can only imagine how you must be feeling about Jake's..." She nibbled her lip. "Maybe I could get one of the other partners to cover for me."

I snorted. "Mom, I'm not going to slit my wrists tonight, okay?" When her face crumpled a little at my harsh tone, I sighed. "I'm sorry that I sounded like an asshole. But I'm seventeen years old, not a baby."

Giving me a hesitant smile, she cupped my chin in her fingers. "You'll always be my baby, remember?"

"Yeah, yeah," I mumbled. Even though I fought it, I really did enjoy it when she wrapped her arms around me and squeezed me tight. Nothing felt as good as my mom's hugs—the smell of the light vanilla lotion she wore and the strawberry shampoo.

As she pulled away, she ruffled my hair. "If I didn't wake you, why are you up?"

I shrugged. "I just couldn't sleep."

"Want me to get you something from my goody-bag?"

I laughed. "Yeah, you got something to knock me out?"

She nodded. "But just this once." I followed her downstairs to the kitchen. In the bottom rack of the pantry, there was a bag full of medical supplies—you know, the really good stuff that only doctors had access too. She dug around in the bag for a

53

few minutes before snatching out a bottle. "Here you go."

I took the blue pill from her hand.

"Sweetie, why don't you stay home from school tomorrow? You know, take it easy before the wake and all."

I almost choked as the pill slid down my throat. Since Mom never advocated for me skipping school, I thought it was best I took her up on the offer. "Um, yeah, sure. Why not."

"Good. Sleep in and get your rest."

When I leaned over to give her a quick peck on the cheek, she threw her arms around me, hugging me tight. "Jeez, Mom, you been taking the roids lately?" I joked, trying to lighten the somber mood enveloping us. Tears sparkled in her eyes when I pulled away. Oh shit. "Mom," I warned.

She shook her head as her hands came to cup my cheeks. "I need to say this, sweetheart." She drew in a shaky breath, and I could tell she was fighting hard not to lose it. "I just keep thinking over and over again in my mind how I couldn't bear if something happened to you like it did with Jake. After seeing Evelyn tonight and the pain she was experiencing..." Mom closed her eyes as a shudder rippled through her body. "My heart just shatters," she whispered.

Our roles shifted, and I took on the comforter by pulling Mom into a big bear hug. "Stop thinking those things. I'm right here, and I'm okay. Nothing is going to happen to me."

I let Mom weep for a few minutes before I pulled away.

"Come on now, you need to be strong for patients. Somebody is counting on you to get their baby into the world tonight."

Mom bobbed her head as she wiped her eyes. Her hand then brushed against her abdomen for a second. At my confused expression, she jerked away from me. "Okay then. I guess, I'll see you tonight then."

"Okay."

"Get some rest, sweetie," Mom urged while kissing my cheek one last time.

"I'll try," I replied." As Mom started out the garage door, I headed back upstairs. I started to feel the effects of the magic blue pill almost the second my head hit the pillow. Thoughts whirled through my mind like debris in a storm and spat out bits and pieces of random conversations. Suddenly, I remembered the ring and song lyrics. I could almost feel the weight of the box in my hand. Even in my woozy state, I tried hard processing the fact that Jake had bought a ring for a girl. Jake, the ultimate manwhore and player, had been serious enough about commitment to buy a ring. Jesus.

Then in the deep recesses of my mind, I had a brilliantly vivid flashback. It was of the last time Jake stayed over. My drug induced state only enhanced the affect, and the scene played out in my mind like a movie.

It was a week until Spring Break, and with all the craziness going on his life and mine, he hadn't stayed over in a while. It

55

was almost noon when we dragged our disheveled asses downstairs. We'd been up most of the night playing games on the Wii, texting chicks, and inevitably watching titty flicks on HBO. Hey, don't judge. We were just two unattached, horny dudes.

Mom, outfitted in her pink tennis skirt and white shirt, was at the stove taking up blueberry pancakes. I gotta hand it to her, the one meal she didn't ever screw up was breakfast. As we collapsed at the table, she came over to us. "Hi guys! Did you sleep well?" She reached over to ruffle my hair, but I ducked away.

Jake perked up the moment he saw Mom. He flashed his megawatt smile at her. "Good morning, Maggie." Sniffing the air appreciatively, he then said, "Wow, something sure smells good! Did you cook for us?"

Mom smiled. "I sure did. I figured I better do something special for you because it's been so long since you stayed over."

"Aw, thanks. That's so sweet of you."

She set a small feast of culinary goodies down in front of us. As she poured a glass of orange juice, she eyed Jake. "So what's been keeping you away?"

He stopped shoveling in pancakes for a moment. "I've just been busy that's all."

"Hmm, has someone special got you running in circles?"

Mom asked, desperately hoping Jake would abandon his manwhore ways.

"Not really."

Mom gave a disappointed sigh. "Well, don't stay away so long next time. You're always welcome here."

A knock at the back door interrupted us. Mom practically skipped over to answer it. Greg blew into the kitchen in his tennis shorts and Polo shirt. Jesus, he and Mom looked like two Neapolitan ice cream cones standing together. I fought my gag reflex.

"Noah, Greg and I are going to play tennis."

"You don't say," I mumbled. Mom shot me a look, and I ducked my head.

"I should be back by five or six."

"Okay."

"You and Jake behave yourself, okay?"

"We will," I said.

"I'll keep him in line, Maggie," Jake said, with a broad grin.

Mom laughed. "All right then."

As they started to the door, Jake leaned back in his chair to stare at my mom's ass in her tennis skirt.

I grabbed the newspaper next to me and whacked him in the head.

"What the hell was that for?" he asked.

"For scamming my mom, you pervert!"

Jake grinned. "Sorry, I couldn't help myself."

"Well, you better try."

He continued staring at the door. "She seems happy," he mused.

"Yeah, whatever," I grumbled, suddenly losing my appetite.

Jake cocked his eyebrows at me. "Don't you think she deserves a little happiness?"

"Yessss," I hissed.

"Oh, I get it. You just don't like him."

"The guy's a tool!"

Jake snorted. "No dude, my dad is a tool. That guy," he jerked his head towards the door. "is a decent guy."

"Whatever."

"You think they're pretty serious? Like getting married serious?"

"I don't wanna think about it!" I shouted. I shot up from my seat and stalked over to the sink. I tossed my plate into the sudsy water, which sloshed onto my shirt and the floor. "And what the hell do you know about marriage or relationships? It's not like you've ever been faithful to a girl for two seconds."

"That's not true," he argued.

"It so is, man. You wouldn't have the first idea about how

to be in a relationship."

Jake's eyes narrowed. "Take that back."

"I will not."

I'd turned to get a dishcloth to mop up the water when Jake appeared at my side. "Listen man, I'm not just some player who doesn't care about anyone but myself!"

"I didn't say you were."

Out of nowhere, he shoved me hard against the counter. "Not in so many words, but you did."

I shook my head in disbelief. "Dude, what the hell is the matter with you?"

Jake's face softened. "Nothing...sorry."

"Man, you're acting weird today. Maybe I better call Mom back to examine you."

He snickered. "Um, last time I checked, having a vagina wasn't one of my problems."

"No, screwing too many is!" I joked.

Jake laughed but shook his head. "There you go again. I told you last night I was changing."

"I'm sorry. I didn't know if you were serious or not."

"Well, I am. No more one night stands or random hookups for me."

"How come?"

Jake didn't answer me. Instead, he walked out of the

kitchen to the living room. I followed him and plopped down beside him on the couch. "Jake, you didn't answer me."

He glanced up from the remote and gave me a smile—a truly sincere one. "Because I think I'm in love."

I almost fell off the couch. "You're what?"

"You heard me, asshat!"

"I'm sorry, man. I just wasn't expecting that from you."

"Well, I'm sorry to shock you, but it's the truth."

I stared at him in astonishment. "Wow, that's intense."

Jake laughed and propped his feet on Mom's antique coffee table. "It feels intense man."

Eyeing him warily, I kicked Jake's feet away. "Yeah, well what happened to you telling me when I was in a relationship that love's for pussies?"

With a grimace, Jake replied, "I was wrong. And I'm sorry."

My eyebrows practically shot off my forehead. "Excuse me? Did you just not only admit that you were wrong about something, but you also apologized?" When Jake bobbed his head, I reached for my phone. "Okay, Mom definitely needs to check you out!"

"I told you, I'm fine."

"So when did it happen?"

He was thoughtful for a moment. "I don't know. It's been

coming on for a while. I guess I just didn't notice. But for sure like a month ago."

Then it hit me that I hadn't asked the most crucial question of all. "So who is the lucky chick?"

"I'm not telling you," Jake replied.

I shot up off the couch. "What? That's bullshit man!"

He slowly shook his head. "Nope. Not going to tell you."

"Why not?"

He tossed the remote control to the side of the couch and then stared at me. "Because I haven't told her yet. I think she deserves to know first, don't you?"

I rolled my eyes as I started pacing in front of him. "So you're in love with a girl, and you haven't told her?"

"Yeah, that's right."

"Do you think she feels the same way?" I asked.

"Yeah, I think so."

"Do I know her?"

"Maybe," he admitted reluctantly.

I threw my hands up in exasperation. "Okay fine. Keep her a secret."

Jake smiled. "Good, because I plan on it."

Plopping back down on the couch, I grabbed up the remote. "So, let's say she feels the same way about you—in love and all. What does she think about you being a manwhore?"

"I'm a *rehabilitated* manwhore," Jake replied.

I arched my eyebrows. "Seriously dude?"

"Yep."

"And how exactly does one become," I paused to make air quotes with my fingers, "a 'rehabilitated manwhore'? Is there some kind of rehab you studs go to?"

Jake snickered. "No, there's not, you smartass. Basically, it means, I've stopped screwing around."

I gasped and fought the urge to faint off the couch. "Whoa…are you shitting me?"

"Nope."

"Since when?"

Jake raised his eyes to the ceiling while he thought. "Let's see. It was almost four weeks ago with Presley."

My jaw fell to the floor in shock. "You haven't had sex in almost four weeks?"

"I sure haven't…well, not with a girl anyway," he replied, with a wink.

I laughed. "Spare me the details, bro."

"Hey, I gotta do something."

I shook my head slowly back and forth in disbelief. "Man, I'm impressed."

Jake grinned. "Thanks man, that means a lot to me."

"It does?"

"Yeah it sure does," he replied.

"Then I'm glad."

"Now, if we could just find your ugly mug somebody!"

"Hey, screw you!"

Then the vision faded, and drowsily, I turned over in bed. There would be no counting backwards like when they give you anesthesia. As I went under the levels of consciousness, Jake's face was the last thing I saw.

# Chapter Five

With Mom's blessing to skip school, Alex, and I went over to Jake's house to hang out with his brothers and his two cousins from out in the sticks—twins he liked to refer to as "Bubba". Their names were actually Sean and Ryan, but Jake loved to call them just "Bubba".

Jonathan brought a cooler out of the apartment above the garage. We popped a few beers and lounged around by the pool. By noon, we were positively shitfaced. It took us all being drunk off our asses before we dared to bring up Jake.

Bubba, aka Ryan and Sean, were with Jake when he died. After his seventh beer, Jonathan grabbed Ryan's shoulder and slurred, "Dude, can you tell me how the hell it's possible that my baby brother blew his ass up on a tractor?"

My breath caught in my chest, and I slowly eased the can away from my lips, awaiting Bubba's response.

Ryan gulped down his swig of beer and shook his head sadly. "We were all just hanging out in the pasture—bored as hell. Sean and Travis (one of their other hillbilly relations) had brought along some rifles, so we started shooting beer cans off the fence." Ryan glanced around us. "I mean, we tried shooting at them, but we were too fucking wasted to really hit anything."

Sean nodded. "Jake was pretty quiet. He kept mumbling something about falling off the wagon and 'she's gonna be disappointed in me'. About ten, he climbed up on Pawpaw's tractor to get a better vantage point for the cans, or so he claimed. Travis said, 'Hey dumbass, you better get off Papaw's tractor, or he'll wear out your hide!' But Jake just shrugged and started firing over and over again. One nicked the barbwire, ricocheted off, and…"

At Sean's hesitation, Ryan murmured forlornly, "It happened so quick. I mean, boom, and he was gone."

We sat in stunned silence, staring at the sunlight glimmering on the pool water. Jonathan chugged the rest of his beer. Finally, in a strangled voice, he muttered, "Fuck me."

The sound of loud voices snapped us out of our daze. It was Mr. and Mrs. Nelson arguing.

"Did you think you could hide it from me?" Mrs. Nelson shrieked.

"Of course not. I just wanted you to get through the funeral first before I told you."

"And what is that supposed to mean, Martin? Am I such a nut job you don't think I could handle it?"

"No, Ev, that's not what I thought."

As the voices got closer, we threw horrified glances at each other. In a drunken stupor, we stumbled around, hiding the evidence of our binge. Course, anyone with brains would have taken one look or one *whiff* at us and known we were totally plastered. But when you're shitfaced, you're not known for having very many coherent thoughts.

Mrs. Nelson threw open the patio with such a force I thought she'd rip it off the hinges.

"Noah!" she called.

The other guys swiveled their heads toward me.

*Shit. Damn. Hell.* I straightened up in my lawn chair. "Yes, Mrs. Nelson?" I called in the most sober voice I could conjure.

It took me only a second to notice the velvet ring box in her hand. *Double Shit, Damn, Hell....*

"Do you know about this?" she demanded, waving the box at me.

Mr. Nelson joined her at the railing. I exchanged a glance with him before I replied. "Um, yes, Mrs. Nelson. We found it last night in Jake's room." Wanting to stay on her good side, I quickly added, "Mr. Nelson thought it would be best to wait to tell you."

While the Asshole shot me a death glare, Mrs. Nelson bobbed her head. "Good. Then you'll be willing to help me."

"Um, help you?"

66

"Yes," she said, as she started over to us. I would've committed high crimes for a mint at that moment. I covered my mouth with my hand, trying to appear like I was deep in thought to mask my alcohol breath from hell.

"Obviously, there's a girl out there who my Jake truly loved—enough to want to be married to her. I want to know who she is, and I want you to find her."

Forgetting all about my heinous beer breath, I let my mouth drop open in disbelief. "Y-You want me to do what?"

"I want you to find the girl who this ring belongs to. Even though Jake didn't get the chance to give it to her, I want her to have it."

I stopped myself from blurting, "*Are you insane, Mrs. Nelson? I know you loved your little boy, but he was a major panty chasing manwhore! I'd have better luck finding all the girls he deflowered or potentially gave an STD to than the one girl he might actually have had feelings for!*"

But at the desperate look on her face, I drew in a resigned breath. "Sure, Mrs. Nelson. I'll try my best."

She smiled. "Thank you, Noah. I appreciate that." She threw a wary glance at the others before she flounced back in the house and slammed the door. Mr. Nelson rolled his eyes and followed her.

As soon as his parents were safely inside, Jason punched me on the arm. Hard.

"Ow, what the hell was that for?" I cried.

"Man, why didn't you tell us about the ring?" he demanded.

Uh, oh, I hadn't thought about that one. Yeah the Asshole made me promise not to tell Mrs. Nelson, but he hadn't mentioned anything about Jason and Jonathan. At the expectant look on his face, I decided to fudge the truth a little. "You heard me. Your dad said not to tell anyone."

Jonathan snorted. "Figures. The asshole."

Jason rolled his eyes. "Could we focus here for a minute, Johnny Boy? You do realize our brother must've thrown down a hunk of change to buy that ring!"

I knew Jason was right. A ring like that must've cost a small fortune. Sure, the Nelson's were fairly wealthy—the Asshole was an executive with Coke, but at the same time, they weren't giving their sons thousand dollar monthly allowances or anything. With Jake's intense sports schedule, he didn't get in a lot of work hours either.

Suddenly, Jonathan smacked himself on the forehead. "Baseball cards!"

We all exchanged looks. "What the hell are you talking about, bro?" Jason asked.

"Remember like a month ago when Jake decided to sell some of his baseball cards on eBay?"

Jason nodded.

"I bet that's where he got the money. I mean, he had some that were worth a lot of money that Grandpa Nelson had given him."

"I'll be damned," Jason muttered.

Jonathan sighed. "Course, we're forgetting something."

"What's that?" Jason asked.

"Um, how about the fact our baby brother was thinking about marriage? That's pretty damn near shocking if you ask me," Jonathan replied.

Alex, who had been quiet for most of the morning, cleared his throat. "Yeah, I was pretty shocked when I saw that ring. I mean, Jake didn't impress me as the marrying kind—well, at least not until he was thirty or forty."

Jason grunted. "I figured he'd be more like some Hugh Hefner and have about three women living with him."

Jonathan laughed. "Me too, man."

Sean shook his head. "Forget about marriage. I can't believe he was actually in love for once."

The others murmured in agreement. "Knowing Jake, it wasn't about love," Ryan said.

"What do you mean?" I asked. Nibbling my lip, I debated telling the guys about the flashback I'd had the night before about Jake admitting to being in love.

"Probably some chick heard about his reputation and told

69

him she wouldn't sleep with him without a ring on her finger—you know to prove she wasn't just some conquest. Since there wasn't a piece of ass Jake couldn't have, he probably liked the idea of the challenge, so he bought the ring."

"Man, that's a pretty screwed up theory and screwed up view of Jake!" Ryan argued.

Jonathan shook his head. "Yeah, it is, but it also sounds like something Jake would do. Hell, he'd probably let the chick keep the ring in the end, too."

Scratching the back of my neck, I said, "Nah, I don't think so."

Jason raised his eyebrows. "Oh really? You think Jake actually had a conscience and wouldn't do something like that?"

I nodded.

Jason scoffed at me. "Words of wisdom coming from the kid Jake duct taped to his chair in kindergarten."

While the others howled in laughter, I merely shook my head. "He was changing. You know—like maturing or something."

"Are you serious?" Jonathan asked.

I thought of the brilliantly vivid flashback I'd had last night. "I know he was sincere about the ring because he told me he'd fallen in love with a girl."

"Really?" Jason asked.

"Yeah. But he wouldn't tell me who she was because he hadn't had the chance to tell her yet. He thought she deserved to know before I did. So like I said, he really was changing into this caring and compassionate dude."

"Wow, that's deep," Jonathan replied. He stared out over the water. "Deep like the deep end of the pool..."

I exchanged a glance with Alex. "Um, Jonathan, what the hell are you talking about?"

He turned back at me. "No, you're right. Jake really was a good guy sometimes." Jason coughed next to him. "No, man, he was. You and I both know that. He was better than the both of us put together."

Jason sighed. "Yeah, maybe you're right." He shook his head. "Sure as hell doesn't say much for us, does it?"

"So, just how do you propose to find this girl?" Jonathan asked.

I shrugged. "I don't know."

"It's not gonna be easy!" Jonathan remarked.

"I realize that."

"Jake may have been changing like you say, but man was he ever a player. Hell, he got more ass than Jason and I combined!"

Jason nodded. "I don't know what it was about him. I

mean, yeah he was good-looking and all, but man, did he have the way with women!"

Alex started laughing with the others. When I shot him an exasperated look, he abruptly stopped. Once he'd regained his composure, he leaned forward in his pool chair. "So what are you going to do? Start taking depositions from girls like some wacked out *Law and Order* or *CSI* show?"

I refused to answer him. Instead, I fumbled under my chair for the beer I was drinking before Mrs. Nelson's appearance. It was half full. I quickly chugged it down. I cut my gaze over to the guys who were waiting expectantly for my answer.

I sighed. "Look, I haven't a freaking' clue how I'm going to do it, but I do know it'd be nice if I you guys had my back a little more."

Jonathan nodded. "Hey man, you're right. We all need to be in on this for Jake." He grabbed his beer can out of its hiding place. "For Jake," he said and raised his can.

We all brought our cans together—even mine that was empty. "For Jake," we murmured in unison.

# Chapter Six

I left Jake's house around four after I'd sobered up enough. Visitation at the funeral home was to start at six. But instead of heading home to an empty house with Mom at work, I swung by Grammy's because I was sure she'd cook for me.

"Hey Grammy!" I called as I headed side door.

She was bustling around the kitchen in her favorite apron that read 'Kiss the Cook, Sugah!' She glanced up at me, and her face fell. "Noah sweetie, I wasn't expectin' you."

"It's okay. I should've called." I leaned in as she gave me one of her signature wet kisses on the cheek.

Grammy is one of a dying breed of Southern women—right down to her twangy drawl. My Granddaddy's people, who were all Irish 'Yankees' from New York, use to love sitting around listening to Grammy talk. Nowadays there's nothing she loves more than to be in the kitchen cooking or out in the yard working in her flower beds. She still goes to the beauty shop every week to get her bouffant hairdo cemented into place.

After kissing me, Grammy pulled me into her arms. "Oh baby, I'm so, so sorry about Jake. I've done cried my eyes out all day and night after your mama told me." She patted my back, and for that moment, I closed my eyes and let her comfort wash over me. Instead of letting my arms lie limply at my sides, I wrapped them around Grammy's waist and squeezed. "You poor, poor thing. Losing your best friend in the whole wide world. Besides ol' Jake, there wasn't a person you were closer to besides your Granddaddy."

At the mention of my grandfather, I stiffened. It had been two years since he'd died of cancer, and I still missed him each and every day.

With one last pat, Grammy said, "Now you just go on and sit down. I'll whip you up something real quick just as soon as I finish this cake. Okay?"

"Sure Grammy."

I slid onto one of the bar stools and propped my elbows on the counter. Grammy's house was home to me. After all, I'd grown up here since my mom couldn't afford for us to have our own place until she finished medical school. Besides, Mom and I both needed the love and support we got while living with Granddaddy and Grammy.

"So whatta you doin' in the neighborhood? I was expectin' you'd be at school or at the funeral home."

"I was over at Jake's…"

Grammy whirled around from the cake batter she was stirring. Tears eyes welled in her eyes again. "Lord almighty, I don't believe I've evah heard anythang so sad and so tragic as what happened to Jake—to be killed like that..."

I shifted on my stool. "Yeah."

Grammy eyed me. "How you doin', dahlin? I mean, how you holdin' up?"

"I'm fine, Grammy." At her pointed look, I sighed. "Really, I'm fine."

"Umm, hmm," she harrumphed. She continued eyeing me over her shoulder as she snapped on the antique mixer. Its archaic hum echoed through the kitchen. "You still runnin' from your emotions, Noah?"

Grammy was another one who could always see through my bullshit. "I'm not running from my emotions."

"You sure?"

"Yeah."

Grammy pointed her chocolaty spoon at me. "Don't say 'yeah', young man. You sound completely common!" Her worst fear was for me to sound vulgar or common. The poor woman would have probably had a heart attack if she'd heard the way I talked sometimes.

"Yes ma'am," I replied.

I eyed the clock on the stove. "I've got to be at the funeral home at six. You think I could get ready here?"

"Of course, sugah. You go right on upstairs and get ready. I'll just be fixin' you somethin' to eat."

I grinned. I could always count on Grammy. "Okay."

After heading up the familiar staircase, I went into my old bedroom. Grammy had basically kept it the same way I'd left it. Mom had bought us all new furniture—a symbolic gesture for our fresh start at the new house. I still kept a few pants and shirts in the closet.

I took a quick shower and then put on a pair of black dress pants and black shirt. I'd talked to the guys, and we'd all decided to wear black pants, black shirts, and a silver ties. Yeah, we sounded like a bunch of silly girls coordinating what to wear, but at the same time, we wanted to show our unity— the same way the football team was all going to wear their jerseys in honor of Jake being a four year letterman.

Grammy was just taking up the fried chicken—my all-time favorite—when I came back into the kitchen. She'd fixed all my favorites vegetables too with green beans and creamed potatoes. Since I wanted to enjoy my meal, I knew I needed to mention the unmentionable.

When she and I sat down at the table, I held up a hand. "Can we not talk about Jake anymore?"

"Sure honey."

Relief momentarily flooded me as I took a giant bite of

chicken. My elevated mood was only short lived when Grammy went for the throat with another question. "So, whatcha think about Greg?"

I kept my eyes firmly on my plate. Greg was my mom's new boyfriend. Well, he wasn't actually new. They'd been dating for almost a year—she'd waited several months before she sprang him on me. Her excuse was she wanted to make sure they were serious first, but I didn't buy it. He was an anesthesiologist at the hospital. In all honesty, he was one of the few boyfriends Mom had had in the almost eighteen years since my dad. I guess the old Sperm Donor had left a bad taste in her mouth for quite a while when it came to men and dating.

"Didn't you hear me, Noah?"

I fought the urge to snap at Grammy. The last thing I wanted to do before Jake's visitation was to talk about my mom's boyfriend. "Yes, I heard you."

"And?"

"He's fine," I grumbled.

Grammy harrumphed. "By the way you're actin', you'd think your mama was datin' the devil himself. Greg seems like a pretty nice fella."

"Yeah, he's a real peach." I glanced up from my cornbread to see Grammy giving me the stare down. I sighed. "I don't know what you want me to say. I've probably been with Greg six or seven times since Mom introduced us at Christmas.

Whenever I've been with him, he seems nice. Okay?"

She responded by tapping her fork on her plate. "What if they were serious?"

I furrowed my brows. "Serious?" I pondered. "You mean like *marriage* serious?"

"Yeah, that kinda serious."

Suddenly, Grammy's usually mouth-watering chicken wedged in my throat, and I had to take a long gulp of iced tea not to choke. The thought of my mom getting married to Greg or anyone else for that matter wigged me out completely. It'd always been just the two of us against the world, and after all this time, I couldn't imagine her being anyone's wife. Now that I thought about it, she did seem to be spending more and more time with Greg. Whenever he was over, Greg seemed crazy about her. Well, I could have lived without the fact he couldn't seem to keep his hands off of her. That was pretty disgusting.

Grammy stared expectantly at me for an answer. After I swigged some of her sugary sweet tea, I shrugged. "I guess it would be fine."

She slowly shook her head. "Noah Andrew Sullivan, when are you goin' to stop lyin' to me—better yet when are you going to stop lyin' to yourself?"

My fork clattered noisily onto my plate. "Grammy," I started calmly, trying to keep my temper in check so she wouldn't ride my ass. "I would really appreciate you dropping the subject of Greg considering the shi—the stuff—I'm going through right now. I mean, isn't it enough I have go to the funeral home for…" I broke off when my voice wavered at the thought of Jake being connected to Whitfield's.

She sighed. "I've raised five boys, Noah. I've seen evah range of emotion possible since all of my boys are different in their own way. Life is hard, but it's even harder when you don't wanna face it."

"But I am facing things," I protested.

"Facin' means acknowledgement and acceptance." She shook her head. "You're not there yet, baby."

Suddenly, my favorite meal wasn't so tasty anymore. I put my napkin on my plate and stood up from the table. Knowing how she was a stickler for manners, I said, "Excuse me, Grammy, but I've gotta go."

"Wait, you can't go yet." She hopped up from the table and hurried over the countertop. "I want you to take this cake to the Nelson's for me."

"I think you did enough last night," I argued.

Grammy waved her hand dismissively at me. "Grieving bodies need fuel."

My heart constricted a little in my chest when she lifted the lid on the ancient Tupperware container. It was her signature chocolate cake, and it was Jake's favorite. She always made him one for his birthday. Even without closing my eyes, I could

79

see him perched on a stool at the bar with a mixture of a chocolate and milk mustache smeared across his face—even when he was seventeen.

I took the cake from her. "Thanks, Grammy. I'm sure the Nelson's will really appreciate this. And thanks for cooking dinner for me." Giving her a weak smile, I added, "I really needed it."

Grammy smiled. "I know you did, sweetheart." She held the door open for me, and then hurried out to my Jeep to open the passenger side door. I eased the cake down on the floorboard. I wasn't about to tell Grammy that I wasn't going in the funeral home with a cake in my hands. That was the last thing my reputation needed. I doubted anyone would wait around long enough for me to explain my grandmother had baked it. I'd already decided I'd wait until the crowd died down to give it to Jonathan or Jason.

After kissing Grammy goodbye, I buckled my seatbelt. With a heavy heart, I started my pilgrimage over to Whitfield's. The parking lot was packed when I pulled in. It was quite a difference than last night when Maddie and I had come to drop off Jake's things. I eased into a space next to a SUV full of football players. "Noah!" they called as soon as I hopped out of the Jeep.

"Hey guys," I said. I glanced around the parking lot. "You all waiting on somebody?"

The four hefty full-backs eyed each other before staring down at the pavement. "Uh, no," Paul Monroe muttered.

At any other time, it might have been remotely funny that four hulking football players were afraid to go in a funeral home. But I think I'd left my sense of humor back at Grammy's.

"Yeah, well, I think I'll go on in," I said.

They nodded. As I started to the side door, I heard a scuffle behind me. The guys were following me.

The moment I opened the door, I cringed. Weeping wafted out of the viewing room into the corridor. I took a deep breath and pushed on through the doorway.

Jason and Jonathan were stationed at the double doors leading into the room with Jake's urn. They looked quite different than how I'd seen them earlier in the afternoon. Their dark hair was slicked back, and they were wearing our "planned" outfits along with a black suit jacket.

A line formed out of the room and down the hallway. Kids from all groups of the Creekview caste system were lined up to pay their respects. The guy in front of me had dyed black hair and a studded dog collar on.

When Jonathan saw me, he motioned me forward. I felt kinda shitty cutting in line at a funeral home, but I did it anyway.

The crying got louder the closer I got to the room. It came

together like a tragic symphony of sobs, sniffling, and rattling tissues.

I craned my neck to find Mrs. Nelson. She was weaving erratically around the room. One minute she would be laughing with someone after they shared a funny story about Jake, then in an instant, like flicking on a switch, she was sobbing hysterically. Whenever she did that, Mr. Nelson would obediently go to her side. As if he could sense it, his hand would hover at the small of her back until she was overcome. Then he would catch her just before she slumped into the floor.

Jason must have noticed me eyeing his mom's behavior. He eased over to me and lowered his voice. "She's tripping on Valium and Xanex—it's the only way we could get her here."

"And a shot of PawPaw's White Lightning," Jonathan muttered, after the woman he'd been speaking to walked away.

"Wait, he gave her some of that shit?" Jason questioned.

Jonathan nodded grimly. "You were in the shower, I think. I took a spoon full, but she drank a half a cup."

"Fuck me," Jason murmured as he shook his head and stared in awe at his mother. "It's a wonder she's even still standing after all that. PawPaw's moonshine is some serious shit."

"You got that right," I seconded. The most plastered I'd ever been was after drinking a Dixie cup of that stuff at Jake's grandparents. After spending half the night puking my guts up,

I spent the next day practically paralyzed in bed. Whatever it is, those hillbillies sure put some potent shit in there.

The rest of the night seemed to pass in a blur of faces. Like a third brother, I stood with Jonathan and Jason greeting people. It made sense because everybody from school and even Jake's family knew me as well. After a while, my hand started cramping up from shaking so many hands.

It was about eight when Maddie and Pastor Dan showed up. Maddie's dark hair was swept away from her face in a twist—making her solemn dark eyes glistening with tears stand out all the more. She was wearing a straight black dress that should've been demure, but to my horny teenage self, it hugged every one of her curves and showed off her fabulous legs. Just as soon as those thoughts went through my mind, I wanted to smack myself. I mean, who the hell is a horndog at his dead best friend's wake? Deep down knowing Jake, he would have appreciated my thoughts.

After she and Pastor Dan inched forward in the line, she caught my eye by the doorway. She smiled. "Hi Noah."

"Hi Maddie," I said.

We stood awkwardly next to each other—unsure who should make a move and what that move should be. Finally, I stepped forward and briskly hugged her.

She stared past me to where Mrs. Nelson was weeping. "How's she holding up?"

I shook my head. "Not good."

"Poor thing," she murmured. She turned back to Pastor Dan. "Daddy, you should go to her. Do something for her," Maddie urged.

"Sure honey." He bobbed his head at me. "Excuse me, Noah." Like me, he cut in line to go and comfort Mrs. Nelson. No one seemed to mind, or at least they weren't going to call out a minister for line jumping.

Across the room from Jake's mom, tension hung heavy in the air between Avery and Presley. It looked like two rival gangs had set up territory in the room adjoining the urn. You had Avery and her fellow Ice Princesses—the girls who usually rounded out the Homecoming Court. The girls that no one for the life of them could explain how they were popular since no one liked them. Then you had Presley's group—girls whose popularity came from being popular with the guys.

Ironically, as much as each group were staring daggers at the other, their anger seemed to unite when Maddie entered the room. I wouldn't have believed it if I hadn't seen it with my own eyes. As Maddie embraced Mrs. Nelson, a flurry of conversation went up among the two groups.

It was like one of those moments when people are talking about something, and you have no clue what they're talking about. The more you hang around, the more you feel completely out of the loop, and you start to wonder what the hell is wrong with you.

I stared as I watched these two groups of the social elite annihilate sweet, innocent, Honors program Maddie Parker with their eyes. I couldn't imagine why they hated her for being Jake's friend and tutor.

I eased over close to Avery's group—desperately trying to hear their conversation.

"Look at her acting like she and Mrs. Nelson are united in their grief. I mean, who does she think she is?" one of the girls snapped.

"I'll never understand what Jake saw in her or why he wanted to be her friend. I mean, look at her—she's so not his type!"

"Totally pathetic."

Another girl nodded in agreement. "Do you remember how whenever we had a party, he always made us invite her—even though we knew Daddy's Sweet Angel would never come?"

Avery snorted. "Thank God she only transferred in last year. Can you imagine what it would have been like to have had to put up with Jake and her all these years?"

What the hell? That funny feeling crept over me again like I'd missed the great secret. Jake had never mentioned anything to me about inviting Maddie to parties. But then again by senior year, I'd refused to attend most of the parties because I'd always end up plastered with some girl puking on me.

Sometimes you can only have so much fun doing that.

I inched across the room to get the opposite verdict. Maddie was talking to Mr. Nelson as the slutty girls sized her up. Once again, the issue was what Jake had seen in her.

"I heard she was a virgin," one of the girls hissed.

Presley rolled her eyes. "Oh get serious, Melody. Of course she's a virgin! That was her whole allure for Jake—the conquest. I guarantee you if he'd lived, he would've tapped that ass by graduation."

"How can you be so sure? Maddie's one of those ultimate goody two-shoe girls."

"I'm surprised she doesn't wear one of those dorky purity rings."

Presley's eyed narrowed at Maddie. "Trust me girls. I know what I'm talking about. Besides, Jake could charm the panties off anyone!" She gazed around the group. "Am I right?"

All four girls nodded in unison. It put me to wondering if Maddie was the only girl in the entire room Jake hadn't slept with. Well, he and Avery had originally slept together, but then she'd told him she couldn't handle a physical relationship with him. So, basically, he dated her for appearances while being serviced by other girls. I guess it was a win/win situation for both of them.

While I half-heartedly listened to the conversations floating around me, I couldn't help the anxious feeling in my gut. Most of the girls in Jake's life fit into very black and white areas. But I couldn't help worrying that with Maddie, there was some grey area. She'd seen parts of Jake that hardly anyone saw—that had to mean something. I just wondered if it meant she was *her*—the one who the ring belonged to. It was almost too farfetched to even wonder, let alone believe it could be real. But if the last twenty-four hours had proven anything to me, it was to expect the unexpected.

The night wore on, and the crowd started to thin. I was going to be at the funeral home for the long haul since I'd agreed to help 'sit up' with Jake's urn. It was Jake's grandparents who had given us the idea of 'sitting up' with Jake. They were practically mountain people who lived way out in the boondocks up in North Georgia. I'd gone to their farm once with Jake. The further we drove along the backwoods roads, the more uncomfortable I got. I was on edge the entire weekend straining to hear banjo chords and waiting for some toothless hillbillies to come ass rape me like in that movie *Deliverance*.

Anyway, Jake's grandparents said there was a tradition back in the day where family and friends sat up all night when somebody died. I guess it made more sense when there weren't funeral homes, and you would have felt kinda funny turning off the lights and leaving a dead body in the living room.

Jake's brothers were all for "sitting up", so the rest of us decided it sounded like a good idea and a good send off.

It was around eleven when Jake's parents gathered their things to head home. Jason turned to me. "Hey man, Jonathan and I are gonna walk Mom and Dad out, but we'll be right back."

"Okay," I said.

Jake's parents had barely gotten out the front door when the shit hit the fan. It was at that moment that Avery and Presley decided the icy stares and pissed body language wasn't cutting it anymore. They were finally going to duke it out over who was going to be Jake's 'unofficial widow'.

Surprisingly, Avery made the first move. "I just don't know what you're doing staying here, Presley, unless it's to service Jason and Jonathan during the night or some of the other guys here!"

Presley smirked at Avery. "At least I'm in touch with my sexuality, and I could give Jake what he needed."

Avery jerked her chin up. "Yeah, Jake, half the school, and even some of the faculty!" she spat.

"You bitch! You know that rumor about me and Senor Martinez is a lie!"

"Then why did he transfer schools?"

"Because that skanky ho Amanda Montrose gave him a blow job on Cinco De Mayo last year."

A shriek went up in the middle of the crowd. Amanda grabbed her purse and stalked past Avery and Presley in a huff.

"Whatever," Avery grumbled.

Presley stepped forward to stand toe to toe with Avery. "Let's get this straight once and for all. *I* loved Jake, and *he* loved me. He only dated you for appearances."

"No, Jake loved *me*."

"Oh yeah, then why didn't he go to prom with you?"

"Because I was already going with Caleb Evans."

"No, it's because Jake didn't ask you. He asked me!"

"Yeah, so he'd be guaranteed to be screwed."

Their voices were getting louder. Some of the others looked at me, urging me to be referee for the fight. I sighed. "Avery, Presley, listen. Fighting like this isn't gonna solve shit. You're both tired and overemotional right now. The whole school knows that Jake cared for both of you, so it's really useless to argue about it," I said, trying to step between them.

Presley knocked me out of the way right before Avery slapped her. Everyone, including Presley, stood motionless, in shock. It seemed Avery's grief had completely dethawed her usual Ice Princess demeanor.

Suddenly, Presley grabbed Jake's urn and pressed it against her ample cleavage. "He was mine!"

"No, he was mine!" Avery countered, grasping at the urn.

The two pushed and shoved back and forth. Suddenly, the urn went flying through the air. It smashed against carpet.

"Jesus Christ!" I yelled.

Jake, or what was left of Jake, lay scattered along the carpet.

Mr. Whitfield rushed into the room. "What in the hell is going on in here?" he demanded.

Everyone refused to answer him. His eyes widened in horror. "My God, don't you kids have any respect for the dead?" he questioned. None of us said anything. "All right, everybody out! Now!" he growled.

Presley and Avery hung their heads in shame as they scurried from the room. I could imagine this was going to be quite the gossip tomorrow at the funeral. Of course, only Jake could manage not only to blow himself up, but to also have a catfight over his remains.

Jonathan and Jason met me at the door. "Dude, what the hell happened?" Jason questioned.

"A bitchfight," I mumbled.

"Huh?" Jonathan asked.

"Presley and Avery were fighting over Jake, and somehow his urn was—broken."

They both glanced past me to where their brother's ashes littered the floor. "Damn," Jonathan murmured his eyes widening in shock.

"Yeah, Mr. Whitfield isn't too thrilled with us, so I'm not sure how well we're gonna be able to 'sit-up' with Jake tonight," I replied.

Jason shook his head. "Well, everybody's pretty exhausted and overwrought, so it's probably good it got canceled." He shuddered as he looked at Jake's ashes. "Well, maybe not because of that."

I exhaled a defeated breath. "Yeah, okay. I'll see you guys tomorrow."

As I strode across the parking lot, I shook my head. God, could this day get any worse? Not to mention I still had to make it through the funeral in the morning. I fought my gag reflex at the very thought.

When I got home, the house was dark. I knew Mom had delivered two babies the night before, so she'd probably crashed early. I eased open the door in from the garage, trying to be as quiet as I could, so I wouldn't wake her up.

Suddenly, I heard music. *Mood* music. I noticed candlelight flickering in the living room.

I skidded to a stop in the living room doorway. "Holy shit!" I cried.

There on the couch in all their naked glory was my mom and Greg. I turned around and tried to flee, but instead, I ran face first into the antique armoire. "Fuck!" I cried.

"Noah!" my mother screamed. With my back turned, I heard her scurry to grab the throw off the back of the couch to cover up.

At the sound of a thump, I figured Greg had fallen off the couch. I heard him furiously throwing on his pants. As soon as I heard a zipper, I whirled around.

"Mom, what in the hell are you doing?" I demanded, even though I was fully aware of what she was doing.

"I-I thought you were going to be s-siting up with Jake tonight, and it was one of the few nights Greg and I were both off," she stammered. Even through the dim light, I could see her face was flushed with embarrassment.

"Yeah, well, sitting up turned into a fiasco, and I decided to come home."

I glanced over at Greg who refused to meet my gaze. I snorted. "Sorry to have interrupted. I'm going upstairs to bed now, and I promise I won't be coming back downstairs until hell freezes over!"

Without another word from my mother or Greg, I whirled around and stormed up the stairs. I rushed into my room and slammed the door. Slowly, I slid down the frame and into the floor.

I fell asleep on the floor in my clothes.

# Chapter Seven

The next morning I woke up to a gentle rapping at my door. "Noah, it's eight o'clock. If you're not up, you better get a move on, sweetie," Mom's muffled voice urged.

I opened my eyes, and then I immediately snapped them shut. I couldn't believe today was my best friend's funeral. If that wasn't bad enough, my mind raced with the prospect of having to sing. I covered my eyes with my arm and let the emotions wash over me.

The events of the previous night played over and over in my mind. I couldn't forget the image of Jake's urn smashed on the funeral home floor. Nor could I forget the image of Mom and Greg getting busy on our couch. Damn, I loved that couch, too. Now I'd never be able to sit on it again.

No son should ever have to imagine his mother having sex least of all see it. Yeah, I know she's only thirty-five, and she has needs and all, but seriously. I didn't know how I was going to look at her in the same way. I mean, all my life it's just been the two of us against the world. I had the sneaky suspicion that Greg was hell-bent on wedging his ass into our family—our little alliance against the world.

I slowly rolled into a sitting position and sniffed the air appreciatively. Something smelled good downstairs. My stomach growled. I decided to wait on my shower until after I got something to eat.

When I got into the kitchen, there was quite a spread of food on the table. It wasn't surprising that Mom had made my favorite breakfast of French Toast. I peered around the kitchen for Greg, but I didn't see him.

I caught her gaze and raised my eyebrows. The moment I did, pain shot through my forehead. "Ow!"

Mom hurried over to me. "What's wrong, sweetie?" She reached out to touch my eyebrow, but I flinched away from her. Her face fell.

I realized right then I could continue acting like a prick because of what I'd seen last night, or I could be a little more adult about it and move on. Deep down, I knew today was gonna be a bitch, and I'd need her—you know to get through it.

"Sorry," I mumbled.

"You've got a cut place above your eyebrow." The moment the words left her lips, she blushed. I knew she realized how I'd gotten the cut. It'd come from running into the armoire to escape the sexcapade in the living room.

"Yeah, well, why don't you fix it, Dr. Sullivan?" I said, trying to change the subject.

She smiled weakly and nodded. Then she hurried into the pantry for her medical kit. When she came back, she motioned for me to have a seat. I eased down in one of the kitchen chairs, and she got to work. Suddenly, I was laughing.

Mom jerked her hand away and gave me an odd look. "What's so funny?"

"Remember all the times Jake got "hurt" while he was over here? I swear, there wasn't a time he didn't come over to play when we were little that he didn't end up with some wimpy little cut or scrape that he needed *you* to 'make better'."

Mom laughed. "Oh gosh, I'd forgotten all about that. As soon as he was old enough to realize I was in medical school, he was all about my healing."

"Yeah, I don't think it was your healing he was interested in," I muttered.

"Noah!" Mom exclaimed, her face flushing again.

"Oh come on, Mom, you know he had a huge crush on you. I swear, Jake must've come out of the womb a little hornball!"

Mom shook her head. "Well, I don't know about that. I just used to think he needed a little extra attention, you know? Being the youngest boy with two very demanding older brothers. And Mr. Nelson certainly isn't the most caring individual—"

"The man's an asshole."

"Language, Noah," Mom warned.

I snorted. "You know it's true."

Mom grinned. "Yes, it's true, but I don't want you talking like that." When Mom touched the alcohol swab to my cut, I jumped. "Sorry sweetie."

"It's okay. Just stings a little." I would dare admit that it hurt like a bitch. Once Mom finished doctoring my eye, I fixed a heaping plate of French Toast, bacon, and eggs.

With a pained expression on her face, Mom sat down next to me. "I'm so, so sorry I won't be able to be with you at the funeral today, sweetie. I tried everything to get out of this C-Section, but I can't."

"It's okay," I mumbled, through a mouthful of food.

"Grammy will be there, and so will Uncle Mark and Aunt Eva," she informed me.

All through my childhood, Grammy had been the 'stand-in' when mom couldn't make it to things. But there were few times that I didn't remember my mom being there. I don't know how in the hell she did it, but she did.

"It's okay, Mom. I mean, you spent all of yesterday at the funeral home with the Nelson's. I'm sure they understand, just like I do."

Her brows creased in worry. "I hope so." Her expression then turned quizzical. "Are you nervous, you know, about singing?" she asked.

"Yeah, a little," I lied. She didn't need to know I could

practically hurl the entire contents of my stomach up at the thought.

"You're going to do great, Noah," she replied. When I didn't answer, she patted my hand. "It's going to be fine, sweetie. I know it'll make Mr. and Mrs. Nelson very happy." I shot her a look, and she smiled. "Well, maybe Mrs. Nelson at least since the Asshole probably won't care one way or the other!"

I laughed. "Nice language, Mom."

With a wink, she replied, "I try." She glanced at the clock on the microwave. "Better hurry up and eat. You need to get ready."

The talk of the funeral had completely wiped out my appetite. I laid my fork down and pushed my plate away. "Yeah, I think I've had enough," I said.

Mom nodded. "Okay then."

"Thanks for fixing my eye."

She didn't blush quite as much this time. "You're welcome."

"Oh yeah and for fixing breakfast."

"Once again, you're welcome."

I smiled at her and then hopped up from the table. I headed upstairs to take my shower. After I got out, I eyed the black suit my mom had laid across my bed. If it's possible to actually hate a piece of clothing, I did that suit. Mom had bought it when my grandfather died. That was the only time I'd worn it. Now two years later, I had to wear it to Jake's funeral. Who would have ever imagined? Of course, I'd had to get new pants since I kept shooting up. Another reason for Mr. Nelson to think I was a total fruit since what self-respecting 6'2 kid didn't play basketball?

Asshole.

When I slid the jacket on, I cringed. Like most guys, I guess I'd never really dealt with my grief over Granddaddy's death. I'd stepped up to the plate and been a man—you know, the strong, stoic one who everyone could count on, not the grieving grandson whose heart was shattered in jagged shards. My mom needed me desperately since she'd gone to pieces after Granddaddy died. As I slid on my tie, I tried to remember if I'd shed one tear since he died. The harder I tried, I still couldn't remember the last time. I could feel the sobs rising slowly from the pit of my stomach—the same kind that had overtaken me at school. But I wouldn't let them—not now. I had to keep it together.

I could almost hear Jake's voice echoing through my head. *Fuck dude, I'm really touched at this emotional shit-storm you're going through just for me. Who knew you'd turn into such a sentimental pussy over my death? You're one step closer to growing a vagina!*

Those thoughts brought a welcomed smile to my lips and a burning pain through my chest. Even though Jake ragged the hell out of me, I missed it—I missed the jokes and teasing at my expense. That was just who he was—as Grammy would say, 'It was all part of his charm.' I paused in straightening my tie to rub my chest. Glancing up at the ceiling, I nibbled on my bottom lip for a minute. "Hey man…Jake…if you're up there and you're listening, I could really use some help to get through today. I wanna do right by you—I mean, your funeral is the last thing on earth we all can do for you. So give me a little of your swagger to tackle today, okay?"

Silence echoed back at me, but I slowly began to feel lighter—like peace was chasing away the heavy feeling. I cocked my head and grinned up at the ceiling. "Thanks man."

I then hurried out of my bedroom and pounded down the stairs. After giving Mom a final kiss and hug, I hopped in my Jeep and headed to the funeral home. Instead the of the mini-panic attack I braced myself for when I pulled into Whitfield's, a sense of calm washed over me and stayed with me through the next two hours before it was time to start to the church for the funeral.

Even though Jake had been cremated, his parents had selected eight guys to be honorary pallbearers. It ended up being Alex, me, Bubba-Sean and Ryan, and several of the football players. We each had a blood red rose on our lapels.

We rode in a separate car behind his parents and brothers. As we got ready to pull into the church, I had never seen such a crowd. Cars were even parked along the highway. I shuddered at the thoughts of all those people—all those people I'd have to sing in front of. But more than anything, it was all those people I had to try to keep a hold of myself in front of.

The car pulled in the front of the parking lot, and we all hopped out. The funeral director started lining up the family members, and then he positioned us in front. I drew in a deep breath as he threw open the double doors.

The sound of everyone rising to their feet rumbled through the church like distant thunder signaling a storm on the horizon. As we moved towards the opened door, the aisle to the church altar stretched out endlessly before me. Jake's urn sat on a pedestal at the top of the altar. It was bathed in multicolored light from the stained glass windows and surrounded by baskets of flowers. I could practically hear Jake's voice in my ear. *"Damn, makes me look kinda fruity, don't ya think?"*

Pastor Dan started in first—somber-faced and outfitted in his black mourning robe. The pallbearers were to go next. From all the way outside, I could hear the weeping. That same weeping had remained a constant ringing in my ears for the last forty-eight hours. It closed in around me, shrouding me in darkness.

I just wanted out.

I wanted to turn and run just like I had that day in the counselor's suite. I was under water again—fighting to reach the surface, fighting for air, and most importantly, fighting for life.

A hand on my shoulder jolted me out of my thoughts. It was one of the funeral directors. "It's time, son," he whispered.

I nodded but putting one foot in front of the other turned out to be harder than I thought. Alex, who was walking beside me, gave me a little tug on my suit sleeve. Finally, I was able to lift my feet and start the march down the aisle.

The first pew on the left was reserved for us. The funeral director moved the red velvet rope blocking it off the same way a bouncer would at a club. Jake's parents, brothers, grandparents, and slew of aunts, uncles, and cousins would be sitting on the right side. Once all the family had filed into the church, Pastor Dan motioned for everyone to be seated.

He gazed into the crowd and cleared his throat. "It is with heavy hearts that we come together today to say farewell to Jacob Anthony Nelson. Jake is survived by his father, Martin, who always supported him on the sidelines of sports and life."

"Asshole," I muttered under my breath.

Alex shot me a look.

"His loving mother, Evelyn, who…" I tuned out as the nerves overcame me. After the opening introductions and prayer, I was up. A sickening knot twisted in my stomach. I wasn't ready for my first real performance to be in front of almost a thousand grief-stricken mourners. I tried to remember my mom's reassuring words, but in the end, it didn't help.

"Now, I'd like to ask our associate pastor to lead us in prayer. Let's all bow our heads."

I lowered my head, but it was a sham. I twirled my guitar pick anxiously between my fingers. I must have been pretty jerky because Alex leaned over and put his hand over mine. I didn't realize I was practically bouncing the entire bench.

"Amen," echoed throughout the church, and I jerked my head up.

"And now Jake's best friend, Noah Sullivan, is going to sing Jake's favorite song," Pastor Dan said.

I practically bolted up from the bench—overcome with nervous energy. A hush came over the mourners as I strode across the pulpit. For once the cacophony of sniffling and sobbing ceased, and the sound of my shoes tapping along the floorboards echoed off the walls. Easing down in the chair, I propped the guitar on my thigh and adjusted the microphone. I drew in a ragged breath—trying to fill my lungs and steady my already out-of-control nerves. The irony that I was singing a song by a band who had lost members in a fiery plane crash wasn't lost on me.

As I strummed the opening chords, I could almost see Jake

102

in my mind—lighter in hand and a wide grin on his face. "*FREE BIRD!*" his voice screamed in my mind.

I pinched my eyes shut—fighting back the tears. I willed myself to focus on the chords—they were the only things keeping the melody and my sanity in check.

"*If I leave here tomorrow, would you still remember me?*" I sang. While the words flowed out of my mouth, I detached from the crowd and even myself. I wasn't singing in front of a mass audience. I was somewhere else like in a weird out-of-body experience. It was truly freeing, and it was the only way I think I would have ever gotten through that song.

After I finished, the last chord still echoed off the walls. It was kinda an awkward moment because I don't think people knew what to do. Should they applaud? Wouldn't that be disrespectful? In the end, I just eased the guitar back onto the holder at the edge of the pulpit and went back to my seat. Alex gave me a reassuring smile and thumbs-up sign. I mouthed a quick, "Thanks."

Once I got settled, Pastor Dan stood up again. "I've been asked by the Nelson family to say a few words about Jake. You know, it's never an easy thing delivering a eulogy, especially for one so young. Jake and I came to know each other under some interesting circumstances…" Pastor Dan paused and smiled as a murmur of laughter rang through the crowd. Everyone remembered that a drunken ride on a lawnmower had brought the pastor and the hell raiser together.

"But I have to say the Jake I knew was quite a remarkable young man. During those two years, I saw him grow and change. He was truly evolving into a spiritual warrior."

I slowly swiveled my head to look at Alex. He wore the same dumbfounded expression on his face as I did. Did Pastor Dan know the same Jake we did? Jake a spiritual warrior? He was more a Viking warrior—you know, pillaging and raping through villages. But with Jake, all of his women came willingly.

Yeah, it was true in the last few weeks that Jake appeared to be changing, but it would be hard for me to say I saw some 'spiritual warrior' in him.

Pastor Dan continued on. "I'll never forget the smiles he brought to the faces of the children on the Pediatric Oncology floor, or the pride he felt when he helped rebuild homes in Mississippi damaged by terrible storms."

I turned back to Alex. "What the hell? He told me he went to Mississippi to hook-up with this college girl he'd met through Jason," I whispered.

Alex nodded. "Same here."

I didn't dare look around at the other guys. I knew they were all experiencing the same "WTF?" moment I was, and if I saw their faces, I might lose it and start laughing hysterically.

Admittedly, in the last six weeks Jake had suggested he was

turning over a new leaf. Making a vow to give up drinking and partying was one thing. But to work with sick kids on the cancer floor and rebuild homes in Mississippi was completely out of my realm of understanding and belief.

Pastor Dan did manage to hit upon some "truthful" things about Jake. He mentioned his gift at sports, his charming smile, and his ability to make girls swoon. I guess saying swoon was as G-rated as Pastor Dan could make it. I guess deep down he knew that Jake was a manwhore, but I'm pretty sure he would never admit it. I'm not sure why he ever let a guy like Jake spend so much time with his very unworldly daughter.

"And now, Mr. and Mrs. Nelson have asked my daughter, Maddie, and myself to sing *Go Rest High On That Mountain*." Pastor Dan motioned behind us where I assumed Maddie was sitting.

At the mention of Maddie's name, I straightened up on the pew. She came by me in a cloud of Noa perfume. I waited to see who would be joining them on the piano or guitar, but no one did. They sang the entire song a capella, and it was amazing. Their voices blended with such harmony that you felt like you were listening to seasoned professionals—not just a preacher and his kid. As a musician, I was floored, as a grief-stricken friend, I was totally moved, and as a red-blooded male, I was moved in an entirely different way by Maddie.

By the time they finished, the chorus of sniffling had

returned. "Now we shall move on to the Rolling Hills Cemetery where Jake remains will be interred," Pastor Dan said.

The funeral director motioned for the congregation to rise. Then he motioned for us. We all quickly hopped to our feet and started down the aisle. As I glanced at the faces, I was amazed at all the different groups of kids who had shown up for the funeral. I'd heard Dr. Blake had made an announcement that all students attending the funeral would be excused without penalty. I don't know if some of the kids were there truly because of their feelings for Jake or if they were really there just to get out of school.

As we came out of the double doors, sunlight blinded our eyes. Even though I was outside in the fresh air, I still couldn't get the sickening, sweet smell of funeral flowers out of my nose. We were ushered to the car the funeral home provided for us.

The moment we pulled into traffic, Blaine cleared his throat. "So, uh, that was a nice funeral, wasn't it?"

All of us stared at him. I guess he was one of those people who couldn't stand silence. I decided to take pity on him. "Yeah, it was."

"Noah, I gotta ask something," Andy Hiller said.

"What is it?"

Andy looked at the other guys before he responded. "Uh,

did Jake really do all that stuff that Pastor Dan said, or was he trying to make Jake sound better—you know cause he died?"

Alex and I glanced at each other before I responded. "I really can't answer your question. I mean, Jake never told me about any of that stuff, but Pastor Dan is a religious dude, so he wouldn't have lied."

The other guys nodded their heads in agreement.

"Maybe there was a lot about Jake that we didn't know," Alex suggested.

"He seemed pretty straight forward to me," Tyler Mitchell mused.

"Yeah, parties, girls, and good times—that was the Jake I knew," Blaine replied. He glanced around at the other guys and shook his head. "I'm not sure I'd even want to believe that Jake Nelson was doing all those things Pastor Dan claimed he was doing. Hell, I liked him just the way he was!"

A chorus of "Damn rights!" rang through the car. Next to me, Alex remained silent, obviously overwhelmed by the drama of the 'Two Jakes'. I kept my mouth shut as well, and so did Bubba, aka Sean and Ryan. I guess we all realized that driving home the point about Jake's transformation would be meaningless to this crowd.

The cars wound around the circular main road of Rolling Gardens. It was a relatively new cemetery in town that was close to the interstate. High on a hill overlooking a pond was a

107

mausoleum that held 'Cremains'—a term that I'd never heard of until Jake died.

The driver parked the car. While the other guys hopped out quickly, it took every last shred of strength and sanity to pull myself from the tinted glass limo. Once I put my feet on the ground, I fell back against the side of the car, shielding my eyes from the intense sun. Why the hell was it such a cheerful day outside? It was almost like the weather was mocking the emotions I felt. Dark clouds should be rolling in on the horizon while icy pellets of rain beat down on my back. Lightning, harsh and jagged as the pieces of my broken heart, should cut across the blackened sky.

Instead, a cloudless, cornflower blue sky stretched overhead. Birds chirped happily from their perches in nearby trees. It was all a fucking sham.

I drew in a ragged breath. So this was it—the final finish of Jake's funeral. I wasn't sure I could stand idly by as they put what was left of my best friend into a mausoleum vault. Mr. Whitfield walked by us, reverently holding Jake's urn. Suddenly, my mind wandered back to Jake's cremains littering the floor of the funeral home. I wondered how in the world Mr. Whitfield had gotten Jake back in there. I hated to think of him whipping out his Dust Buster and vacuuming Jake up.

Tugging on my suit sleeve, Alex jerked me forward from both the car and my morbid thoughts. The massive crowd enveloped the marble mausoleum. Once everyone was assembled, Mr. Whitfield gave a nod, and Jason and Jonathan stepped forward. They both said a few words about their brother. It was mainly funny stuff that had the crowd roaring with laughter about Jake's antics. After they finished, each of us pallbearers took off our boutonnieres. One at a time, we walked over to the open vault and laid our flower next to Jake's urn. Then we stood and watched as the vault was closed. A marble tile already bore Jake's name, birth and death dates, along with a saying: *The life of one we love is never lost. Its influence goes on through every life it ever touched.* Yeah, that summed up Jake pretty well.

When the crowd started breaking up and heading to their cars, Blaine stopped me. "Hey man, you're coming to the party, right?"

I nodded. "Yeah, I'll see you in a little while."

"Good deal. Alex, you comin'?"

Blaine and I both turned to Alex who continued being uncharacteristically quiet.

"Uh, no, I gotta go make sure my passport is being renewed—you know, for our trip."

Since freshman year, we'd all been planning on going to Brazil—Rio De Janeiro to be exact—when we graduated high school. My Aunt Eva's family was from a small village outside of there, and Alex didn't get to see his Brazilian relatives much. There were five of us going: Alex, Jake, Blaine, Tyler and I. Jake had been thrilled by the prospect of what he deemed 'international ass'. Now, there would be only four of us unless we invited someone else.

"Bummer. Well, I guess I'll talk to you later," Blaine said, then went off to talk to some of the other members of our group.

I cut my eyes over to Alex. "What's up with the bullshit story?"

"What do you mean?"

"You took care of your passport renewal months ago. You did it when I went to get mine, remember?"

Alex shuffled on his feet and refused to meet my gaze. "Oh yeah, that's right."

"So what the hell is going on?" I demanded.

"I just don't think it's right—partying and drinking right after Jake's funeral. There's something kinda disrespectful about it, okay?"

That wasn't exactly the answer I expected from him. But I understood what he meant. Jake would have thought we were both pansy party poopers, and I'm sure if it had been me that had died, he would have been leading a full charge to the nearest beer keg.

"Yeah, that's okay, cuz," I replied.

Alex looked relieved. "So we're cool?"

I smiled. "We're always cool, man."

"Good," he said. He saw where his mom was waving at him. "Shit, I guess I better go. Talk to you later?"

"Yeah sure."

# Chapter Eight

The Monday following the funeral, I decided there was no time like the present to get busy, so to speak, with my detective work. I had no idea in hell how I was supposed to find *her*. So, I decided to start with the most likely of suspects or one of the girls who knew Jake the best.

On and off again Girlfriend #1 Avery.

I met her at her locker after first period. "Hey, Avery."

"Hi Noah," she said, in her usual voice devoid of emotion.

"Listen, I was wondering if I could come over this afternoon."

She raised her eyebrows and peered questioningly at me. Geez, I guess she thought now that Jake was dead, I was gonna start hitting on her or something.

"To talk. Just to talk."

"Yeah, that's fine. How about right after school?"

"That's good."

"Okay, see you then," she replied and slammed her locker. She walked off down the hallway holding her head regally like a queen. I sighed. This wasn't going to be easy.

The rest of the day went by in a slow haze. Maybe daze was a better word. I couldn't concentrate on anything. We were in the home stretch towards graduation, and most of us were feeling the burn out. That coupled with Jake's death meant we didn't give a shit about anything anymore. I knew my college acceptance was good to go, and there wasn't much I could do to screw it up.

When the bell rang at the end of the day, I bolted out of my seat and practically sprinted to the parking lot. I made the familiar drive through the tree-lined suburbs of Governor's Ridge, one of the richest areas of town. Avery lived in a house you might see on an episode of *Cribs*. Her parents even had one of those crazy televisions in the bathroom mirror. It was insane. She was an only child, and her dad was some multi-millionaire. I'd been to her house for parties before. But the house was most memorable to me because I'd had a pretty hot hookup there with Avery's cousin from out of town during our February break.

As I pulled into the driveway, the opening dum, dum music from *Law and Order* played in my head. I could see it flashing across the screen now: *Tuesday. 3:45 PM. The home of Avery Moore.*

God, I seriously needed a life.

After she let me in, Avery led me upstairs to her room—in

the East Wing of the mansion. I couldn't help but remember the comments Jake had made about Avery's pageant crowns and trophies. He always teased her by calling her Honey Boo-Boo, even though Avery was the farthest thing from a redneck diva. He'd always snort back a laugh and say, *"Man, the second you step in Honey Boo-Boo's room, you're blinded by the light radiating off the rhinestone tiaras."* Then he'd grin his wicked grin and say, *"Sometimes it's kinda sexy because you can almost catch your reflection in the trophies while you're doing it!"*

He hadn't been lying. Well, at least about the tiaras. From the looks of it, Avery had participated and won every single pageant imaginable since she was a toddler. One entire wall of her room was dedicated to her winnings. It was intense.

"So what did you want to talk to me about?" Avery asked.

"Jake."

"I thought so." She sat down on the leather love-seat and motioned for me to join her. "Noah, I'm really sorry about what happened at the funeral home—you know with the urn and all." She shook her head. "I don't know what came over me."

I snorted. "I do. It was jealousy."

She pulled her shoulders back and then shot me a death glare. "Yes, I realize it might initially appear like jealousy, but you have to understand that I was also under a lot of stress at the time. Do you know what it's like to love someone like Jake?"

With a smirk, I replied, "Well, no, actually I don't."

She dismissed my smartass comment with a wave of her hand. "I did love Jake. And I know he loved me…in his own way. It's just when he died, everyone…" She glanced at me. "Every *girl* was fighting for a piece of him. I just wanted to protect mine."

"I'm not here about that night, Avery."

"Yeah, well I just wanted you to know that."

We sat in silence for a few minutes. Time was ticking, so I cleared my throat. "So did you guys have a special song or something?"

She gave me an odd look. "Why do you ask?"

"I just wondered. You know, I'm just trying to gather as many memories as I can of him," I replied lamely. Damn, I sounded like a complete tool. Peeking up through my shroud of hair, I tried to gage whether Avery believed me. Her skeptical expression spoke volumes.

"I've heard a rumor, Noah."

"You have?"

"Yeah, about some things that were found in Jake's possessions."

*Oh shit.* "And?" I prompted.

She narrowed her eyes determinedly at me. "I want them."

I eased away from her since she appeared like she was ready to pounce. "Well, Avery I'm not sure they're yours—"

Avery stared at me in shock. "What do you mean it's not mine? They're pictures of me!"

The world around me tipped and then spun at her revelation. Finally, I replied, "Wait, what?"

Avery glanced down at her hands folded in her lap. "We were fooling around the weekend after New Year's. I let him take some pictures—you know of *me*."

When I got what she meant, I gasped. "Um, okay."

"He may have deleted them, but I just want to make sure."

"Oh," I replied, my chest deflating.

"So you think you can get them for me?"

"Yeah, um, it shouldn't be a problem."

She sighed with relief. "Good. The last thing I need is for them to fall into the wrong hands and end up on the internet or something."

"That would suck," I said. She still hadn't answered the song lyrics question. "So it's a real bummer you guys didn't have a special song—you know that meant something to the two of you."

Avery rolled her eyes. "I guess that's because Jake only listened to ridiculous rap music without any deeper meaning than 'I want to screw you nine different ways'."

At her totally exasperated expression, I ducked my head to avoid laughing in her face. Geez, she had such a stick up her ass that I wondered how Jake had ever managed to spend more than ten minutes with her—especially considering for the latter part of their relationship he wasn't getting any from her. He'd respected her wishes when she'd told him she couldn't handle a physical relationship anymore. Now that I looked back, it was probably one of the most decent things he had ever done with a girl.

I stood up from the couch. "Yeah, I guess I better get going. I'll get those pictures for you as soon as I can."

Her eyes widened as she shook her head wildly back and forth. "I don't want to keep them. I want you to delete them!" she shrieked.

Holding my hands up in defeat, I replied. "Okay, okay, I'll delete them."

Avery exhaled noisily. "Good. I'm glad to hear we're on the same page." She then followed me down the winding staircase into the marble floored foyer. She smiled at me. "Thanks Noah. You know, for being a good friend to me and Jake."

"Sure. And thanks for letting me come over."

"Yeah, anytime," Avery said, listlessly before closing the door behind me.

I walked to my Jeep, content in the knowledge I could cross

one girl off the list.

# Chapter Nine

After I left Avery's house, I ended up back at Rolling Hills Cemetery. It was like an unseen force was drawing me there. I didn't want to believe Jake had that kinda power from the grave, but I went anyway.

I made the slow drive around the circle to the mausoleum. When I got out of the Jeep, I noticed someone was sitting on the grass in front of the building.

It was Maddie.

At the sound of someone behind her, she sighed. "Daddy, I said I'd call you when I was ready to come home."

"Um, it's Noah," I muttered.

She whirled around, her face flushing a little. "Oh, I thought you were my dad."

"That's okay."

"I didn't expect anyone to be here."

"Yeah, me either," I admitted.

She nodded and motioned for me to have a seat on the grass next to her. I eased down and stared at the vault holding Jake's remains.

"Hey, I didn't tell you how great you sounded the other day at the funeral. That song was really beautiful," I said.

She smiled. "Thanks. You sounded great, too."

"Yeah, I guess *Free Bird* was an odd choice of a funeral song, but—"

"It was Jake's favorite," she murmured. "It was exactly what he would have wanted."

I flicked a random blade of grass with my finger. "Maddie, I'm trying to understand all this stuff that's been going on. You know, the 'two Jakes'."

She nodded. "He had a hard time with it, too."

"He did?" I asked.

"Of course he did. Don't you know how hard it was to be two people? The guy everyone expected him to be and the guy he really was deep down?"

It felt kinda strange to be having this conversation with Maddie about my best friend, but there was a part of me that was desperate for answers.

Finally, I shook my head. "But he shouldn't have felt that way," I protested.

"Why do you think so?"

When I didn't respond, Maddie sighed. "He was looking forward to graduation you know."

"Yeah, he thought college was going to be a blast."

"No, that's not it at all. He was going to "come out" so speak."

My breath caught in my chest. "Wait, are you trying to say Jake was….gay?"

Maddie laughed. "No, Jake wasn't gay. I mean, he was going to truly turn over a new leaf. He had been looking forward to leaving town so he could do that. He'd even talked to his football coach about working with the volunteer organizations on campus."

Okay, it was one thing contemplating Jake might be gay, but it was a totally mind blowing to think he was looking forward to turning his back on partying to be a do gooder.

"I'm sorry, but I just can't imagine Jake doing much volunteer work," I said.

Maddie smiled sadly. "Well, he was."

"Whatever," I mumbled. I thought talking to Maddie would give me answers, but I was starting to feel more and more confused.

She must have sensed my confusion because she said, "You know, it was like Jake was honorable to a fault. He did everything he could to please others—even if it was misguided."

Seriously? Jake did things to please others? Since the moment we'd met, he'd been one of the most selfish assholes on the planet. It was me, me, me, all the time. I shook my head incredulously. "But Maddie…"

She looked over at me. "I know what you're going to say."

I raised my eyebrows. "You do?"

"To you and to everybody else, he was a jerk 90% of the time."

Well, I wasn't expecting that. But it was certainly closer to the truth. "Pretty much."

"But to me and my family, he was a perfect gentleman 90% of the time."

Once again, that was totally out of character for Jake. "I just don't get it," I replied. I glanced back up at the vault. "I still don't understand why he felt like he had to be two people to me."

"Well, think about it for a minute."

I sat deathly still, trying to collect my thoughts. "What I meant to say is, I was his best friend, and I don't understand why if he could be that way with you and your parents, then why in the he-," I caught myself as Maddie arched an eyebrow at me. "the *heck*, he couldn't be real with me."

"Maybe he was real with you, and you just didn't realize it."

"Huh?"

"In all the years that you guys were friends, you're telling me you never saw a different side to him?"

I closed my eyes in thought. My mind whirled in a mosaic of colorful memories. I thought about the camping trip when Jake saved my life. I thought about the Father/Son camping trip in Scouts that Jake refused to go on just because I didn't have a dad to go with me. And then I thought about the six weeks when my grandfather was sick and how he stayed by my side like a brother. How could I not see before how self-less he truly was? I mean, sure he had his epic douchebag moments, but even before he was 'changing' into a so-called better person, he did kindhearted things. Deep down, I guess he was a truly giving person, but I'd just been too blind to always see it.

A knot formed in my throat. I swallowed several times before murmuring, "Yeah, I guess you're right."

Maddie smiled. "He talked about you a lot."

I snapped my head to stare at her. Oh, holy hell. "He did?"

She smiled. "Yeah, all the time."

I didn't respond for a few minutes as I contemplated all the wild nonsense he could have said. "What did he...say—you know about me?"

"That you were a good guy and a good friend—too good of a friend than he sometimes deserved. Oh, and he told me the duct tape story!"

I rolled my eyes. "Of course he did."

Maddie laughed. "Don't worry, I told him what a jerk he

was to do that to you."

I laughed. Miss Choir Priss was full of surprises. "You did?"

"Uh, huh, and you know what he said?"

I shook my head.

"He said, 'Well, I didn't know how else to get him to be my friend'."

A strange burn radiated through my chest. It continued up my throat to where I choked. "Yeah, he had some issues, but he was a good friend," I finally said.

We sat in silence for a few minutes. Maddie cleared her throat. "Um, I guess I better call my dad. He dropped me off on his way home," she said.

"I can give you a ride," I suggested.

"Are you sure?"

"Yeah, I don't mind."

I held my hand out and helped her up off the grass.

"Thanks," she replied, with a smile.

"No problem."

When I opened the Jeep door for her, I wanted to slap myself. I didn't have a freakin' clue what had gotten into me. I had *never* done that for a girl in my life. I shrugged the thought away.

Maddie told me how to get to her house. She lived in a nice

subdivision only a few streets over from where I lived.

After I eased the Jeep behind her dad's car, I turned to look at her.

She smiled. "Thanks for the ride."

"No, problem. I was glad to do it."

She hesitated for a moment and then asked, "Would you like to come in for a while?"

I don't know what I was more surprised about. The fact she asked me in, or the fact I agreed. Seriously, I was ready to cue the music from *The Twilight Zone*. As Maddie walked ahead of me, I eyed her suspiciously, contemplating what kinda weird hold she had over guys. A part of me was tempted to run back to the Jeep and bail. I mean, Jake's miraculous conversion happened sometime after getting involved with Pastor Dan's rehabilitation program. Maybe he had some weird brainwashing wing, and she helped him by luring in unsuspecting teens.

Yeah, I was losing it!

When she breezed through the front door, Maddie called, "Hey guys, I'm home!"

Pastor Dan poked his head out of the kitchen. "Wasn't I supposed to pick you up? Don't tell me you hitched or something?" he asked with a smile.

Maddie laughed. "No Daddy, Noah gave me a ride home."

"Hey, Mr. Parker," I said.

"Hi there, Noah. Thanks for being so kind."

"I was glad to, sir." *Sir?* Okay, something had seriously gotten in to me. I rarely if ever referred to anybody as *sir*. I swallowed nervously as the brainwashing cult idea flashed in my mind.

"We've ordered a pizza for game night, Maddie. Noah, would you like to stay?" Mrs. Parker asked.

I glanced over at Maddie. She nodded and smiled. "Okay, that sounds great. Just let me text my mom to let her know where I am," I replied.

Pastor Dan smiled. "Good, we'll be more than happy to have you." He looked over at Maddie. "Will you go get Josh and tell him the pizza is on its way?"

"Sure," she said.

For some reason, I followed Maddie up the stairs. Maybe it was because I was afraid to be alone with Pastor Dan. Like I was afraid he'd really whip out the religious hoodoo on me if we were alone.

When we got to the top of the landing, Maddie stopped. She turned back to me and bit her lip. "Um, Noah. There's something I should tell you about my brother before you meet him."

Before she could say anything else, a kid, who looked about seven or eight, came bounding out of a room at the end of the

126

hall. "Hey Maddie!" he cried.

I froze in the hallway. The kid had chalky white skin, and he was bald. He couldn't have been more than seven, so I knew he didn't have male pattern baldness at an early age. He was sick.

Well, I guess he wasn't too sick because he came hurtling down the hall to us. He peered up at me. "Hi, I'm Josh!" he exclaimed, thrusting out a pale hand.

"Hey there, I'm Noah," I replied. I took his hand gingerly into mine, afraid one hardened shake might rip it completely off.

"Nice to meet ya," he said. He didn't release my hand. Instead, he started dragging me down the hall towards his room. "I wanna show you somethin'," he said.

"Josh," Maddie's voice warned.

He whirled me into his room. I did a double take. "Jes-" I began before I quickly looked down at Josh. "I mean, geez," I replied.

My dad's face was plastered all over Josh's room. His rookie poster hung over the bed, and then his MVP poster was over the closet door. It was intense. "Wow, you sure do like Joe Preston."

Josh rolled his eyes and grinned. "Duh, he's like the most awesome baseball player ever!"

"Yeah, I guess."

He stared at me. "Don't you like him?"

"Uh…." I didn't know what to say. *"No, Josh, I don't like him. He's a major asshat who knocked up my mother and ran off. I've had little contact with the prick."* Nope, that wouldn't work. Josh would probably pass out.

Maddie joined us in the doorway. I glanced from her to Josh who was waiting for my response. "You see, Joe Preston is my…" I choked on the words a little, "my dad."

Josh's hollow eyes widened to the size of dinner plates. "Nun-uh," he protested.

"No, it's true." I swept my hand over my chest. "Scout's Honor."

"Wow…" he shook his head slowly. Then when the realization finally sunk in, he started bouncing around. "Wow, I can't believe this! *You're* Joe Preston's son. That is *so* cool!" He then ran across the room to his desk and grabbed up an autograph book. "Can I have your autograph?"

"Josh," Maddie scolded.

"What?" he questioned.

"Maybe Noah doesn't want to sign your autograph book."

"No, it's fine," I said.

The doorbell rang. "Pizza's here!" Josh cried and then ran out of the bedroom.

Maddie smiled at me. "I'm sorry about that."

"No, he's fine."

"Can I ask you something?"

"Sure."

"If Joe Preston is your father, why do you go by Sullivan?"

Oh Jesus. She just had to ask that question. I didn't know what I was going to tell her since she had no realm of understanding. I mean, her parents were the ideal couple. But, she wanted an answer, so I drew in a deep breath. "Because I don't really have a relationship with my father. He was twenty-one when he got my mom pregnant, and he really hasn't had much to do with us. Don't get me wrong, he's not a total deadbeat. He does pay a little child support."

"Oh, I see." Her face flushed the color of the red spread covering Josh's bed. It made me feel like an ass. "Then I'm really sorry for what Josh did—and for all this," she said, gesturing around the room.

"It's okay. You don't have to apologize." I cleared my throat. "Um, can I ask you something?"

"He has leukemia," she replied anticipating my question.

I grimaced. "I'm sorry."

"Thank you." Maddie stared at the door. "It's been really rough on him. He's had two rounds of incredibly aggressive treatment. The doctors say his prognosis is pretty good."

Pretty good? I didn't want to say that I didn't like odds that were *pretty* good. You might as well say you had a shot in hell.

"Did Jake…?"

"Yes, Jake met him, and he was really good to Josh. He even skipped basketball practice to sit with Josh during one of his treatments."

I tried not to let the surprise show on my face. I did remember Jake bitching about having to run suicides until he puked because he'd cut out on a practice. Of course, he never told me why he skipped out.

"Was he at the funeral the other day?" I asked.

"Yeah. Mom and Dad weren't sure about him going, but he finally wore them down."

We were interrupted by Josh's voice. "Guys, come on!"

I followed Maddie down the stairs. Mrs. Parker was setting the dining room table while Pastor Dan was putting ice in glasses. Maddie ushered me to the table, and before I could sit next to her, Josh shook his head. "No, I want Noah to sit *here*," he insisted. Maybe there was some kinda religious hoodoo hanging over the house. Normally, I would've recoiled at the very idea of Josh. But instead, I smiled at Maddie and moved to sit next to Josh.

The Parker's were the real deal. After we bowed our heads over paper plates, Pastor Dan gave thanks. I started to feel like I was in an episode of that old show *7th Heaven*. Then we started making a dent in the two large pizzas they'd ordered from Dominos.

For a sick kid, Josh sure could put the food away. I mean, he seriously could've put Blaine and some of the other football players to shame with the way he devoured his pizza. For dessert, Mrs. Parker had homemade chocolate pound cake. I thought I'd died and gone to Heaven.

After dinner, Mrs. Parker and Maddie quickly cleared the table for game night. No shit, they seriously had a game night once a week where they played board games together. You know, all that jazz that it's not about playing the game but spending quality time together and all. This particular night was Monopoly.

Maddie glanced over at me, anxiously gauging my reaction to game night. I smiled. "I'm a killer Monopoly player. I used to always win when I played with my grandparents and my mom."

"Oh really?" Pastor Dan questioned, with a grin.

Josh leaned over to me. "Watch out for Dad—he cheats!"

Pastor Dan laughed. "Now son, don't you be telling lies to our guest."

"Daddy, you know Josh is telling the truth," Maddie exclaimed, a grin etched across her face.

"It's sad that two children would accuse their father of such a thing," Pastor Dan replied, and then he gave me a wink.

Maddie and Josh weren't lying. We had barely gotten

started when Pastor Dan tried to pull one over on us. "No offense, sir, but should a minister be doing that sort of thing?" I asked.

I thought I might have offended him, but instead, he roared with laughter, and so did Mrs. Parker. "That's a wonderful question, Noah," Mrs. Parker said. "I've often thought the very same thing."

"All I have to say is sometimes you need a little something to repent for, and I know He forgives me!"

We all laughed. Fortunately, I was able to outwit Pastor Dan's schemes to end up the Donald Trump of the night.

"Good job, Noah," Maddie said.

"Yeah, way to beat Daddy!" Josh chimed in. It was the first thing he'd said in a long time, and I'd noticed for the last few minutes he'd been propping his head up on his elbows. He yawned, and Mrs. Parker nodded.

"All right, that's enough for tonight. Josh is getting tired."

"I am not!" Josh protested.

Pastor Dan shot him a look, and he piped down.

"I'll clean this up, Mom," Maddie said.

Mrs. Parker smiled. "Okay, I think I'll let you. I'm going to take my coffee in the living room."

"I'll join you," Pastor Dan said.

When Josh dallied at the table, Pastor Dan gave a short

whistle and a jerk of his head. Josh hopped up and followed into the living room.

I started helping Maddie pick up the game pieces when the thump, thump of a jacked up stereo interrupted us. Even with her dark hair shrouding her face, I could see Maddie had flushed scarlet. "What is that?" I asked.

"My dad and his oldies," she murmured.

"Maddie, get in here!" Josh shouted.

In the living room, Pastor Dan and Mrs. Parker were dancing together. Josh was doing crazy dance moves around the living room. I recognized the song. It was *Smokey Joe's Cafe*, and it had been one of my grandfather's favorite tunes from the 50's. A slow burn radiated in my chest, but I did my best to ignore it. I wished that it was possible just once to think of Granddaddy or of Jake without the same debilitating chest pain.

Pastor Dan saw Maddie, and his eyes lit up. Without missing a step, he motioned to her from the living room.

Maddie's face glowed with mortification.

"Come on and dance with me, Maddie," he urged.

"No Daddy!" Maddie hissed.

"Madeline Elizabeth Parker, get your uptight tail over here this instant!"

I couldn't help laughing as Maddie stalked over to her

father. He grabbed her into his arms and did a fast waltz around the living room. I had to admit, Pastor Dan had some serious moves. While he and Maddie cut a rug, Mrs. Parker did some old moves from the 60's with Josh—the Twist, the Alligator, you name it—they were doing it. I think they even started doing the Sprinkler.

Pastor Dan dipped Maddie, and then spun her over to me. "Your turn, Noah," he urged.

Maddie blushed as she tried to catch her breath. "You don't have to."

Since no one from school was going to see me and possibly give me shit, I decided what the hell. I grinned. "No, it's okay."

"Really?"

"Sure."

She smiled with surprise when I pulled her to me. I quickstepped her across the room like Grammy had taught me. We had our own *Dancing with the Stars* moment in the Parker's living room.

"Nice footwork, Noah," Pastor Dan complimented.

"Thank you, sir."

I cleared my throat and stared into Maddie's eyes. "So did Jake ever…"

"Dance like this?" Maddie responded.

"Uh-huh."

Maddie shook her head. "No, he didn't."

Hmm, I guess there was one thing I'd done that Jake hadn't. I didn't know if that was a hollow victory or not. I mean, he might not have ever had the opportunity. But what I really wondered is if given the opportunity would he have shot down the chance.

When the large grandfather clock struck ten, Mrs. Parker turned off the stereo. She gave Josh a look. "Okay, I know it's way past somebody's bedtime."

"Aw, Mom," Josh whined.

"Upstairs, now," Mrs. Parker replied.

I glanced at Maddie. "I guess I better be heading on, too." I smiled at Pastor Dan and Mrs. Parker. "Thanks for having me for dinner and game night."

Pastor Dan smiled. "You're very welcome. Come back anytime."

"Thanks."

Maddie walked me to the door. As I started off the porch, I looked back. "So I'll see you at school tomorrow?"

A small expression of surprise flickered in her eyes, and I felt like an ass. Maddie must've been thinking I'd be behind the scenes friends with her or something. "Um, yeah, sure. See you at school."

"Okay, then. Thanks again for everything."

"You're welcome."

As I dug my keys out of my pocket, I grinned. It wasn't the way I'd envisioned the night—board games with the $7^{th}$ *Heaven* gang and dancing around the Parker's living room, but all in all, I had a fun, G-rated time.

# Chapter Ten

On Tuesday, I stopped by the Nelson's house. Luckily, Mr. and Mrs. Nelson were at work, and Jonathan was the only one at home.

"Hey man, what's up?" he asked.

"I came by to look for Jake's camera or maybe his phone."

Jonathan grinned. "Oh, like, for the *ring* investigation?"

"Yeah, I guess you could say that," I replied.

"Good idea. Man, I bet it'll have an assload of chicks on there!"

I laughed. "Yeah, I'm sure it does."

Jonathan led the way upstairs to Jake's room. On the bed were a couple of duffle bags. Jonathan started unzipping some of them. "This was the stuff he had with him up at PawPaw's. Mom hasn't had the heart to unpack it yet," he informed me.

I nodded. Something about seeing those bags weirded me out a little, and I backed away from the bed—fully content with letting Jonathan find the camera.

"Jesus," Jonathan murmured.

My gaze fell on a plastic bag in his hand. It was Jake's iPhone. He must've had it on him at the accident because it had clearly been bagged by the police—not Jake's MeeMaw.

I gulped. "Does it work?" I croaked.

Jonathan shot me a look before he unzipped the bag. "I dunno, man. It looks fine." He grimaced. "It must've been in his truck and not on him when..." Neither of us wanted to think about the rest of that statement. The battery clicked off, so Jonathan dug in the bag for the charger.

Luckily, Jake had never felt the need to lock his phone, or we would have been shit out of luck. *"Lock it? Hell, I could never remember the password, so screw that!"* he'd said.

Once the phone came up, I started scrolling through the pictures—paying particular attention to the dates. Finally, I found the ones Avery was talking about. "Whoa!" I didn't know if I would ever be able to look at her again, considering she was not only naked, but in some very, very provocative poses.

Jonathan leaned over me. "Holy shit! Is that Honey Boo-Boo?"

I laughed. "Yeah, that's her—a lot more than I'm used to seeing"

"Damn, I bet she doesn't show all that at the pageants."

"I sure as hell wouldn't think so," I mused.

"What are you going to do with them?" he asked.

"I promised her I would delete them."

"Man, that's a pity," Jonathan said.

I quickly sent the five naughty pics to the recycling bin. Then I emptied it. "Okay, problem solved."

"Yeah," Jonathan murmured with a wistful look in his eye.

I slapped him on the arm. "Dude, quit memorizing the pictures of Honey Boo-Boo—I mean Avery—for your spank bank!"

He grinned wickedly and waggled his eyebrows. "Sorry but some pictures can't ever be erased!"

"Yeah, that sounds exactly like something Jake would've said," I replied.

The mention of Jake brought us back to ourselves. An awkward silence hung in the air. I eyed the phone and then looked at Jonathan. "Hey man, would you mind if I took this phone? You know, for evidence and detective bullshit."

"Sure. Mom and Dad won't mind—they probably won't even miss it for a while."

"Okay, cool." As I weighed the phone in my palm, I glanced up at Jonathan. "So do you have any idea who the ring chick might be?"

Jonathan rocked back on his heels before shaking his head. "I mean, I didn't know of any specific girls in Jake's life besides Honey Boo-Boo and that Presley chick."

While I bobbed my head in agreement, Maddie's face once again entered my mind. "What about Pastor Dan's daughter?"

With his blonde brows furrowing, Jonathan gave me an epic WTF? look. "The girl who tutored Jake?"

"Yeah, Maddie."

"Dude, I don't think so. I mean, Jake might've mentioned her once or twice to me, but he never sounded like he had a jonesing for her."

Chewing on my bottom lip, I thought about the many faces of Jake that Maddie, Pastor Dan, and even myself had seen. "But what if he was keeping his feelings for her a secret? Like he was hiding them away just like this ring?"

Jonathan snorted skeptically. "When did Jake ever hide anything? He said and did exactly what he wanted to."

"Um duh, the ring?" I argued.

He pursed his lips in thought. "Well, maybe it could be her. Who knows. I'll just say I'll be shocked as hell if it actually turns out to be her."

"You and me both," I murmured. I then started for the door. Jonathan's voice stopped me. "Hey Noah?"

I turned around. "Yeah?"

"Blowing up is pretty quick, right? I mean, you don't think Jake felt anything on that tractor, do you?"

Anguish swam in his dark blue eyes. I didn't know what

Jake felt in that last moment—that last second. I hoped he hadn't felt anything—that he was here one minute and gone the next. Maybe in the end it didn't matter if you knew for sure— maybe you could just choose to believe what you wanted.

So, I shook my head at Jonathan. "No man, you heard Bubba when they said it was quick. I'm sure Jake didn't feel a thing."

Jonathan weighed my answer for a few seconds before nodding. "Yeah, that's what I thought, too. Thanks, man."

"No problem," I replied.

On Tuesday and Wednesday, I began the task of working my way through Jake's phone. His address book was a symbolic black book like from back in the day. I started with the girls Jake had labeled "Butter Faces"—meaning everything was hot *but* the chicks' faces.

And it was a bodacious bevy of hot bods I 'interviewed' that week. Long legs, fabulous racks, Jennifer Lopez like asses, but none of them had a song with Jake. Well, Libby Petersen did, but it was *Let's Get Drunk and Screw*, not *You Were Always on My Mind*.

I started to get discouraged. What if I wasn't able to find *her*? Jake had dated and screwed extensively not only through Creekview, but also at some of the other high school in our county. It was almost an unending journey—one I might still be on in my old age where I finally tracked down the girl to a nursing home.

Thursday as I sat zoned out at the lunch table, I felt a hand on my shoulder. It was Maddie. The moment I saw her, I couldn't help the beaming smile that spread across my face. "Hey," I said as I hopped up from my chair.

"Hi," she said shyly.

"I haven't seen you around this week."

"Yeah, I've been at All-State Chorus competition."

"Oh really?"

"Uh, huh."

Maddie and I stood awkwardly at the table. I could feel the expectant gazes of the guys at my table bearing into my back. "So did you, like, uh, win?" I stammered.

"We came in third as a group, and I came in second as an individual."

"Wow, that's awesome," I replied. The back of my shirt was practically peeling off from the burn of the guys gaping at me and Maddie.

Maddie must've sensed my awkwardness. "Well, I just wanted to say hello and see how you were doing," she said, a slight blush creeping across her cheeks.

My heart jolted a little in my chest. Damn. She was worried

about how I was doing with my grief—so much so she'd risked being embarrassed or annihilated by the A-Crowd just to check on me. She started to turn away, but I grabbed her arm. "I'll walk you out."

Maddie raised her eyebrows in surprise, but then she smiled. "Okay."

Without a word to the guys, I grabbed my books and followed Maddie out of the cafeteria.

"What about you?" I asked, as we headed through the double doors. "I mean, how are you doing?"

She shrugged. "I'm okay, I guess." Her big dark eyes widened. "Oh Noah, I'm sorry. I shouldn't even be talking about how I feel. I had so little time with Jake, and the two of you were best friends since you were kids." She rubbed my arm tenderly, causing the hairs on my arm to rise. "I bet you're really lost without him," she said.

Damn, she'd really hit the nail on the head. I hated to admit that without Jake around, I did feel lost—like I didn't know who I was anymore. Having those type of feelings running around in my head made me feel like a total pussy. The world I'd known had shattered around me in an instant, and now everything seemed so surreal. People went on doing exactly what they'd done before while I tip-toed through this new reality.

Once again, the dull ache in my chest radiated at the

thoughts of Jake. "Yeah, I am," I murmured.

Maddie smiled sadly at me. "I can't even imagine how much you miss him, Noah. I wish there was something I could do—"

"No, it's okay. Just being here and talking about him—that helps me," I answered.

The bell rang shrilly over our heads. "Well, I guess I better go. It was good seeing you," Maddie said.

"Yeah, same here."

"Bye," she said.

"Bye," I murmured.

As she walked away, it once again hit me like a ton of bricks or a swift kick to the balls. I'd been through most of the girls in Jake's phone and zilch. When I'd gotten to Maddie's number, I'd skipped over it. Why? Because wasn't she just the preacher's goody daughter who was merely a friend and a tutor? But then I thought about what she'd said at the cemetery, and the things he'd confided in her—things he'd never told me when he was shitfaced or sober.

The more I thought about it, the more some of the pieces starting coming together. The more the pieces started coming together, the more I felt like a giant dumbass for not seeing it before. I made a mental note to rule out any form of detective work in my future since I was pretty suckasstastic at it.

Maddie could be *her*. The more I allowed myself to think it,

144

the less I wanted it to be true. Something within me didn't want Maddie to be Jake's or most of all that Jake was Maddie's.

# Chapter Eleven

It had been a hell of a week. To get my mind off of Jake, his harem of women, and Maddie, I decided to go to a party at Presley Patterson's house. I knew it was probably a mistake, but at the same time, I was ready for a little refreshment to take my mind off things.

By the time I got there, the party was in full swing. Presley lived in one of the nicer houses on the shitty side of town. The rumor was many years ago Presley's mom had a fling with Elvis Presley right before he died. Then she'd made her rounds during the 80's being a groupie for most of the heavy metal bands—the bigger the hair the better. But I guess she never lost her love for Elvis because when Presley was born, she named her after him.

I found most of "the crowd" at the party. I wasn't too surprised to find a game of practically naked Twister going on. Presley's parties were notoriously risqué, even for our crowd. "What's up, Noah!" Blaine called to me, his voice muffled from underneath a couple of girls stripped to their bra and panties.

"Hey, Blaine," I replied. I looked around the room. "Where's the beer?"

"Kitchen," he mumbled.

I called hello to some of the other party goers as I made my way down to the hall. In the kitchen, I found the mother-load with two coolers of Budweiser. Before I knew it, I'd guzzled three beers. Unfortunately, it had the opposite effect than the one I desired. I got a raging pain in my head like someone was stabbing me with an ice pick behind my right eye. The insane thumping of the party music only made it worse. I couldn't focus on any of the conversations, and I certainly couldn't get into a curvy freshman who was chatting me up while trying to feel me up.

With my head pounding, I snuck into Presley's bedroom. I quickly scanned the room for any couples using it to hook up. Fortunately for me, the coast was clear. I was well acquainted with Presley's room since it's where I'd lost my virginity to Presley's cousin at a New Year's party sophomore year. Jake had reacted like a proud father—thumping me on the back and congratulating me. Of course always the player, he'd lost his when we were in the eighth grade to one of Jonathan's ex-girlfriends.

I rummaged in Presley's medicine cabinet for some Advil, Tylenol, anything. Finally, I found some next to a bottle of Midol. Popping pills and chasing them with beer is never a good idea, but I did it anyway. I was willing to do anything—including cutting my head off— to be rid of the pain.

I didn't bother turning on the lights. Being in the dark was better on my head. I eased down on the bed and draped my arm over my eyes. Just as I was about to dose off, I heard a noise next to the door.

"Noah? Noah, are you in here?" a voice whispered.

"Yeah," I moaned.

Light from the hallway momentarily flooded the room as someone entered. They closed the door behind them. I didn't know who it was until the lamp beside the bed flicked on.

It was Presley.

"Hey," she said, with a crooked grin.

"Hey."

"What's the matter?" she asked.

"My head hurts like hell," I groaned.

Presley sat down beside me. "Oh, you poor baby. I'm so sorry."

The next thing I knew her lips were on mine. I jerked away. "Presley, what the—"

"Shh, Noah. Let me make you feel better," she whispered, as she pushed me back against the bed. Since my headache was almost gone and she was an incredible kisser, I gave in, and we made out for a few minutes. My hand traveled up her shirt when I finally released her lips, desperate for air.

As I gasped and panted, she grinned seductively at me. "I've got a secret."

"Yeah, so?"

Her breath was hot over my earlobe. "I'm not wearing any underwear," she whispered, as she crisscrossed her legs.

"Um, yeah, good for you."

Her hand trailed up my calf to my thigh. Uh, oh, this wasn't good.

"You've got a secret too, don't you?" she asked.

"No, I'm wearing boxers as a matter of fact."

Presley rolled her eyes playfully at my response. "No silly. I mean, you've got a secret about Jake."

My eyes widened. How the hell did she know about that?

Suddenly, her hand was inching further up my thigh. "Wonder what color boxer shorts you have on?"

I silently willed that traitorous part of me to be still, but it wasn't hearing anything about it—especially after Presley's fingers found my zipper.

"Look, you're drunk, and we really shouldn't be doing anything," I protested.

Her head shook wildly back and forth. "I haven't had a drop to drink. I swear. I just…" When she nibbled her bottom lip, my erection jumped in my pants. "I just don't want to be alone tonight." Her hand was inside my jeans now. Fuck me. I had a freight train running through my head, and a wildfire burning in my crotch. But with just one sniffle from Presley, my hard-on began to wither. When I gazed up at her, tears sparkled in her dark blue eyes. "Noah, I don't know what to do without Jake, and I need to be with someone who loved him like I did."

At her words, a shudder ran through me. Just the thought that she wanted a connection to Jake through screwing me was like a douse of prickly ice water crashing over me. What the hell was I doing? Presley was Jake's girl—at least one of his girls. More importantly, she was the last girl he had been with before he gave up sex. Now here I was being the ultimate backstabbing douche by making out with her and getting a partial hand-job.

I knocked Presley's hand away. "Stop it."

Her blonde brows rose in shock. "Don't you want me?"

Running my hand through my already disheveled hair, I grunted. "Of course I want you. You just brought me from half-mast to raging hard-on." I shook my head. "But don't you realize how incredibly fucked up this is? You were Jake's…girl, and I'm his best friend. We can't screw each other to make our grief go away."

My mouth fell open when embarrassment tinged Presley's cheeks pink. I don't think I'd ever seen her blush in my life.

150

"Yes Noah, I know." She jerked her chin up to stare sadly at me. "I'm perfectly aware how incredibly fucked up I am without Jake. I don't sleep. I barely eat, even though I know I should. I'm so scared and alone. I need some way to deal with it, and this—" she motioned to the bed and our rumpled clothes. "*This* is all I know to do to make things better—to feel anything with someone."

Mascara blackened tears ran down her cheeks, and her shoulders began to rise and fall with her sobs. That familiar suffocating feeling crept on me, but I fought like hell not to let it overcome me. Reaching over, I handed Presley the box of tissues off her nightstand. After she'd wiped her eyes and blown her nose, she stared intently at me. "Have you heard that there's some big secret going around about something Jake had in his room?"

Uh, oh. "Well, yeah, maybe."

Presley's brows rose in surprise. "Do you know what it is?"

"I was there when it was found."

She gasped. "What is it?"

"Nothing much," I lied.

"Please tell me. I promise, it'll be our little secret."

Trying to keep her from riding my ass, I teased, "Like your lack of underwear?"

She laughed. "Ugh, I'm sorry. I can't believe I said that to you earlier. But hey, me not wearing panties isn't that huge a

151

secret, but sure, we can say we'll keep it between us."

My mind whirled with thoughts. I knew I probably shouldn't tell Presley, but at the same time, it was probably the quickest way to find out if she was the one. "Um, they found a ring," I admitted.

Presley stared at me in disbelief. "A ring? What kind of ring?"

"Just a ring," I replied.

"Come on, Noah. You can tell me what kind of ring it was."

I sighed. "It was an engagement ring, okay? A one carat engagement ring."

What she said next floored me. "That's it?"

"That's it?" I repeated dumbly. I shook my head. "Yeah, that's it. Did you expect something else? Like a car or a yacht?"

She laughed nervously. "No, I wasn't thinking that." She shrugged. "Do you know who it's for?"

"Nope."

"Hmm."

I drew in a breath. "So did you guys have like a song or something?"

"Huh?"

"Like a song that meant something to you."

When she nodded, my heart surged in my chest. This was it.

152

"It was *Crash* by Dave Matthews."

I exhaled like a deflated balloon. "Are you sure?"

Presley laughed. "Yeah, I'm sure. We played it every time we…were together."

"I see."

She shifted on the bed and stared down at her manicured nails. "Noah, I really want to thank you for putting the brakes on us tonight and for comforting me."

"You don't have to thank me. That's what friends are for."

Presley smiled. "And since you were such a good friend to Jake and now to me, there's something I want to tell you."

"Oh?"

"Yeah, I-uh, it's—" she began when the bedroom door flung open and Blaine and a freshman girl fell inside.

Blaine stared at us with eyes swimming in booze. "Whoops! I thought this room was free." He glanced at the two of us before wiggling his eyebrows at me.

I stood up. "Yeah, I was just leaving."

"Hey, no need to rush. We can all party together," Blaine argued.

"No, man, I don't think so." I turned to look at Presley. "I'll talk to you later."

"Yeah, catch you later."

As I started to the car, I realized that I'd learned two things that night....Presley wasn't the girl, and after learning about *Crash* and their sex habits, I would be forever scarred from Dave Matthews.

# Chapter Twelve

After my escapade on Friday night, I spent most of Saturday partially hung-over and in a shitty mood. Luckily, Mom was on call, so I had the house to myself. With everything that had been going on with the headache that was the investigation into *her,* I hadn't had time to focus on my personal life, or more importantly, the specter of Greg. Mom and I skirted around the issue—especially after the couch incident. I could tell she was still mortified because whenever she would glance at my wounded eyebrow, she'd blush.

Things were tense between us in many ways. Some days she cooked breakfast for me, and we made small talk over pancakes or French Toast. She always tip-toed on eggshells around the subject of Jake, but eventually she always brought him up. I could tell Mom was worried to death about me. There were the sleepless nights, sheets drenched in sweat, and dark circles under my eyes from the nightmares that she pretended not to notice to let me save face.

But there was also something else—a thickness hung heavy in the air—like something dark looming over the horizon with him. I couldn't quite put my finger on it, and to put it bluntly, I was freakin' tired of playing Sherlock Holmes all the time.

So instead of feeling like I had the fucking rug jerked out from under me, I should have been prepared for what happened on Wednesday afternoon. But I wasn't. The moment I breezed through the garage door after work, heavenly aromas filled my nostrils. I gazed around the kitchen, and I saw something truly shocking. Not only was Mom home relatively early, but she was cooking.

And not just that. She was taking bread out of the oven. *Homemade* bread. Oh, something was definitely going on.

"Hey sweetie," Mom said.

"Hi," I replied hesitatively. I glanced past her into the dining room where the table was set conspicuously for three. "What's going on?" I asked.

Mom laughed. "It's called dinner, Noah."

I rolled my eyes. "Yeah, I know that. It's just you very rarely cook, least of all set the dining room table."

Mom didn't answer me. Instead, she slipped on some oven mittens and grabbed the lasagna off the counter. I followed close on her heels into the dining room. "So, I'm gonna ask one more time. What the hell is going on?"

She whirled around. "Language, Noah!"

Geez, she sounded just like Maddie. I couldn't catch a break. When Mom started back into the kitchen, I stepped in

156

front of her. She sighed. "All right fine. I need to talk to you about something."

She ushered me into the living room. I side stepped the now infamous couch and plopped down into the chair.

Mom stared at me before drawing in a deep breath. "Noah, Greg has asked me to marry him, and I've said yes."

The wind left my body in a long, exaggerated whoosh. Kinda like the time I fell off the monkey bars in first grade. Well, I didn't actually fall. Jake pushed me off because I was taking too long to get across them, but that was another story. "Wait, what?"

Mom fiddled with the hem of her skirt. "I'm engaged to Greg."

Christ Almighty, could this be happening at a worse time? "When did he ask you?"

"A couple days ago."

My gaze flickered toward the ceiling as I tried taking a few calming breaths.

"Noah?"

"Huh?"

"There's something else."

I met her gaze. "You mean something even better than you're getting married?"

She winced before lowering her eyes. "I'm pregnant."

I tore out of the chair in an instant. "You're what?"

Peeking up at me through her eyelashes, she murmured, "You heard me."

Oh no. Oh, *hell* no. This couldn't be happening. Wasn't it bad enough she'd found another man? Now she was going to have another kid. I was practically being phased out of my own family.

"When are you due?" I demanded.

"October."

My eyes widened. "Bullshit! You're that far along, and you didn't think you should tell me?"

"Yes, and I'm sorry," she replied. She stood up and slowly stepped over to me. "Honey, I know you're upset."

"Really? What makes you say that?" I snapped.

"I'm sorry I didn't tell you sooner, but at my age, I wanted to make sure everything was okay before I told you. Then just as I got the green-light out of my first trimester and with the Amnio, Jake got killed, and I didn't want to spring it on you then." When I refused to acknowledge her, she sighed exasperatedly. "Noah Andrew Sullivan, stop acting like a two-year-old throwing a tantrum and talk to me about what you're feeling!"

I snorted as I jerked my head up to glare at her. "Oh, I'm terribly sorry I'm being 'childish'. It's just I'm not really sure how to act when I get the fucking rug snatched out from under

158

me!"

"Nothing will change between you and me—"

"Are you shitting me? *Everything* will change! How can you be so blind as to why I'm not thrilled at your news? Of course, after it's just been the two of us all these years, I want you to bring a total stranger into our house and into our lives. What could be better? No wait, there's more? Ah, you're going to have another kid. Fabulous! Then you'll have a whole new family. Even better, maybe it'll be a boy, and then you won't even need me!"

My two-year-old tantrum had turned into an acid filled teenage rant. I truly felt shitty when Mom's chin trembled. "The Amnio showed it's a girl," she said softly.

"Well, isn't that sweet?" I snapped.

The tears pooling in Mom's blue eyes spilled over her cheeks. Although I did feel instant regret for hurting her feelings, the sadistic part of me was glad she was able to see how much I was hurting. In the end, I didn't know why I was being such an ass, but just the very thought of her being pregnant infuriated me.

Mom drew in a few deep breaths before she spoke. "Look, I know this baby and my marrying Greg is going to bring huge changes to your life—to *our* lives. But I hope you can see that they're going to be good changes, sweetheart. Your happiness means more to me than anything in the world, and I hope you

159

can believe that. I wouldn't do anything to hurt you, ever." A small smile curved at her lips. "I want you to be happy for me and happy for you."

I crossed my arms over my chest. "Oh, I'm happy."

"You are?" she asked tentatively, as if she feared I would go off on another one of my Dr. Jekyll and Mr. Hyde bipolar episodes.

"Sure, I am. Why wouldn't I be glad that you found a guy who'd actually marry you when you got knocked up this time!"

The moment the words left my lips I regretted them. Mom appeared momentarily stung. But then in a quick, fluid motion that took both of us off guard, she slapped me.

Hard.

Her eyes widened in disbelief. She hadn't hit me since I was ten years old when Jake and I ran away from home...for ten hours. When I'd finally shown back up, she'd been a weeping, snotty shell of the Mom I'd known. I figured she'd hold out her arms for me to rush into, but instead, she had first smacked my cheek. "How could you scare me like that?" she'd shrieked. Then she'd burst into tears and held me for two hours.

But I wasn't waiting around for hugs this time. "Thanks a hell of a lot, Mom," I mumbled. I spun on my heels, grabbed my keys off the counter, and stormed outside.

I stalked out to my Jeep. When I climbed inside, I slammed

the door. "Fuck!" I cried, banging my fist on the steering wheel. As I cranked up the engine, I squealed out of the driveway intent on going to one place. And then it hit me so hard I slammed on the brakes, causing my neck to whip back.

There was no place to go.

Because Jake was dead.

That one thought caused my stomach to heave, and I scrambled to fling open the door. I puked the entire contents of my stomach and my tumbled emotions onto the pavement. Defeated, I wiped the back of my hand across my mouth and contemplated where the hell to go.

Since we were kids, we had always used each other as a refuge. When his dad was acting like a bastard, he'd hop on his bike and pedal over to my house, or when I thought Mom was being too strict, I'd escape to his. Then if we truly wanted to tell the world to fuck off, we'd hide out in emerald thicket of trees behind Grammy and Granddaddy's house.

And then a feeling came over me so strong that it took my breath away. I put the car in drive and sped along the road. Instead of turning onto Grammy's street, I by-passed it and kept on going. I didn't want a lecture at her house, and I didn't want Alex or any of my other guy friends.

Instead, I pulled in Maddie's driveway. Throwing the car into park, I felt a wave of both relief and anger wash over me. I was angry that I couldn't go to Jake's, but I was also relieved that there was someone as kind and considerate as Maddie to go and talk to.

Then my grief fueled anger changed over as thoughts of my previous conversation with my mother and her slap caused me to storm up the walkway, stomp up the front steps, and pound on the front door. Fury caused me to dig into my pocket for some money because I knew I wanted to be prepared for Maddie's 'Cuss Can' antics.

When Maddie swung open the door, I thrust a five dollar bill in her face. "Look, I'm fucking pissed off right now, so put this in your damn cuss can!"

Her eyes widened. "No, that's okay. You keep it."

I shoved the money back in my pocket. "You're not going to believe what my mom just told me!" I rushed past in her in the house. When I whirled around to find her still standing in the doorway, I threw up my hands. "What?"

A sheepish expression filled Maddie's face. "It's just that my parents aren't home. They've taken Josh to the doctor…"

"Yeah so?"

She looked down at the foyer floor, toying the rug with her flip-flop. "I'm not allowed to be alone in the house with a boy when my parents aren't home," she said softly.

I rolled my eyes toward the ceiling. Jesus, Maddie had to always play by the rules. I stalked back across the living room and peered at her. Then I snorted exasperatedly. "You know we

162

could just as easily *fornicate* on the front lawn if we were so inclined."

Color flooded her cheeks. Great, now I was being an ass to her as well. "Dammit, that was a jerk thing to say. I'm really sorry, Maddie. I'm just really upset right now."

"It's okay," she replied. Without any more pressing from her, I headed outside and onto the front porch. After she closed the door, she motioned for me to have a seat in one of the rockers. I flopped down in one with a grunt while she cautiously sat down next to me.

"So what happened with your mom?" she asked.

"She's getting married."

Maddie's dark brows furrowed. "Oh, is her fiancée like mean or something?

"No, Greg's a pretty decent guy," I replied. I refrained from telling her the couch incident—I was afraid she might pass out.

"Then what is it?"

I shrugged. "I guess that I'm afraid of the changes that are to come. Like having some dude I barely know in the house or if we have to move…"

"But mainly you're afraid of losing your mom's love, right?"

Grimacing, I replied, "Yeah, but that's going to happen regardless of whether she gets married or not."

"How could you say that?"

"She's pregnant."

Maddie's dark eyes widened with excitement. "Oh Noah, that's wonderful. I'm so happy for her!" she squealed.

I shot her a look. "Thanks a lot."

Maddie frowned. "I don't understand."

With a sigh, I replied, "Neither do I."

"Let me guess. You're afraid with your mom getting married and having a baby she's going to completely replace you in an instant and totally forget that for seventeen years of her life she had a wonderful son to love and be proud of?"

After Maddie said it aloud, I felt like a complete dickwad. It sounded so childish and stupid, but at the same time, it also sounded completely feasible. "Maybe."

She smiled and linked her arm through mine. "Your mom could never replace you. Think about it, you're her first born. A new husband and new baby aren't going to change that."

I stared into her big brown eyes, and I realized I wanted to be as honest with her as I could. "Then everything is worse because Jake's gone when I need him most." I kicked at a nail on one of the wood floorboards. "I guess deep down, all I keep thinking of is that everyone leaves me—my real dad, my grandfather, Jake...how can I be sure my mother won't too?"

Maddie's hand came to cup my cheek. "Aw, Noah, how

could you ever think that? She's never going to leave you." She shook her head. "Besides your jerk of a dad, no one has left you because they wanted to—not your grandfather or Jake. The people who love you and care about you aren't going anywhere." She smiled. "Myself included."

"Really?"

Nudging me playfully, she said, "Now I want you to think about something for a minute. Next fall, you're going off to Tech, right?" When I nodded, she continued on. "You'll meet all these new people, go to lots of parties that you probably shouldn't—"

I chuckled. "Hey now."

She grinned. "You have a whole new life ahead of you. But what would your mom have done without you in the house?"

In all honesty, I hadn't thought of that. *Wow, Noah, what a way to be a selfish prick.*

When I didn't answer, Maddie patted my arm. "It's okay if you didn't. Just think about it now. I mean, she was going to be all alone, and now she'll have somebody. Two somebody's actually."

"It's a girl," I suddenly blurted for no apparent reason.

"Really?" Maddie squealed.

I rolled my eyes. "Yes."

"Oh, if she looks anything like your mom, she'll be so

beautiful," Maddie said.

"There's something else."

"Besides your mom getting remarried and having a baby?" she asked, smiling slightly.

"She slapped me."

Maddie's eyes widened. "She did?"

I nodded.

"But why?"

Instead of answering her, I hopped out of my seat and walked down the length of the porch, gazing out at the flower beds.

"Noah?" Maddie prompted.

"Well, um, it's the way I acted when she told me. I-I said some pretty hurtful things."

She rose out of her chair and came over to me. "What did you say?"

I turned back towards her and inwardly groaned. There was no way in hell I wanted to tell Maddie the awful thing I'd said. But when she tenderly took my hand in hers, I crumbled. "I was the biggest asshole in the world. I told her I was glad she'd found some guy who'd finally marry her. You know, after he knocked her up."

Maddie gasped and dropped my hand. "Noah, how could you?"

I threw my hands up. "I don't know why. I mean, why do we ever say or do the things we do?"

"You have to apologize right now!"

I stared at her. Jesus, was she pushy! She never stopped trying to make me be a better person. It made my blood boil as I crossed my arms over my chest in a huff. "Tell me something I don't know, Einstein."

Suddenly, she narrowed her eyes at me, and I wasn't expecting the response I got. "Don't get smart with me! I'm just trying to help." She whirled around and started back inside the house.

Shit.

"Maddie, wait!" I called. When she kept walking, I dug deep and said the word most guys loathe. "Please!" She stopped and turned around. I'd already hurt the woman I cared about most in the world today, so I didn't want to screw up with anyone else, especially not Maddie. Deep down, I didn't know why I cared so much about what she thought of me. Normally, I wouldn't have given a shit. But after Jake, she meant something to me—more than I was willing to admit sometimes.

I sighed and raked my hand through my hair. As she stared expectantly at me for the other two words guys hated to say, I stuffed my hands into my pants pockets. "Um…I'm sorry."

The corners of her lips turned up like she was fighting a

smile. "Thank you." After I had groveled to her satisfaction, she came back over to me. "You know, you probably need to take her some flowers when you apologize."

"Okay, I can do that."

"Want me to help you pick them out?"

As I gazed at the sweet expression on her face, I wanted to kick my own ass. I didn't want to go flower shopping with her. I wanted to grab her in my arms and lay a big one on her. Better yet, I wanted to go for a sex romp with her through her parents immaculately kept flower beds. But I knew I couldn't.

"Yeah, I'd like that," I lied.

She smiled. "Then I will." Suddenly, she brought her hand to her forehead. "Oh, I almost forgot. It's Wednesday night."

"So?"

"It's church night." She quirked her eyebrows at me. "Do you ever go?"

I shook my head. The truth was I hadn't gone to church since my granddaddy died. I guess you could say I was still a little pissed at God.

"Wanna come with me?" she asked enthusiastically.

Truthfully, the last thing on earth I wanted to do was go to church. But at the same time, I was up for anything that meant being close to Maddie. I also wanted to check out Pastor Dan's place a little more to see what it was that had such a hold on

Jake.

"Yeah, but I don't want you guys doing anything weird to me," I said.

"Don't worry. You don't get to handle snakes on your first visit," she said.

My eyes widened in horror. "Snakes? What the hell!"

She burst out laughing. "I'm just kidding you, Noah!"

"Oh, right, sure," I replied, although I sounded a lot more convinced than I felt.

# Chapter Thirteen

There was quite a crowd for a Wednesday night. Maddie led me up the aisle to a bench full of teenage girls—and one or two Bible toting guys. It had never crossed my mind about Maddie having friends. I mean, our sole connection was Jake, and besides him, we ran in very different circles. But once we got in the church, I saw she was the Queen Bee of the Godly Circuit. Her friends all sized me up. Some of them I recognized from school. I couldn't help noticing that a few gave me disapproving looks like I was the Big Bad Wolf leading Maddie astray.

"Hi guys, this is Noah," Maddie introduced.

"Hi Noah," they said together before the younger ones dissolved in giggles.

"Hey," I replied giving a lame wave. Maddie urged me to take a seat. Thankfully, it was next to one of the guys. When he glanced over at me, he stiffened and readjusted his glasses on his nose. Suddenly, I remembered he was one of the kids Jake used to pick on to get homework out of. I wanted to hold up my hands and say, "I come in peace."

Instead, I flashed my most convincing grin and said, "Hey man, how's it going?"

"Fine," he squeaked. He turned his head and began talking to the girl beside him, and I didn't blame him one bit. Now that I was on his turf, it was my turn to shift nervously in my seat. Thankfully, my slight heart palpitations eased when Maddie sat down beside me. Her delicious perfume filled my nostrils, and I sighed with contentment.

A wiry looking man with glasses stood up and motioned for Maddie's mom. She came up from her place on the front row to play the piano.

"Let's look to page seventy-two," the man's voice boomed. The members of the choir rose from their benches behind the pulpit. Pastor Dan came out in his robe, and once again, I felt like cuing the *7th Heaven* music.

Maddie handed me a song book out of the holder from the bench in front of us.

I shook my head. "Uh—I, I don't think I—"

"I think you can," she replied with a smile.

Reluctantly, I flipped to page seventy-two. When I saw the title of the song, it was like every molecule in my body shuddered to a stop. It was my Granddaddy's favorite song. He used to sing it all the time. In church. Out fishing. Mowing the lawn. I closed my eyes as the deep timber of his voice echoed through my mind. He put his heart and soul into every line,

171

giving inflection on the parts that meant something to him. Although he loved Frank Sinatra, Dean Martin, and Perry Como, he never sang them like he did this song.

Mrs. Parker struck the first few chords, and the congregation raised their voices in song. It felt like my lips were cemented together with Crazy Glue or something. I couldn't for the life of me sing. Hell, I could barely breathe. I felt like I was in a tripped out flashback. All I could think about was my granddaddy.

Since I'd never known my real father, Granddaddy was the only father I'd ever had. When he died two years ago, it shattered me. I know he loved all his grandkids, but he made me feel like I was the most special. Maybe he felt sorry for me because I didn't have a dad, or maybe it was because I was "his Maggie's" little boy.

Whatever it was, it was the most fucking special thing I've ever experienced on this earth.

Granddaddy was the one who bought me my first guitar and taught me how to play. I practically pissed my pants with excitement when I moved from sitting next to him, eyes wide with wonderment as his fingers strummed the chords, to balancing on his lap with the guitar in front of me. I never felt happier or safer nestled his strong arms while his calloused fingertips directed my tiny ones along the frets. Damn, the patience that man must have had. Needless to say Grammy didn't, because after a few days of lessons, she banished us outside to the porch.

Granddaddy never lost his smile as he listened to me work the chords into a melody. "You've got God given talent, son. Don't you ever forget that," he'd say before spitting a wad of tobacco into his cup.

With a shrug, I'd protest, "But I'm not good at sports, Granddaddy." After all, each and every one of his sons and grandsons were involved in some sport. For years, he practically lived at either the baseball diamond, the football stadium, or the basketball gym.

Granddaddy's worn and wrinkled hand would come to stroke his weathered chin thoughtfully. "Being athletic is a good talent to have, son, but one day it is of no use to you. My boys shone as bright stars once upon a time, but now all that has dimmed. It served them well with scholarships, but not a one is still using their talents. But music..." His face would break into a wide grin. "Music is timeless. I've played all the days of my life, and I'll play until my dying day."

My conversations with Granddaddy always felt kinda like Forest Gump and his mama. He always had a way of explaining things to me to where I could not only understand, but I could also get the bigger meaning out of. He could make me feel ten feet tall with just a look.

I'd just started tenth grade when he started acting funny.

He'd forget things, or he'd make off-the-wall statements. Mom and Grammy got worried that he might have the beginning stages of Alzheimer's Disease. So, they finally convinced him to go to the doctor.

But he didn't have Alzheimer's. Instead, a MRI revealed he had a brain tumor. Something called Glioblastoma. A real badass tumor that's like a spider. It has a fat body that surgery can remove, but it's the spider-like legs that get imbedded in your brain and fuck up your life.

Granddaddy's diagnosis was one of those life-altering moments when you're sure the earth skidded to a stop on its axis. It would have to, wouldn't it? How was it possible for the world to keep right on turning when my Granddaddy was going to die?

Yet somehow it did. Within my family, it was a hellish blur of agony. Grammy brought Granddaddy home, and Mom and her brothers rallied around to take care of him. They moved a hospital bed into the living room, so there'd be more room for him to be surrounded by his family. My uncles took turns staying nights. They didn't want to leave Grammy or my mom by themselves.

One night, I stayed up with him. It was close to the end, and he'd been sleeping most of the time. I was trying to read a book for my literature class when he opened his eyes and glanced over at me. "Noah," he whispered.

"What's wrong, Granddaddy? You need something?"

He shook his head. With a weak flick of his wrist, he beckoned me closer. "Want to tell you somethin'." His voice was gravely and weak as if it took everything in him to speak. I leaned forward as far as I could on my chair beside the bed. My elbows pressed into the metal railings of his hospital bed.

"I'm right here, Granddaddy."

He smiled. "You know, I was so angry when your mama got pregnant. I didn't want her to keep you. I wanted her to give you to a family who could provide for you better than she could."

I gasped as his words stung me. I couldn't imagine these were the final thoughts he wanted to tell me.

He gave a little rattle of a laugh. "I ain't finished, son."

I gave him a relieved smile. "Oh, okay."

"But the minute you were born, your mama called for me. I went into that room still bound and determined for her to give you up. But there she was holding you to her chest, and the love she had for you was written all over her face. She handed you to me, and I took you in my arms..." Tears welled in Granddaddy's dark eyes. "And it was instant love. The same love I'd had for my boys and for your mama. I knew right then and there you were meant to be with your mama and with our family."

Although I tried fighting them, tears pooled in my eyes and

spilled over my cheeks. Damn them! I didn't want his last sight of me to be that of a blubbering pansy.

As if he could read my mind, Granddaddy shook his head. "Don't be ashamed of your emotions, Noah. Experience them and embrace them. They're what make us alive and strong."

I nodded. "I'll try."

"There's something I want you to have, and I've told all the boys."

"What is it, Granddaddy?" My mind whirled with possibilities. He wanted me to have his rifle with the silver casing, or the pinky ring his mother had given him. I was off by a long shot.

"It's the Sullivan family Bible." The look on my face betrayed me again because Granddaddy chuckled. "Thought I had a treasure for you, huh?"

"Maybe."

He grinned. "It *is* a treasure, Noah. It came all the way over from Ireland with my father. It's been passed down through many generations. It's supposed to be given to the first son of every family, but I want you to have it."

"But why me Granddaddy?"

"Because you need it. Mike is already the strong head of his family. But you're missing part of yourself because of your father. This Bible will show you that no matter what happens with him, you're whole. When you've got family who love you

176

and care about you like our family, Noah, you're a rich man."

"Then I'll take it."

He smiled. "Good. And one day years from now, you'll turn to the words themselves for answers, and when you do, you'll find more treasure there within its pages."

"We'll see," I said.

"Give me a hug, Noah."

I leaned over the bed and gathered up his withered form as best I could. I kissed his cheek weathered with age. "I love you, Granddaddy," I murmured in his ear.

"I love you, too, Noah."

He died the next morning. I cried for two days straight. But when I got to the funeral, I was as stoic as a soldier, even when Alex and my other cousins wailed and boohooed all around me. Of course, I'd been shadowed the whole time. Someone never left my side. We even slept side by side in my bed for the first time since grade school.

That person was Jake.

I questioned him why he would want to give up his Friday and Saturday nights to sit at home with me while we took care of Granddaddy. "Dude, that man," he said, gesturing towards the living room where Granddaddy lay in his hospital bed, "has treated me like I was one of his family since I was five years old. Hell, sometimes he's treated me better than my own father. I love him just as much as I do my PawPaw."

His words had touched me. But it was his actions that were truly heroic. One night, Granddaddy started having seizures, and we had to stay up round the clock to give him medicine under his tongue. Mom and Grammy were worn out by 2:00am, so Jake and I stayed up. Every hour we got up from the couch we shared to give Granddaddy his medicine.

But now Jake was gone, and the pain was overwhelming. It tore through my chest and into my throat. A suffocating pain like a giant's hands were squeezing and constricting my lungs. I was ten and under the surface of the water again, and this time there was no Jake to save me. I was going to drown sitting right there on the bench. I had to get out of there—I could no longer breathe or keep this inside me.

Without a word to anyone, I bolted up from my seat. "Noah?" Maddie asked before I scrambled over her. Even though I wanted to haul ass, I knew I would draw attention to myself if I ran out of the church, so I did my best speed walking down the aisle.

Bursting through the double doors, I sprinted off the steps and started weaving through the cars in the parking lot. At the edge of the property was an old brush arbor where the church had sometimes met. Old wooden benches were laid out under a wooden awning.

I collapsed onto one of them. I clamped my hand over my mouth to stop the sobs, but they wouldn't be contained. They spilled through my fingers and filled the air around me. It was like a dam had collapsed in my mind, and thoughts and emotions coursed through me.

*Suck it up! Be a man!*

*It was instant love.....I love you, Noah.*

*Don't let the emotions out. Keep them buried.*

*Hey man, don't make me duct tape you again. You know, I'm here for you no matter what. We're best buds, remember?*

*No one wants to see the real you. Keep it hidden. They won't love you if they see the real you.*

Suddenly, someone gently touched my shoulder. I jerked away, but the hand found me again. "Noah, I'm sorry. I'm so, so sorry," Maddie whispered into my ear.

Instead of the comfort I should have felt, mortification flooded through me so hard I shuddered. No. No. No! She hadn't seen me like this. This was a fucking nightmare. As much as I hated admitting it to myself, I'd felt a flicker of something for her—something I didn't know what the hell it was, and I hoped she was feeling something too. But how could she now after seeing me a blubbering pansy?

Finally, I dared myself to look up at her. Tears streamed down her cheeks. There was such acceptance and understanding of me along with my pain in her eyes that I didn't want to run away. Instead, I reached out to grab her hips, pulling her to me. Without hesitation, I buried my head in her

179

waist. She cradled my head in her arms, running her fingers through hair.

I didn't run away from my emotions. I let them envelop me. I wept openly and without shame, and for the first time in a long time, I felt safe.

When I finally finished, I wiped my eyes on the back of my hand. Maddie eased down beside me on the bench. "Are you okay?"

"Yeah, I'm sorry about spazzing out like that."

"Oh Noah, you don't have to apologize. You've just lost your best friend. It's totally understandable," Maddie argued.

"It's not just about Jake..."

Her dark brows rose in surprise. "Oh?"

I nodded. "My grandfather was the only dad I've ever known. He passed away two years ago. That was his favorite song you guys were singing," I explained.

Reaching over, Maddie took her hand in mine. "I'm so sorry."

"Thanks," I murmured. Feeling revived, I squeezed her hand. The smile she gave me warmed my heart. We sat in silence for a few minutes before Maddie hopped up. When I glanced up at her, she grinned wickedly at me. "Come on, let's get out of here."

My eyebrows jerked up in surprise. "What?"

"You heard me."

"Yeah, but what about your parents?"

She shrugged. "They'll understand."

With a force that surprised me, she grabbed me by the hand and dragged me off the bench. I led her over to my Jeep, and within a few seconds, we were pealing out of the church parking lot like runaway sinners. "So what exactly did you have in mind for our mad escape?" I asked.

Maddie cut her eyes over at me. "I wanted to do something that would get your mind off things. So what's something you usually do when you're upset?"

"Get drunk."

I expected her to gasp and immediately start praying for me. But she only raised her eyebrows. "Is that right?"

"Yeah."

"Hmm," she murmured. She gazed out the window and then pointed. "Pull in there."

It was Baskin Robbins. I whipped it into a parking space and turned to look at her.

Maddie motioned to the building. "Well, you have your way of coping, but this is what I do when I get upset."

I couldn't help but grin back at her. "Wow, I don't know if I should get involved in hard stuff like ice cream."

"Whatever," she murmured as she hopped out of the Jeep.

I followed her up the walkway to the store and held open the door for her. Sugary sweet aromas filled my nose as we strolled up to the counter.

"So what are you getting?" Maddie asked, as we peered up at the menu.

"Probably a chocolate cone."

Elbowing me playfully, Maddie asked, "Just a cone? Where's your sense of adventure?"

I grinned. "Like I said. I don't want to go all hardcore—I hear it's easy to get addicted. I wanna say outta Ice Cream Rehab if you don't mind!"

Maddie giggled. "I guess you're right. Better stay on the safe side with your itty, bitty cone," she teased.

"Hey now," I countered as the guy cleared his throat to take our orders. I motioned for Maddie to go first. "I'll have a build your own sundae with vanilla, chocolate chip, and strawberry ice cream with hot fudge, wet nuts, sprinkles, and whipped cream."

"Good lord, you're really going to eat that?" I asked.

"Mmmmm, hmmm," she answered.

"I'll be surprised if you don't go into a sugar-induced coma first."

"I just might." She then nudged me. "Wanna try it with me?"

I shot her a skeptical look. "Are you kidding?"

"Nope."

"All right."

"Great!" she exclaimed. "Will you give us two spoons please?"

The cashier nodded. Before Maddie could reach into her purse, I thrust a five into the cashier's hand.

Maddie shook her head maniacally back and forth. "No, Noah, I meant to treat you," she protested.

"No, I don't think so."

"But—"

Maddie continued to argue, but I interrupted her. "It's a treat just being with you," I quipped.

"Whatever," she laughed.

Her laugh, coupled with her expression, sent warmth tingling over me. I don't know what it was about her laugh that got to me. I'd never given former girlfriends' laughter much thought. Of course, no girl seemed as amused or entertained by me as Maddie did.

I took our massive sundae over to a table while Maddie got us napkins. I'd barely gotten my spoon raised when she was already devouring her side.

"Hey now, you gotta pace yourself!" I cried.

She grinned sheepishly. "I know. I'm just hungry that's all."

"Oh, I interrupted your dinner, right?"

"No, you didn't," she said. I could tell she was lying by the way she ducked her head and refused to meet my gaze.

I smiled. "You should have said something. I would've taken you to get something to eat."

"I'm fine." When I started to protest again, she shook her head. "Wednesday's dinner is always potluck at the church. It's nothing exciting, I promise."

"If you're sure...I mean, we can still get dinner."

Maddie gave me a dimpled smile. "We'll see."

We enjoyed the sugary goodness in silence for a few seconds. Then Maddie cleared her throat. "So...I was just thinking about what happened earlier and was wondering if you wanted to talk about your grandfather?" she tentatively asked.

Once again, she was Miss Pushy with the feelings stuff. I guess I couldn't blame her. Her dad was a minister, so she was used to problem solving. Even though she had made me feel better earlier, I wasn't really up for anymore soul searching.

I shook my head. "No, not really."

She gave a quick bob of her head. "Okay, we don't have to."

But I as looked up at her, there was something so accepting in her eyes that I suddenly found myself talking. Seriously, it

184

was like I was purging myself of word vomit. It came spewing out of my mouth, and I couldn't stop. I told her about him taking me fishing, learning how to play guitar, and even about our last conversation. That's when I saw the tears glistening in her dark eyes.

"Those are really beautiful memories, Noah," she said softly.

I shrugged. "Whatever," I mumbled as we finished off the sundae. "So what about you?"

Maddie raised her eyebrows. "What do you mean?"

"What's your story?"

"I don't really have a story."

I snorted exasperatedly. "Sure you do. Everyone has a story."

"I'm kinda boring, I guess," Maddie said.

"I doubt that."

"No, really I am."

"Then tell me what's boring about you," I urged.

Maddie cleared her throat. "Um, well, I'm not like other girls my age, but I'm okay with that."

"So why aren't you like other girls?"

She twisted her napkin nervously in her hands. "Well, I don't party, I don't drink, and I don't believe in having sex until you're in a longstanding, committed relationship or at least engaged."

Ouch, that last answer literally hit me hard below the belt. "You really don't?"

She shook her head. "No, but you do, don't you?"

Her question caught me off guard. "Well, yeah, I mean I have done it if that's what you're asking."

I expected her to blush, but instead, she laughed. "No, that's not what I was asking, but thanks for letting me know."

With a grin, I replied, "Sure."

Maddie cocked her head at me. "Did you at least love them?"

I shifted uncomfortably in my chair. "Not the first girl. But the others, yeah, I guess so. I mean, I was in a relationship with them at the time. I've never been a player like Jake."

Maddie's expression momentarily darkened at the mention of Jake, but she quickly recovered. "I can understand it when you love someone. It's having sex with a stranger or someone you hardly care about that I can't imagine. For *me*," she emphasized. "I just look at sex like a gift."

Instantly an R-rated fantasy flickered through my mind that featured her wrapped in nothing but a giant, red bow. After shimmying it off her creamy, white shoulders, her perfect Double D's would be exposed. I shifted in my seat at the thought of taking them into my hands and my mouth. Then I would bring my fingers to her—

186

"Noah?"

"Huh?"

Her dark brows furrowed. "I asked if you were okay. You were moaning."

Oh fuck. My eyes widened in horror. "Sorry. I was just...um..." Shit, how the hell was I going to get out of this one? "I guess I was just groaning more than anything when I thought about how your beliefs on sex must have seemed to Jake."

"Well, I can't say he agreed with me, but he did respect my beliefs," Maddie replied.

"He did?"

"Yes. He knew we were never going to be friends with benefits or anything like that."

"I'm sure that bummed him out greatly," I said, with a grin.

Color flooded her cheeks a little. "I guess so."

My last statement unsettled both us. Maddie must've been desperate to change the subject because she suddenly started gathering up our trash while I couldn't help but wonder if her reaction had anything to do with Jake's true feelings and the ring. Once again, I couldn't help wondering if Maddie was *her*. That caused a slow burn to radiate through my chest.

Maddie snapped me back to attention when she rose out of her seat. "Come on, let's go get your mom some flowers."

"Okay."

All the florists were closed, so we headed to the Publix across the street. I eyed the colorful bouquets before glancing over at Maddie who was inhaling the roses. Suddenly, I found myself blurting, "Why do chicks dig flowers so much?"

Maddie grinned. "It's not just 'chicks' who dig them. I mean, you send flowers for all kind of reasons."

"Fruity reasons," I said.

"Now that's not true. The winners at the Kentucky Derby get flowers and the Gold Medal winners get roses at the Olympics," she protested.

"I guess you're right."

"Flowers just say things that words sometimes can't say."

A funny feeling rippled through my chest. "Kinda like song lyrics, huh?"

Maddie gave me an odd look. "Yeah, I guess so." She glanced back at the bouquets. "So which one of these says, 'Mom, I'm sorry for being a mega-sized, selfish jerk'?"

"Hey, watch it now," I argued.

She laughed. "Do you want my opinion or not?"

I raised my eyebrows. "Do I have a choice?"

"Probably not."

"Then let me have it."

"I'd go with a dozen red roses with baby's breath—classic,

elegant, and very apologetic."

I eyed the price tag. "Uh, huh, looks like you also go for what straps my wallet the most too!"

Maddie held up her hands. "All right, it's your decision." She gave me one last look over her shoulder before she strolled away.

I sighed and rolled my eyes before I snatched up the bouquet of roses and went to pay.

It was after ten when I dropped Maddie off at her house. "Are you sure your parents won't be mad at you…and me?" I asked.

Maddie shook her head. "I texted them to tell them what was going on. They were worried about you, so they told me to take my time."

"So, you can't be alone in the house with a boy, but you can run away from church and stay out half the night?" I asked.

Maddie cocked her head at me. "My parents knew what I was doing out with you."

*Figures*, I thought. "They trust you that much?"

She nodded. "And why shouldn't they?"

"I dunno."

"I've never given them any reason to distrust me. Like I told you earlier, Noah, I'm not like other girls. I don't sneak out of the house to hook up with random guys, and I don't go to parties where there are drugs or drinking. I respect my parents and their wishes."

I held up my hands in mock surrender. "Okay, okay, I get you. You're a good, church going girl who gets her kicks inhaling ice cream sundaes, not Jello shooters!"

Maddie smiled. "Hmm, once again, I sound totally boring."

I shook my head. "Trust me, Maddie. You're anything but boring."

Her mouth dropped open in surprise. "Really?"

"You're selling yourself short. Trust me, Jake didn't spend time with boring girls, and neither do I."

Maddie blushed. "Thanks, Noah. That means a lot to me."

"Well, you're welcome. And thanks for tonight—I really appreciate you listening to me and helping me through all of this," I said.

She smiled. "You don't need to thank me. I was happy to do it. And I had a good time, too."

I returned her smile. "So did I."

She hopped out of the Jeep. I watched her bounce up the walkway to the front door. She waved at me before heading inside. I then eased out of the driveway and made my way home. My palms were sweaty, and my skin felt clammy when I turned onto my street. I felt like an absolute pussy for having such a physical and emotional reaction.

I clutched the bouquet in my hands as I tentatively stepped through the garage door. The house was quiet except I could hear the television on in the living room. When I got to the doorway, I saw Mom asleep on the couch. A quick glance into the dining room showed the uneaten dishes and empty plates. From the looks of it, she'd canceled on Greg after my bitch fit. That made me feel even worse that she'd deprived herself of having time with the man she loved all because she had an asshole for a son.

I knelt down beside the couch. "Mom," I said softly.

She stirred, but her eyes stayed closed.

"Mom, it's me. Please wake up. I need to…I want to apologize."

Suddenly, her eyes snapped open, and she gazed over at me. There was a guilty look in her eyes that told me she still hated herself for hitting me. It was then replaced by one of relief. She was glad I was home. "Noah," she said, as she as she pulled herself up on the couch.

She started to say something, but then she saw the flowers in my hand. When she caught my gaze, I smiled. "These are for you."

"They're beautiful."

I drew in a deep breath. It was now or never time. "Mom, I was a real jerk to you earlier. I wish I could take back what I said and did, but I can't. I want you to know I didn't mean it, I promise."

Mom refused to look at me. Instead, she kept her eyes on the flowers.

"And I think it's great that you've met a guy as nice as Greg, and I'm sure you're going to be very happy."

Her head jerked up, and she stared incredulously at me. "You do?" Mom questioned.

"Yeah."

She reached out and touched my cheek. "I'm so sorry I hit you, Noah. I shouldn't have done that."

I shook my head. "Yes, you should have. In fact, you should have decked me one. I mean, I said a real shitty thing to you!"

"Language," she half-heartedly admonished as a smile crept on her lips.

"Okay, it was a really crappy thing to say."

"That's better." She reached over and hugged me. In her arms, I felt safe again like I had earlier with Maddie.

"I love you, Noah," Mom whispered in my ear.

"I love you, too."

That night when I got ready to get into bed, my eyes fell on the bookcase across from me. More specifically, they honed in on the Sullivan family Bible. I got out of bed and slowly walked over to the bookcase. I pulled the ancient book off the shelf. As soon as I held it in my hands, the smell of age and dust filled my nostrils. I opened it and started thumbing through the pages. Suddenly, it flipped open to the Book of Genesis with the part about Noah, and an envelope fluttered to the floor.

"What the hell?" I murmured. I quickly bent down and scooped up the envelope. Scrawled across the front was my name, and it was in Granddaddy's handwriting. With trembling fingers, I opened it. The only thing inside was a check for five thousand dollars. On the subject line, it read, "Noah's Treasure".

I stood dumbfounded in the middle of my room for a few minutes, just staring at the check dated two years ago. Then I threw open my bedroom door and ran down the hall to Mom's room. I knocked on the door. "Come in," she called.

Propped up in bed reading, she stared at me in surprise. "Honey, what's wrong? You look like you've seen a ghost."

I strode over to her bedside and thrust the check into her hand. "I—I just found this in the Sullivan Bible."

"Uh, huh," Mom replied.

My mouth hung open. She didn't seem a bit floored. "Um, hello, it's a check for five thousand dollars!"

"Yes, I see that, sweetie."

I raised my eyebrows. "Did you know about this?"

Mom nodded.

I snorted. "Then why didn't you tell me?"

"Because Daddy told me not to. He wanted you find it yourself when you were ready—more precisely when you went searching in the Bible."

"And what if I hadn't?"

Mom smiled. "He knew you would." She handed the check back to me. "And so did I."

I couldn't believe it. "But it's been so long. Won't the check be void?"

"No, Grammy has the money waiting on you."

"Grammy knew about it too?"

"Of course, she did," Mom said. She gave me a pointed look. "Where exactly did you find it?"

"In Genesis with Noah."

The corners of her lips turned up in a pleased smile. "I thought he might put it there—course Romans was his favorite book. Do you know why I named you Noah?"

"Cause it was Granddaddy's middle name?"

"Yes, but I also knew you were going to face a lot of struggles in life—not having a father and being what people would label 'illegitimate'."

"More like bastard, isn't it?" I questioned, with a grin.

194

Mom rolled her eyes. "Whatever. I just wanted to name you after someone who was looked at negatively by the world but who was favored by God."

I shook my head. "Aw, Mom, you're so deep," I mused, trying to avoid the serious look that was creeping in her eyes.

She smiled. "That's right. Be a typical man and change the subject—anything to avoid the touchy feeling stuff, right?"

"Maybe," I admitted.

"Okay, I think I'll let you this once and not push it."

"Good." I leaned over and kissed her on the cheek before heading into the hallway to my room.

When I finally collapsed into bed, my mind was whirling. It'd been a hell of a day, and I was pretty sure there was more to come.

# Chapter Fourteen

The rest of the week flew by. Everything was winding down at school—talk of graduation practice and parties were on everyone's lips. Then on Monday afternoon when I breezed through the garage door, I found our kitchen had been transformed into Wedding Central. I raised my eyebrows as Mom and a dude I'd never seen before were hunched over the kitchen table buried in a mountain of books. Grammy was sitting across from them furiously taking notes. I cut my eyes over to the stove where Greg stood, arms folded over his chest.

I grabbed a bottle of water out of the refrigerator and went over to him. "Dude, what the hell is going on?"

"Your Mom's scaled back her hours for the next few months, and I traded with Dr. Sanchez to have this afternoon off to discuss… the wedding plans."

I leaned over and lowered my voice. "Um, who's that?"

Greg rolled his dark green eyes. "That would be Gerard, the wedding coordinator," he grumbled.

I eyed the guy in the pale pink suit with a fake rose in the

196

lapel. "Wow," I murmured.

Greg nodded. "I totally understand that Maggie has waited her entire life to have the wedding of her dreams, but him," he paused and gave me a look like he wanted to hurl at any minute. "I don't get *him*."

Stifling a laugh, I nodded. "Dude, I feel your pain."

Greg grinned as he held out his fist for me to bump. Normally, I would have thought he was a total douchebag, but I rethought my strategy and decided to give him a chance to try to be my future step-father. I knocked his knuckles with mine and smiled.

Mom glanced up from the pile of papers and magazines to see me. "Noah, come here and let me introduce you to Gerard."

"Okay," I said, reluctantly before shooting Greg a look.

As I walked over to the table, Gerard jerked his head up to take me in. A smile widened across his lips shimmering in pink lip gloss. "Now look at this fine piece of male specimen!" he exclaimed. He turned to my mom. "Maggie, when you told me you had a seventeen-year-old son, you didn't tell me he could've hopped right off the runway at Fashion Week!"

Mom beamed in appreciation of his compliments of me. I, on the other hand, wanted to slap the shit out of him. I didn't like the way he was ogling me—like I was a pretty piece of flesh or something. Ugh.

"Noah, it's a pleasure to meet you. Your mother is one of

197

the most promising clients I've had in years. Why her wedding just might make it into *Atlanta Brides* or another magazine," Gerard drawled.

"Oh, um, wow. Great. Thanks," I muttered since I was totally unsure of what to say.

He gingerly shook my hand, and then he turned back to my mom. "Isn't he going to look absolutely divine in his tux, and when I think about him giving you away—" Gerard flapped his hand in front of his eyes, trying to calm himself. "I just want to weep at the moment!"

Dumbfounded, I stared in surprise at Mom. "You want me to give you away?"

She smiled. "Of course, I do. You will, won't you?"

Wow, I hadn't expected that at all. My heart did a funny flip-flop in my chest. "Yeah, course I will. It's just you hadn't mentioned anything, and I don't know—I guess I thought Uncle Mark might do it since he's your oldest brother."

Mom shook her head. "Nope, it's you all the way, sweetheart."

"Oh, that's just precious!" Gerard gushed.

I glanced over my shoulder at Greg who was doing his best to stifle his laughter behind a dish towel. He removed the towel and held his hands up in self-defense.

"Okay. I'd love to," I said.

"And I'm sure there's probably a hundred girls vying to be your date at the wedding, you yummy little dream," Gerard said.

Then he did the unthinkable. He. Pinched. My. Cheek. He better be damn glad it was the cheek on my face and not my ass, or he would have been picking himself up off the floor. Involuntarily, my fist curled, and I had to fight not to smack him regardless. When I shuddered violently, Greg turned a laugh into a cough. I shot him a death glare to which he winked in response.

Mom tried not to laugh at the expression on my face. Instead, she cocked her head. "So, who are you going to bring?"

I was still contemplating my revenge on Gerard. "Huh?"

"You don't have to bring a date, but I was just thinking you might."

A date? Huh, I hadn't even thought of that. The truth was even though I was more accepting about the wedding, I still wasn't too thrilled to think or talk about it. But I'd probably look like a big loser showing up dateless to my mom's wedding.

"Yeah, I'll find someone."

Mom smiled. "Oh good." Then she bit her lip like she always did when there was something she wanted to say but wasn't sure she should.

"What is it, Mom?" I questioned.

"Well, I was just going to tell you that I've asked Pastor Dan to marry us."

My eyebrows shot up. "You have?"

Gregg nodded as Mom replied, "Yes, we did."

"But you barely know him," I countered.

"That's true, sweetie. But after Pastor Phillips died last year, I really haven't connected with any of the other ministers at our church, and I don't know, there was just something I really liked about him that night at the Nelson's. Plus, he's so good to visit the sick, and he always comes to the hospital to pray over the new babies."

I didn't really know what to say. "Then I think that's a good idea."

A pleased expression came over Mom's face. "Oh good, I'm glad you think so."

Gerard clapped his hands. "So sorry to interrupt this family moment, Maggie, but we've really got to press on with the details. We're on a tight schedule here you know."

"Hey, people who are already pregnant get married all the time!" I exclaimed, jumping to Mom's defense.

Trying to hide a smile, Mom shook her head. "Gerard wasn't talking about my pregnancy, Noah. He's talking about how Greg and I have moved up the wedding because of our schedules," she explained.

"Oh," I murmured. Gerard raised his eyebrows at me. "Sorry," I said.

He smiled. "No problem, sugar."

On that note, I started backing out of the kitchen. "Where are you going?" Mom asked.

"I—uh, I gotta see about my date," I replied.

She nodded, and I gratefully escaped out the door. As I climbed into the Jeep, I couldn't help thinking about how Jake would have reacted to Gerard. At the insane things he might've said or done, laughter started bubbling out of my mouth. As I wiped the amused tears from my eyes, I couldn't help thinking that Jake would be proud for Mom. He would have certainly enjoyed partying at the rehearsal dinner and wedding. He also would have probably made some lameass excuse that he should be made my baby sister's godfather—like any of us would want that. With my spirits raised, I headed over to Maddie's.

When she answered the door, I couldn't help myself, and I broke into a goofy grin. "Hi!"

"Hi Noah," she said. Her expression was strained, and suddenly, I felt like an idiot for just showing up on her doorstep.

"Um, I'm sorry for not calling. Is this not a good time?"

Maddie hesitated. "It's just, um, Josh had a treatment today, and he's not—"

A small voice interrupted her. "Is that Noah?" Josh called.

"Yeah, it's me," I answered.

"Tell him to come in and visit me," he said.

I looked at Maddie, and she nodded. She stepped aside, and I walked into the foyer. In the living room, Josh stretched out on the couch. He was so pale he could've passed for an albino. I hesitated at first, and then I sucked it up and headed over to him.

I eased down on the couch and smiled. "Hey Little Man, how's it going?"

"Not good."

"I'm sorry."

Maddie stood behind the couch. "Hey, how about some ice cream?"

"Yeah," Josh replied, with as much enthusiasm as he could muster.

Maddie smiled. "Okay, I'll go fix you some." She headed into the kitchen leaving Josh and me alone.

"So treatments suck pretty bad, huh?" I asked, trying to make conversation.

Josh widened his eyes. "You're not supposed to say words like that."

"Oops, sorry."

He grinned. "That's okay cause they really do suck!"

I laughed. I reached into my pocket and pulled out a dollar. "How about you taking this money instead of the cuss can?"

"Really?"

"Sure."

"Okay," he said, and he grabbed the dollar out of my hand. "I haven't gotten anything for a treatment in a long time."

"What do you mean?" I asked.

"Mommy and Daddy used to buy me a present for each treatment I had to do. But they can't afford it now."

"Why not?"

"Cause we don't have a lot of money now cause my medicine and stuff costs so much."

"Oh," I murmured. Damn, not only did the Parker's have to deal with the emotional pain of Josh's illness, but they also had to get kicked when they were down with the financial part. It just wasn't fair.

A panicked look entered Josh's eyes. Before I could ask what was wrong, he jerked forward and puked all over me.

I sat in shock as my mind processed what had just happened. Part of me was utterly disgusted and wanted to race out the door and never look back. Then another part felt awful for Josh—especially after the expression of pure horror came over his face at the sight of me drenched in his vomit.

Maddie rushed back into the room. "Oh no!" she cried.

"I-I'm s-sorry, Noah," Josh stammered.

My heart dropped at the sight of tears pooling in his big dark eyes along with his chin trembling.

"Hey, Little Man, don't cry. It's okay."

"N-No, it's n-not," he whimpered.

"Yes, it is. It's totally fixable, okay? I promise."

I stood up, which caused the vomit to slide down my shirt onto my jeans. Maddie rushed over to the couch. She yanked the blanket covering Josh and quickly started patting me down. When her hand dipped below my waist and brushed across my crotch, I gasped. Raising my gaze to the ceiling, I silently willed my dick not to get the wrong idea and spring into action.

Maddie flushed bright red from her cheeks all the way down to her neck while stumbling away from me. "Oh, um, I'm s-sorry."

"It's okay."

She quickly turned her attention away from me and started patting Josh down. Luckily for him, he only had a little on the top of his Scooby Doo pajamas. The rest had managed to hit me and the blanket.

Once Josh was cleaned up, Maddie turned to me. "Why don't I get you something to change into?"

"Okay."

"Come on," she said, motioning for me to follow her. We

left Josh for a moment as we headed down the hall to her parent's bedroom. She flicked on the light in the closet and started rifling through her father's things. Pastor Dan was a big, muscular dude, so the clothes were gonna be a little awkward.

Maddie handed me a shirt. "I'll find you some shorts, too,"

"Thanks," I replied. Without thinking, I tore my puke-stained shirt off. Maddie momentarily stopped searching the racks to stare at me. Not just the way you'd look at somebody who happened to be undressing in front of you, but more like somebody you *wanted* to be undressing. I'd never seen that look in her eyes before, and I had to admit, I totally dug it. A whole reel of fantasy images flickered through my mind of her running her hands over my bare chest or kissing a wet trail down to my…*FUCK! Get a grip, Pervert! Her sick brother just puked on you, and she's just trying to help you, not screw you!*

My sex-fiend thoughts were forgotten as Maddie's face turned beet red when she finally realized she was openly ogling me. "S-Sorry." She thrust a pair of gym shorts at me.

"Thanks."

Because she looked so cute and sexy when she blushed, I brought my hands to the button of my jeans. Her eyes widened, and she flushed all the way down her neck. "I better go check on Josh," she muttered and then quickly breezed past me. Inwardly I groaned as the delicious and dangerously sexy scent of her perfume invaded my nostrils. It was like a jumpstart to

205

my groin each and every time.

She practically sprinted out in the hallway before I could say anything. I smiled as I changed into the shorts. When I got back to the living room, she'd already gotten Josh a change of pajamas and a new blanket was covering him.

"All better?" I asked.

"I think so."

"So where's your mom and dad?" I asked.

A funny look came over Maddie's face. "They, uh, had to take care of some business—um, church business, so I told them I'd watch Josh."

I could tell there was something she wasn't telling me, but I let it go. I noticed Josh was peering up at me. "What is it, Little Man?"

"Will you sing for me like you did at Jake's funeral?"

"What?" I asked in surprise.

"It's just Daddy always sings to me after I have a treatment—you know so I can go to sleep."

I glanced over at Maddie, and she smiled. "Well, I don't know…"

"Please?"

Geez, what could I say? "*No, Little Man, I'm just not feeling it this afternoon?*" Yeah, that would make me an unimaginable asshole.

"Okay, I guess I could. What do you want me to sing?"

"Know any John Lennon?"

I raised my eyebrows. "Course I do—do you?"

Josh gave me a wide grin, showing the gap from one of his newly lost teeth. "Yeah, he's one of my daddy's favorites."

"Is that right?"

"Uh, huh. You know *Beautiful Boy*?"

"Yeah, I know it," I replied. Warmth filled me because it was one of my mom's favorite songs. She loved for me to play it because she said it was exactly how she felt about me. She also had me change all the times John mentioned "daddy" to "mommy".

"Will you play it then? Daddy plays that one for me a lot."

"Okay."

Maddie went to her dad's office and came back with a shiny Gibson Southern Jumbo. "Wow, nice," I mused.

She smiled. "It's Daddy's treasure."

I gently took it from her. "I promise to be very careful." After I eased down in the chair next to the couch, I took the pick out of the top and then stared down at the strings. My body shuddered as I realized the last time I'd held a guitar in my hands was at Jake's funeral. If I closed my eyes, I could almost hear the symphony of weeping and or smell the sickening aroma of all the flowers.

"Noah?" Maddie questioned.

"Uh, I'm sorry…I haven't played in a while," I replied as I started strumming a few opening chords. As I focused on the music, I tried desperately to push away the suffocating pain ricocheting through my chest at the thought of Jake and his funeral.

Instead, I focused on entertaining Josh. With rapt attention, he kept his eyes on me for most of the song. Of course, they started drooping by the end of the first chorus, and by the end of the song, he was asleep. I glanced up at Maddie. A strange look flickered in her eyes before she smiled at me. "Thanks," she whispered.

"No problem," I replied.

She motioned me towards the kitchen where we could talk. "I'm really sorry about your clothes and all. I can wash them for you if you want," she offered.

"Really, it's not a big deal at all, so please don't apologize. Things like that happen when you're sick."

"Yeah, they do."

I shifted on my feet before nervously raking my hand through my hair. "Listen Maddie, I came over here because I wanted to ask you something."

"You did?"

I nodded. "My mom is getting married two weeks from Saturday, and I wanted to know if you'd like to go with me."

Her eyes widened as she gazed skeptically at me. "As your date?"

"Of course."

"Sure, I'd love to," she replied with a smile.

"Great."

"So does this mean you're okay with the wedding and all?"

Leave it to Maddie to always play Dr. Phil. "I'm still not thrilled with the prospect, but I'm learning to deal with it."

"Because you know your mom will be happy?"

"Yeah, something like that."

She nodded. "I know what you mean. My parents have so much going on with Josh and with…" She hesitated like she was going to say something but then thought the better of it. "I just try to think of things I can do to make them happier, but it's hard." She smiled ruefully. "That's why I work so hard to keep my act together—the last thing they need is me worrying them."

I bit my lip before I finally asked her what was on my mind. "Um, Maddie, is there something besides Josh's illness going on?"

Playing with the hem of her t-shirt, she asked, "What do you mean?"

"You're just acting a little funny—like about your parents being gone. I just wondered if everything was okay."

She sighed. "No, it's not okay. It's about my brother."

"Josh?"

"No, my older brother, Will."

My eyebrows rose in surprise. "I didn't know you had another brother. Is he away at college or something?"

Pain flickered on Maddie's face. "No, he's in Charter Peachford for drug addiction."

I swayed a little on my feet. Pastor Dan had a son who was a drug addict? The idea was almost too hard to comprehend. Maddie and Josh were practically Stepford Children. It was hard believing there was a bad seed in the perfect Parker gene pool.

"I'm sorry, Maddie. I didn't know."

"It's okay."

"How long has he been an addict?" I asked.

"On and off for five years. He started experimenting when he was fifteen, and it went from there. He hit the really hard stuff about a year and a half ago. After he lost his scholarship and he dropped out of college, we finally did an intervention, kinda like that show on TV."

I nodded.

"That's when he went into treatment. But he'll stay for a while and then leave. He comes home and tells us he's better, but he's really not. Mom and Dad refuse to let him come around anymore because it's too hard on Josh—both physically and emotionally." Maddie sighed. "It's hard on all of us."

I reached over to tenderly rub her cheek. "I'm so sorry, Maddie."

The moment I touched her, she jumped like she'd been shocked. We stared at each other, barely blinking or breathing. Finally, Maddie murmured, "Thanks."

I wanted to say more, but I didn't know what. "If you ever need to talk, I'm here."

She gave me a weak smile. "That's sweet of you, Noah. I appreciate it."

I nodded, but my heart ached for her at that moment. I wanted so much to help her—to take the worry and burden off her, but I didn't know how. More than anything, I wanted to draw her into my arms—to somehow physically shield her from all the sorrow surrounding her. But I didn't. Instead, I shoved my hands in my pockets to keep from touching her.

"Well, I guess I better go. Tell your mom and dad I said hello, okay?"

"I will. Thanks again for everything." She handed me the bag with my puke clothes that were utterly reeking.

As I headed out to my Jeep, my mind was whirling. Josh's face flashed before my mind, then Maddie's, and then the Parker's. The more I thought about it, the more I wanted to do something for Josh. I wanted to be his personal *Make a Wish*

*Foundation.* I tried thinking of something that would blow him away, and then it hit me.

He was a baseball fanatic, and there was nothing more he would want than to meet his idol. The more my mind raced with emotions, I thought about the cash strapped Parker's, and I wanted to do something for them. In the end, all roads led to Mr. Baseball himself, Joe Preston.

The last time I'd seen my father I was seven. He was on a four-day game stint in Atlanta and staying at a friend's house on Lake Lanier. He'd asked Mom if he could have me come and stay with him. It was the longest I'd ever been with him. Up until that point in my life, he'd drop in for a couple of hours at a time, play with me a little, and then bail.

I remember being absolutely beside myself with excitement as Mom packed up my clothes in my Power Rangers suitcase. Even Jake was pumped about my dad's visit. "Will you get me his autograph?" he'd asked.

But as bouncing off the walls as I was, I didn't notice that Mom wasn't sharing in my excitement. I would never forget the look on her face when my dad came to pick me up in a BMW convertible with a curvy blonde in the front seat. I might've been a kid, but I did appreciate the fact Tiffany wore low cut shirts and short skirts the entire weekend!

It was a whirlwind four days that would've been any kids dream—going to the baseball park every day, staying up late, going to the zoo, the movies, getting to swim in the lake, and riding through the city with the top down.

My dad took me to meet the team, and I even got to hang out in the dugout during batting practice. It was the first time in my life someone said, "Damn, Joe, he's the spitting image of you!" I did look like my father, but it was something no one in my family would ever acknowledge. Poor Mom—it must've been a double edged sword to love someone so much who looked like someone you hated.

I ate my weight in junk food. Unlike Mom, my dad never harped on me to eat vegetables, and I got ice cream at every meal—even if I didn't clean my plate. It was absolute heaven, and I didn't want it to end. When it was time to go, I pitched a fit and cried like a spoiled little brat.

My dad knelt down beside me. "Hey kid, don't cry. We'll do this again real soon, I promise."

I nodded my head, but I was unsure if I really believed him. Mom came to pick me up at the lake house. Dad leaned over and kissed her on the cheek and told her how beautiful she looked. He said something about the two of them getting together the next time he was in town, but Mom didn't reply. Now that I'm older, I realize what the douchebag was alluding to about getting together. Yeah, nothing like a booty call with the mother of your child.

On the way home, I talked ninety miles a minute, filling my

mom in on every detail—well, everything that wouldn't get me in trouble like the ice cream and staying up late. She would smile and nod as I described every moment of the four days. Finally, when I was finished, I looked over at her. Huge, silent tears dripped off her face.

And then something turned over in me. I wasn't mad at Mom for crying at all my excitement. Somehow even at seven, I realized how much he'd hurt her. She wasn't trying to be selfish—she was just a twenty-three year old girl still desperately in love with the prick who'd knocked her up and dumped her.

The more I thought about it, I realized she'd been the one who'd gotten up with me during the night, who'd rocked me for hours when I was sick or cranky, who'd sing to me when I was scared, and kiss the bruises to make them go away. She'd sacrificed everything for me—her friends, her dating life, stretch marks…the whole nine yards.

So I vowed then and there that unless my father wanted both of us, I'd never speak to him again. Mom argued with me over and over again. "Noah, Mommy is okay with you going to see your daddy, I promise. Please don't do this!" she'd beg when I'd refuse his phone calls. She even forced me to talk to him a few times, but Granddaddy told her it wasn't a good idea to do that to me.

Finally, my dad stopped calling me. He would talk to Mom

214

occasionally. So, like I did with everything else, I pushed the pain deep inside. I turned to my Granddaddy and to my uncles, and they became everything I needed—for a while. But I couldn't run anymore. I was almost a man, and I needed to face the skeletons of my past.

When I got home, I found the house dark. I breathed a sigh of relief to find the cheek pincher gone. There was a note on the counter.

*Noah,*

*Greg and I have gone to have dinner at the Country Club and to finalize the menu for the*

*reception. There's some leftover chicken casserole in the fridge if you get hungry.*

*Love ya,*

*Mom*

I was kind of glad I had the house all to myself. I needed absolute quiet and privacy for what I was about to do. Without turning on any lights, I padded down the hallway to the office. On the desk was my mother's black address book. Flipping through the pages, I stopped when I got to the P's.

My heart pounded in my ears, and my fingertips were so sweaty I could barely dial the numbers. When I finished, I shakily brought the receiver to my ear. He answered on the third ring. "Hello?"

For a moment, I couldn't find my voice. I sat paralyzed in

the desk chair, trembling all over like a little girl. *Get it together, dickwad*! I thought to myself.

Finally, I mustered my strength. "Uh, hey, you don't really know me, but this is Noah—your son."

# Chapter Fifteen

I'd barely eased to a stop in the Parker's driveway when Josh came sprinting up to my Jeep. He was outfitted in a baseball cap, and he was wearing my dad's jersey. I couldn't help but laugh at the way he was squirming all over like a puppy.

"Hey, Little Man, ready for the game?"

"Oh yeah!"

Maddie came out onto the porch. "Josh, you better get back here. You know what Mom and Dad said about putting on sunscreen."

Josh rolled his eyes. "All right," he grumbled before starting back for the porch.

Damn, she looked fine as hell in her Sporty Spice game mode attire. Her long dark hair was pulled back in a ponytail. Praise God it was hot as hell outside because she was wearing a rather revealing tank top and short-shorts. I glanced down at my crotch while thinking, *"Down boy, don't even think about it!"*

Maddie started lathering Josh down with SPF 50—first all over his arms and legs, and then finally, she took his cap off and started on his bald head. I couldn't help snickering.

"What?" she demanded.

"Don't you think you're overdoing it a little? He looks like he's wearing a cream colored toupee!"

Josh giggled, but Maddie shot me a death glare. "No, I don't think I'm overdoing it."

"Okay, okay," I said. I winked at Josh, and he tried to stifle his laughter.

Once Maddie had sufficiently slathered two or three coats of sunscreen on Josh, we were ready to go. I helped him get in the back of the Jeep, and then I held the door open for Maddie.

"Thanks," she said.

"You're welcome."

Finally we got on the road. It wasn't long before we were cruising down the interstate towards Turner Field. As the skyscrapers came into view, Josh unbuckled his seatbelt and leaned forward. "We're almost there!" he squealed.

"Josh, put your seatbelt back on. It's not like you've never been to Atlanta," Maddie ordered.

He reluctantly slid back and fastened it again. It was kind of fun having someone so enthusiastic along for the ride. It was certainly easing my nerves a little since today I would be seeing my dad for the first time in ten years.

The call had set a lot of things in motion. It just so happened that my dad had a few upcoming games in Atlanta. When I told him about Josh, he offered to meet me at the stadium, and I'd agreed. He said he would take care of the details like the tickets and all, and then we could see each other after the game. Like a true egomaniac, he'd picked the one he was pitching in of course for us to come to.

As Turner Field came into view, Josh could barely contain himself. "There it is! There it is!" he cried.

"Yeah Little Man, we're almost there," I said.

I exited off the interstate and followed the line of cars to a parking lot. A guy flagged us inside, and I rolled down the window and handed him a ten. By the time I pulled the Jeep into a spot, Josh was already out of his seatbelt and impatiently waiting for Maddie to get out.

"Geez, Josh, calm down!" Maddie cried, as she grabbed her purse.

Her feet barely hit the pavement when Josh leapt out behind her. "Come on," he urged, as he hurried around the side of the Jeep. I grabbed his hand before he started to cross the road.

"Whoa, Little Man. You gotta hang tight and stick with us, okay?"

He reluctantly nodded.

It was a typical scorching Saturday, and I was already

breaking into a sweat by the time we reached the ticket window. "Yeah, I'm Noah Sullivan—Joe Preston has some tickets waiting on me."

The lady gave me a quick once over and then her eyes widened. I guess she saw the resemblance. "Even though I can tell it's you, I need to see your driver's license for verification."

I dug out my wallet and showed her. "Here you go. Enjoy the game!" she exclaimed, as she slid the tickets out to me.

I've gotta say the Sperm Donor really went all out. He scored us tickets in the air conditioned box where the extreme VIPS usually sit. Not only did we have an excellent view of the field, someone even came by to take our drink or food orders. It was tight.

We'd barely eased into our seats when Josh hopped up and pressed his nose against the glass pane. "Look there he is!" he cried.

My dad was striding out of the dug-out towards the pitcher's mound to warm-up. At the mere sight of him, my heart fluttered a little in my chest, and my stomach tightened into knots. Geez, if I was going to have this type of reaction to just seeing him, what was it going to be like when I met him? Would I puke or piss my pants?

The minutes ticked by to game time. Finally, we rose for the National Anthem. The entire time I kept my gaze focused on my dad. I couldn't help it. I scrutinized every motion he made—the way he brought his hand over his heart, the way his lip shuffled back in forth like he was impatient about something. I couldn't help noticing that was one of the little quirks he had that I had inherited too. I guess I was searching his face for all the answers I desperately wanted to know about him—all the unanswered questions that had piled up over the years.

It turned out to be an edge of your seat kinda game. Then in fifth inning, my dad gave up a home run. "Uh-oh," Josh murmured, as the coach came out to the mound. "Think he's done?" he asked me.

"I don't know. He might have a little left in him," I replied.

In the end, he did, and he managed to strike out the rest of the batters. The next inning the Padres caught up, and my dad's sacrifice bunt helped them to take the lead. I don't think I'd ever enjoyed a baseball game so much. The final score was Padres 5 and Braves 4. Josh danced around the box—which got us some strange looks from some of the Braves' fans.

When the game was over, an usher came up to us. "Mr. Preston asked me to bring you down for a tour of the field."

"Wow!" Josh exclaimed, as he shot out of his seat.

Maddie grinned as we followed the usher out of the box. "Wait right here, please," he instructed as we got down to the field.

"Okay," I replied.

Maddie leaned over and whispered in my ear. "How are you holding up?"

I jerked my gaze to meet hers. I didn't know how she was always able to tell exactly how I was feeling. It was freaky, but it was also comforting. "I'm fine," I lied.

"Hang in there. It's going to be fine, you'll see," she reassured me.

We watched as some of the remaining players were being interviewed by news reporters, and a couple of players were giving autographs. Because of our VIP passes, they came over and talked with Josh and signed caps and posters.

But my dad was nowhere to be seen. Then I turned around to see him striding towards us. It was one of those moments when your heart stops, and you have to struggle to breathe. I might've been almost eighteen years old, but there was a part of me that was still that seven-year-old kid inside, desperately wanting a father.

Joe smiled and extended his hand. "Noah, it's great to see you again."

When I shook his hand, I almost laughed when I found it as nervously clammy as mine was.

He glanced over at Maddie and Josh. "And who are your friends?"

"Oh yeah, this is Maddie Parker and her brother, Josh." I ruffled Josh's cap a bit. "I think he might be your biggest fan."

Josh stared open-mouthed at my dad like he was seeing a superhero or something. At my comment, he slowly bobbed his head in agreement.

My dad laughed. "Well, you're awfully small to be my biggest fan!"

Normally Josh would have protested at being called small, but he was too stunned by "greatness" to argue. "I-It's nice m-meetin' you, Mr. Preston," Josh stammered.

"It's nice meeting you as well."

Thrusting out the jersey that had come with the VIP package, Josh asked, "Can I have your autograph?"

"Why, of course. Actually I think I can do much better than that. Why don't you all join me for dinner tonight?"

Josh seemed more surprised than I was. "Really?"

"Of course." He reached in his pocket and brought out his wallet. He thrust a fifty into Josh's hands. "First, why don't you and your sister go check out the souvenir tables? Maybe even get a milkshake. If they give you any trouble, tell them Joe sent you."

Josh beamed. "All right!" he cried.

Maddie glanced up at me through her long dark lashes and then smiled knowingly. "We'll see you later," she said and then she hurried behind Josh who was already bounding away.

My dad watched them go and then he turned back to me

with a sly grin. Always the pimp and player, he mused, "She's very beautiful."

"She's just a friend," I replied.

He acknowledged my comment with a skeptical look before saying, "You know, this might sound a little strange, but she reminds me of your mother."

I'd thought the same thing myself, but I sure as hell wasn't going to admit it. I didn't like the sort of weirdo Oedipus thing it said about me that I was attracted to a girl who reminded me of my mom.

"Maybe," I said.

He motioned for me to have a seat. We sat in silence for a few minutes, watching the crew clean and repair the field. Finally, he sighed. "Noah, I just want you to know that I'm really glad you got in touch with me."

I raised my eyebrows and fought the urge to spat, *"Yeah right!"* Instead, I managed a much more even tempered, "You are?"

"Yes, I am. There's been many times over the years I wanted to see you. Not a day has gone by that I haven't thought about you, wondered how you were doing, and if you still hated me."

My heart did a funny constricting squeeze in my chest at his words. But before I could stop myself, I blurted, "Yeah, well, you coulda fooled me!" When Joe's brows shot up in surprise, I

224

said, "I'm sorry. That didn't exactly come out right." I shoved my hands in my pockets. "And I never hated you."

He looked at me in surprise. "You didn't?"

I shook my head. "No, not really. I was just pissed off at you."

"Because I didn't stick around after you were born?"

"Yeah, and some other stuff." I stared at him a long minute. "Can I ask you some things?"

"Sure."

I drew in a breath. "My mother...did you ever love her?"

A sad expression came across his face. "You want the truth, right?"

"Yeah."

Joe exhaled a ragged breath. "I wish I could say yes, but I didn't."

Ouch, that comment made me feel like I'd taken a karate chop to the groin. "Why?" I croaked.

"Because I was a twenty-one year old asshole who didn't know what love was! Believe me, it's taken me years to finally find it," he replied. He shook his head. "Noah, I want you to know I admit I was a first rate jackass towards your mother. Since you're older, I think you can understand a little bit where I was coming from—" At the death glare I shot him, he gave a weary smile. "Or maybe not."

"No, I think I get what you're saying. It's just simple biology, right? You were just a horny frat boy alone in the middle of nowhere with a beautiful, innocent girl, right? It must've been a hell of a conquest to be her first."

Joe's expression darkened. "Your mother was never a conquest to me, Noah."

"Then what was she?"

Turning away, he refused to meet my intense stare. "There's no denying she was beautiful—she is still the most beautiful woman I've ever been with."

"Guess that's saying a lot," I growled.

He held up his hand. "But it was more than that with Maggie. I knew she loved me—maybe even adored me. I'd seen it building for years—maybe from the first time I'd met her when she was just an awkward fourteen-year-old girl in braces. Then it was like she blossomed in front of me—"

I rolled my eyes. "That's such a fucking cliché!"

Joe didn't flinch at my language or comment. He merely shrugged. "Well, it's the truth, and you said you wanted the truth." He eyed me before he continued. "During her senior year, things started to change between us. She grew bolder and even flirty—I think it even surprised her. And then that summer we were together every day. We'd go for long walks, swim in the lake, but mostly we talked. She was the only person who had ever really listened to me." Joe stared down at his hands

226

and cleared his throat. "And then it happened. I swear I didn't mean for it to happen—"

I interrupted him by snorting.

He glanced at me. "I really didn't, Noah. When I was young, I went out of my way to seduce girls. But it wasn't that way with your mother. When I crossed that line, I threw everything away I had with your Uncle Mark and your grandparents." A disgusted expression came over his face. "But I did it anyway. I was stupid and selfish, and in the end, I was a jerk who only thought with his dick."

We sat in silence for a few minutes. "How is she?" he tentatively asked.

"She's good. She's getting married."

He smiled. "Yeah, I knew that."

"You did?"

"I've had my spies."

Suddenly, anger boiled in my veins. "Why did you have to have someone check-up on us? Why couldn't your sorry ass come and see for yourself? Better yet, why didn't you come for *me*?"

Holy Hell, I was fighting back the hot, angry tears that scorched against my eyelids. Willing myself not to cry, I bit my lip until the metallic taste of blood rushed through my mouth. I'd be damned if I'd let my father see me cry like a pansy ass Mama's Boy.

"Noah, none of what I'm about to tell you is an excuse for my actions, but I want you to understand why I did what I did." He shuddered. "I'll admit that for many years, it didn't bother me that I had no relationship with you. I was immature and immersed in my own good times. It wasn't until my first daughter was born that I realized what I'd lost with you. By then, I figured it was too late. I imagined you would be so angry and bitter for what I'd done to your mother and to you that you wouldn't want to see me—"

"But I was just a kid. You could have forced me to see you, and I would have come around!" I protested.

Joe shook his head wildly back and forth. "I would've never done that to you. You see, my parents divorced when I was five. Your grandfather was an alcoholic, sometimes abusive. I never wanted to go with him on his weekends. I'd cry and cling to my mother, but he'd unwrap me from her and force me into the car. Several times, she tried to stop him by locking me in the house, but he just ended up calling the police." He sighed and stared down at his hands. "Those are memories that still haunt me, and I've spent years and thousands of dollars in therapy trying to overcome them."

"Yeah, well I'm sorry you had a shitty childhood, but I'm not you!" I snapped.

He raised his eyebrows. "Are you so sure?"

"What are you talking about?"

"Do you remember the last time I saw you?"

"Yeah. You kept me for an entire weekend that you were playing in Atlanta."

"Yes, but do you remember what happened after that?"

At the expression on his face, I realized he knew I remembered it all. I exhaled sharply. "Yeah, I do. But I was just a little boy. I could've changed my mind—I did change my mind."

"But what made you change your mind now?"

I knew full well the reason for calling my dad was rifling through memorabilia and slurping on a milkshake.

When I didn't answer, Joe smiled. "It's not just because of Josh that you called me, Noah."

"Really?"

"I knew deep down there would be a time when you'd be curious, and you'd want to see me." He smiled. "And thankfully my prayers got answered."

I widened my eyes. *Jesus!* Both literally and figuratively flashed in my mind. "You pray?"

Joe laughed. "Is that so surprising?"

"No offense, but hell yes it is. I mean, with the life you've led…" I snapped my mouth shut before I could say anything else hurtful.

He arched his brows at me. "I pray precisely because of the

229

life I've led. The 12 Step Program and AA, do those ring a bell?"

"Oh shit, you are...I mean, you were an alcoholic?"

"Yes, I am a recovering alcoholic."

"Wow."

"Does that change your view of me?" he asked.

"No, I mean, I think it's honorable you did something about it."

Joe smiled. "I'm glad to hear you say that. It means a lot."

Over his shoulder, I saw Maddie and Josh starting back across the field to us. I cleared my throat. "Look Joe, there's another purpose to why I'm here today."

"Oh?"

I nodded. "You see, Josh's parents don't make a whole lot of money, and the insurance isn't covering all of his care. His parents are really in debt. I was wondering if you could—or if you might want to give them some money."

Joe stared at me in surprise. "Really?"

"Um, yeah."

Then as if the day hadn't been shocking enough, he suddenly lunged at me. He wrapped his arms tightly around me and rocked me back and forth. "Uh, Joe," I said, my voice constricted from his bear hug. "Could you please knock it off with the hugs? I don't think we're quite to that level yet."

"Sorry," he muttered before he jerked away. Tears shone in his eyes. "Noah, you don't know how proud you've just made me."

"For hitting you up for money?" I questioned.

He laughed. "No, not for hitting me up for money. Because of this," he said, and pointed to my heart.

"I don't understand."

"No, I don't suppose you do. See Noah, for so many years I was the guy everyone wanted me to be. The winner-take-all jock and the womanizer. But I grew tired of that. More importantly, I grew tired of being somebody I really wasn't. I was ready for a change when I met my wife, Melissa. She showed me it was all right to be me."

A strange feeling crashed from my head to my toes like someone had dumped a bucket of ice cold water over my head. "So it's kinda like 'don't hate the player, hate the game', right?"

Joe gave me a confused look. "What?"

"Like you were a product of what society wanted of you for a long time—even though it wasn't who you really were deep down inside." My heartbeat accelerated as I realized everything that Joe was saying was what Jake had been feeling.

"Yeah, I guess that's a pretty good way to sum it up." He smiled at me. "I'm just so glad you're your own person, Noah. I guess I have your mother to thank for that. Maggie was always her own person. She didn't care what society expected her to be. She always lived by her conscience."

The extreme feelings zigzagging through my body were getting to me a little, so I replied. "Uh, okay…Thanks man."

"No, thank you, Noah," he replied. He stood up from his seat just as Maddie and Josh rejoined us. "So what do you say we go find some dinner?"

I shrugged still dealing with my out-of-control emotions. "Okay then."

Joe offered to take us to Ray's on the River, a pretty swanky place, but in the end, we decided on the Hard Rock Café— which was more for Josh than us. While Josh had Joe talking about baseball, Joe also peppered me for questions about my life. I told him about my music, about wanting to be an engineer, and some of the other parts of my life that he had missed. He gave me his rapt attention through it all and beamed with pride at a lot of my accomplishments.

I had to say I was pretty sad to see the check come. All the awkwardness that I imagined seemed to melt away. It made me wonder what the hell all the conflict had been about to start with. But I knew it was more than that. This wasn't a sitcom where everything was wrapped up in a neat, tidy package in half an hour. It was going to take a lot more time to work through the issues of the last seventeen years. But deep down, I still wanted to try. In a weird way, I think Jake would have wanted me to try as well. His "new" side would have totally dug the acceptance and forgiveness between Joe and me. So for myself and for Jake, I thought I would see where it went.

As we started to the car, Maddie and Josh walked ahead of us with Joe and me trailing behind. Breaking the silence, Joe said, "I hope we won't go ten more years before we see each other again, Noah,"

"No, I don't want that," I answered honestly.

"I'd really like to keep getting to know you. Would you object to getting together when I'm in town?"

Shrugging, I replied, "Sure why not."

"I could even fly you out to San Diego. I could show you the sights, introduce you to your step-mother and half-sisters."

Scuffing the pavement with my shoe, I finally bobbed my head. "I'd like that."

Joe smiled. "I'm glad to hear it."

After silently debating whether or not to ask him, I finally blurted, "Speaking of getting together. I'd really love for you to come to my graduation in a few weeks. I mean, if you can..."

"I'll make it work."

We then hugged each other one last time. "So, I'll talk to you soon," I said.

"I'll be looking forward to it."

# Chapter Sixteen

Josh was out cold by the time we got on the interstate. Maddie looked back at him and grinned. "I can't thank you enough for today, Noah. I don't think I've ever seen him so happy or excited."

"I'm glad he had a good time. I want to thank you guys, too."

"Us?"

"Yeah, I wouldn't have had the courage to call my dad if it hadn't been for you guys," I said.

"Then I'm glad we could help. Your dad seems like a really nice guy," Maddie said.

"Yeah, he does."

Maddie was quiet for a minute. Always playing the peacemaking Dr. Phil she asked, "Do you think you can forgive him?"

I took one of my hands off the wheel to rub my eyes. Once again, she was totally in tune with what I was thinking and feeling. I kept wondering myself if I could forgive Joe and move on—if he could actually have a place in my life as a father. "That's a hard one."

"Yeah, forgiveness is a hard," Maddie murmured.

I sighed. "I really want to forgive him. I mean, he is totally changed from the jerk who knocked up my mom and ran off. It would be nice to have him in my life. I guess we can start over."

Maddie smiled encouragingly at me. "It's never too late." As she turned to stare out the windshield, her expression momentarily darkened. "Sometimes it's easy to forgive. It's forgetting that's harder."

I raised my eyebrows. I wanted to know if she might be talking about Jake, so I pressed her for information. "Who have you had to forgive?"

Maddie didn't answer me. She stared ahead into the dark night. "Maddie?" I prompted.

"My brother Will."

"Oh, I see."

"He's hurt us all so much—my parents especially. Sometimes I want to hit him really hard for what he's put them through." She glanced down at her hands folded in her lap. "But in the end, I always forgive him...I just can never forget everything bad."

"I'm sorry."

She turned to me and smiled. "Thank you."

We spent the rest of the drive in silence with only the muted sound of the radio filling the car. When I pulled into her driveway, Maddie's house was still and dark. "Where are your parents?"

"My dad had a wedding tonight. They won't be home until around eleven, I guess."

I hopped out of the Jeep and pulled Josh to me. He snored slightly as I carried him up the front stairs. Maddie held the door open for me. At the thoughts of taking him up the flight of stairs to his bedroom, I groaned.

Maddie must've read my thoughts because she giggled. "Just put him down here on the couch. He sleeps better there than he does in his own bed."

I nodded and eased him down. When I turned around, Maddie was gone. She returned in an instant with Josh's pajamas.

"Can you help me?" she asked.

"Yeah."

I pulled Josh into a sitting position. Maddie lifted his shirt over his head and then eased the pajama top over him. She noticed my hesitation at his shorts, so she unbuttoned them and slid them off. I had to bite my tongue from laughing. He was wearing Scooby Doo underwear.

Once she was finished, Maddie pulled the blanket over him.

237

A noise in the kitchen caused us both to jump. "Wait, I thought you just said your parents weren't going to be home until eleven," I whispered.

"They're not."

I grabbed the poker off the fireplace and started for the kitchen. Maddie was right behind me, her hand rested on my belt loop. When I flicked on the light, a disheveled-looking figure stood with the refrigerator door open.

"Hey Maddie," a slurry voice said.

I glanced over my shoulder at Maddie. Her eyes widened. "You're not supposed to be here!"

"Who is that?" I demanded.

Maddie blushed. "It's Will."

Speak of the devil. I stared in disbelief at the ragged figure before me. Somewhere in his dirty face I saw some semblance of Josh. I couldn't believe he was really standing in front of me.

She shook her head. "You have to leave, Will."

Cocking his head, he challenged, "Now is that any way to treat your big brother?"

"But you know the rules. Until you get clean, you're not allowed to be around me or Josh."

At the mention of Josh, Will's face flooded with concern. "How is he?"

Maddie sighed. "He's better. The doctors think the treatment is going to work."

Will bit down on his lip a minute before he finally replied, "That's good to hear." He then turned his attention to me. "Who's this? Another punk playing you to get a little ass?"

Maddie gasped, and I stepped forward. "Hey don't talk to her that way!"

He raised his eyebrows. "Wow, another chivalrous little douchebag, huh? Just like that last fucker. What was his name? The one who blew himself up." He chuckled harshly. "What an idiot!"

"Don't you fucking say a word about Jake!" I shouted, shoving Will with all my might.

His dark eyes narrowed at me. "Easy, you don't want to get me riled."

Breathing harshly, I countered, "If you say or do anything to Maddie, I'll break your head in."

Will quirked his brows at me before turning to Maddie. "He must really want you bad if he's willing to take up for you." He then gave me a wink. "I wouldn't waste my time, Ace. Her legs are locked together at the knees like a good little girl!"

"You bastard! Don't you dare say anything shitty like that about my Maddie!" My anger momentarily faltered as I realized my slip-up. I'd called Maddie mine. Was she mine?

My thoughts were interrupted by Maddie's cries. Her

sobbing pierced through to my soul. With clenched fists, I stepped forward. "Look, she asked you nicely to leave, and now I'm telling you. Get out!"

"Fuck you!"

Maddie gasped and stepped in front of me. Tears streamed down her cheek, and she was trembling all over. "Please don't do this, Will? Why do you have to be this person? You're breaking Mom and Dad's heart!" she cried.

Will's eyes flashed stormy. "What do you know of anything? I see you. You're just a cardboard cutout—Mom and Dad's beautiful little princess." He snorted. "You make me sick."

As the tears streamed down her cheeks, Maddie's fists clenched at her side. "Get out!" she shrieked.

I took a step towards him. "You heard her. Get out, man. Right now before I call the cops."

Will's dark eyes gleamed. "Why don't you make me?"

Before I knew what was happening, he'd lunged forward at me. I ducked. Then I popped back up, pummeling him once in the chin and then in the ribcage. He moaned and fell over.

"Now get out," I growled.

When I turned to check on Maddie, Will lunged at my legs, knocking me to the floor. On the way down, I busted my lip on the edge of the table. We started kicking and scuffling on the kitchen floor.

The next sound I heard was the unmistakable click of a gun. Will and I both gazed up to see Maddie standing over us with pistol. "Get out, Will," she commanded.

He shook his head before pulling himself to his feet. "Bitch," he mumbled and then he stalked out the back door, slamming it behind him.

Maddie dropped the gun on the table. "Noah, are you all right?"

I wiped the blood off my lip. "I'm fine."

"No you're not, you're bleeding!"

"It's okay, Maddie. I've had busted lips before."

"Wait, I'll get you some ice."

"Frozen peas or vegetables work better."

She nodded and ran to the freezer.

I was finally coming out of my stupor. "Um, since when do you know how to use a gun?"

"Daddy made me and my mom take a gun class when we were living in Memphis. I was just fourteen at the time, but I was one of the best shots around."

I pulled myself into a sitting position. It was certainly turning into an interesting night.

Maddie came back over to me. With shaky hands, she thrust out a bag of black-eyed peas. "Will this do?"

"Maddie?" Josh's drowsy voice questioned from the

doorway.

I exchanged a horrified glance with her before she replied, "Uh yeah?" She quickly stepped in front of Josh so he couldn't see me on the floor.

Grinding his eyes with his fists, he said, "I thought I heard voices and fighting."

With a nervous laugh, she went to his side. "I think you must've been dreaming. You better get upstairs and get into bed. You don't want Mom and Dad to catch you still up."

"Okay," he replied.

I didn't breathe, let alone speak, until I heard the patter of his feet on the ceiling above me. "That was close."

Maddie rubbed her face with her hands. "Yes, it was." Glancing over her shoulder at me, she grimaced. "You need cleaning up."

She hurried over to the sink and then came back with a wet rag. "Here, let me." Tenderly, she wiped the blood off my lip and cleaned the cut.

"I had no idea Will was that bad," I said. At her surprised look, I replied, "I mean, I know you told me he had been in and out of rehab, but I just didn't expect…"

Maddie gave me a tight smile. "For him to be so awful to me?"

"Yeah." I gripped the bag of peas tight. "Even if he is your

242

brother, I could've punched his lights out even more for the things he said to you."

"My Knight in Shining Armor," Maddie murmured.

"I guess."

She shook her head sadly. "I hate you had to see him like that. He used to be such a good guy."

"Yeah, that happens when you get hooked on drugs," I said lamely.

Maddie didn't say anything. I had wanted to wait for a better time to give her the money, but now seemed like the best opportunity. I reached into my wallet and pulled out the check my dad had slipped me at dinner. Once I'd seen the amount, I knew why he'd given it to me then—I couldn't protest loudly in front of the others at the amount. I did a good enough job silently when my eyes bulged from their sockets.

"Maddie, I want you to have something."

"What?" she asked.

"It's some money from my dad—you know for your parents."

I handed her the money. Her eyes widened. "But Noah, this is too much!"

"I know. But he wanted you guys to have it—we wanted you to."

She shook her head wildly. "But it's too much. We could

never accept it."

"Why not?"

"We just couldn't!" she protested.

"But your family needs it."

"I know...."

"Then take it. My dad was happy to do it, and I-I wanted to do something for you guys."

She stared into my eyes. Then she leaned over and gently pecked my lips.

My eyebrows shot up in surprise. "What was that for?"

She blushed. "A kiss to make the bruise go away."

I smiled. "Thanks."

Just as we stared each other in the eyes, contemplating taking things further, her parents came in the back door and found us on the floor. Thankfully, they made it in just after our kiss. I would've hated to miss even that brief instant of Maddie's warm lips on mine, the heat radiating off of her body, and the smell of her perfume invading my senses.

At the sight of the mess in the kitchen from mine and Will's altercation, Pastor Dan and Mrs. Parker both shot us questioning looks. Maddie merely held up hand and said, "Will." We both then alternated from explaining what had happened to her parents. They were both very understanding and very appreciative that I was there. Of course, I was quick to remind them how level-headed, strong, and tough Maddie had been. Her face had flushed a deep maroon, but she had still given me an appreciative smile.

After I said goodbye to the Parkers, I got in my Jeep and headed home. It had been a rollercoaster day—meeting my dad, Will showing up, and Maddie pulling out a gun. I didn't know how I was going to explain my lip to my mom. For some reason, I didn't think it was right to tell her about Will. In the end, she was too interested in hearing about my day than to even ask.

# Chapter Seventeen

Mom's wedding day dawned sunny and clear. I was eternally grateful since she was barely clinging to the last shreds of her sanity. With all the crazy chaos of planning a wedding coupled with pregnancy hormones, she had turned into a weepy Bridezilla. Greg and I both did our best to step lightly around her—afraid that anything we said or did might set her off into Defcon mode or something.

The wedding was set for two o'clock at The First Baptist Church. Then Mom and Greg were going to take a short four-day honeymoon to Bermuda. It was all the time they could spare, especially with the baby arriving in a few months.

I rolled over and squinted at the clock. It was after ten. "Shit," I muttered, as I hopped up out of bed.

It had been a late night with the rehearsal and then the dinner. We hadn't stumbled in the house until after midnight. Plus, I was partially hung-over after sneaking most of the leftover wine at the table.

Mom and several of her friends and sister-in-laws bustled around downstairs. It reminded me of that scene in *My Big Fat*

*Greek Wedding.* Yeah, it wasn't my usual viewing choice, but Mom had forced me to watch.

"Noah!" she called over the chatter. "We're just about to leave for the salon. You need to be at the church by noon for pictures, okay?"

"All right."

"Greg's got your tux at the church."

"Okay, Mom."

The group made a noisy exit.

"Geez."

I fixed myself some cereal and sat alone at the kitchen table like a prisoner on Death Row eating his last meal. After two o'clock, everything was going to change. There would be no more "Mom and Me". Part of her would belong to Greg, and in four months, a part of her would belong to my new sister, which in the long run wasn't all that bad. I mean, I'd have more of a family now, especially since Joe and I were mending fences with our father/son relationship. Losing Jake and spending time with Maddie had started opening up doors I hadn't quite imagined.

Although part of me was still bitter, I was getting along really well with Greg. He wasn't entirely the douchebag I thought he was. Most of the time, it was funny as hell watching him try to decide whether to treat me like a son or a buddy. I think he was even more nervous about me than I was about him. Of course, we wouldn't have too long together. I'd be leaving for college in August, and Mom and Greg would be moving to a new house. They said they wanted a fresh start. I guess I could see their point. But in a lot of ways, it was going to make me feel even more like a stranger when I came home on weekends to an unfamiliar house.

And once again, there would be no escaping to Jake's. Just thinking of him caused the familiar ache to burn its way through my chest. It was hard imagining the summer without him, least of all my entire future.

Damn, why did everything have to change? I mean, once you got used to something, it had to change. People came into your life, and then they left it. It seemed so pointless.

I didn't have much time to piss and moan since time was ticking. I rushed upstairs and caught a quick shower. Then I threw on some old clothes and headed to the church. I found Greg and some of the other groomsmen getting ready. Mom and Greg's wedding party resembled something out of an extras scene for a major movie! There were ten groomsmen and ten bridesmaids.

After we took some preliminary pictures, the guests started arriving. I pulled duty escorting people to their seats. As I was standing in the church foyer with some of the other ushers and groomsmen, Grammy strode up to me. "Don't you look handsome, Noah!"

"Thanks." In truth, I knew Grammy preferred my tuxedoed self far more than my usual scruffy look.

"Oh, your mama wants to see you."

"Okay."

I headed back to the room where Mom was getting ready. I rapped lightly on the door. "Mom?" I questioned, poking my head in. "We're about ready to start."

"I know. Come on in, sweetheart."

She was standing before a huge three sided mirror. When she turned around, I sucked in a harsh breath as a wave of emotions crashed over me. "Wow!"

I'd never seen her so beautiful in all my life. Her dress was this strapless thing with lots of shiny beady stuff on the top part with a smooth, satin bottom, and it had a long train. I knew it was the dress she'd always dreamed of. Her long hair was swept back, and a glittering tiara sat on top of her head.

Mom smiled. "So, do I look okay?"

"You look more than *okay*," I replied, as I walked up to her. I kissed her on the cheek, trying not to smudge her makeup. "You look breathtakingly beautiful."

Tears shone in her eyes. "Thank you, sweetie. From you, that means the world."

"It's the truth. You're gonna knock Greg's socks off." After I said it, I cringed inwardly. I really didn't want to think about anything like that—I'd already seen enough of their sex life.

Mom stared at her reflection. "I feel so bloated."

I shook my head as her barely visible baby bump was carefully concealed under the fabric of her dress. "Quit fishing for compliments," I joked.

She laughed. "All right."

Grammy poked her head in. "Just a few more minutes."

As soon as she left, Mom turned to me. "Noah, I want to talk to you."

"Um, okay, but didn't you hear Grammy?"

"Yes, I did, but I want to say something to you."

"Okay."

Mom drew in a deep breath, and I got the impression I was about to hear something deeply profound. I shifted nervously on my feet, silently praying she wouldn't start crying. Grammy would kill me if Mom came out looking like an alcoholic raccoon with a red nose and her mascara running down her cheeks.

"Noah, I know that things are about to change, and our lives will never be the same. For almost eighteen years it's been just you and me."

"Yeah, it has."

When Mom took my hand in hers, I braced myself. She was about to lay some serious shit on me. "I just want you to know that I've thanked God every day for giving me you. Even though you weren't planned and the situation was hard, I wouldn't trade any of it for a second. You've been the greatest accomplishment of my life."

Holy shit. I stared at her in disbelief. The woman was a doctor for Christ sake, and she was telling me *I* was her 'greatest accomplishment'. It was almost too much. I started to feel like I was under the surface of the water again as my lungs constricted in panic. Frantically, I took a few deep breaths to calm myself.

"Wow...I, uh, don't know what to say," I mumbled.

She smiled. "You don't have to say anything—I just wanted you to know that. I'm sure things are going to get crazy when the baby comes and you are away at college, so I might not have another opportunity."

Grammy rapped on the door. I squeezed Mom's hand and drew in a ragged breath. "Yeah, well, I'm the one who outta be saying the thanks and stuff. You know, thanks that God gave me such an awesome mother."

Tears sparkled in Mom's blue eyes. "Noah, that's so sweet!" she cried.

I groaned. "Stop, you can't cry now! Grammy will kill me!"

She laughed and gently dabbed her eyes. "Okay, okay, I'll turn the waterworks off."

Grammy didn't bother knocking again. Instead, she threw

open the door. With a broad grin and in her twangy drawl, she exclaimed, "It's time, sugah!"

Mom and I both inhaled deeply. When we got to the doorway, I gave her my arm. "Ready?" I asked.

"As I'll ever be," she murmured. But the moment the doors opened and she saw Greg standing before her, Mom's mouth widened into a radiating smile. And as much as I hated to admit it, the look on Greg's face was one of absolute adoration. And that's the only way I would have had it. She'd been through shit, and so had he. Mom told me about how the only girl he'd ever loved had gotten killed just before their wedding. When he started dating Mom, she was the first real relationship he'd had in years.

Walking your mother down the aisle to get married—it's a really surreal feeling. When we reached the altar, I didn't hesitate when Pastor Dan asked who gave Mom in marriage. I very proudly bellowed, "I do."

It was a really nice service, and I guess I should give Gerard his due. Of course, if he had even tried laying one finger on me, I would have gone apeshit on him. Thankfully, he stayed the hell away from me, scurrying around to ensure everything was perfect for Mom.

Then after we took a million pictures in a million different poses, we started for the reception. Greg had rented a limo, and the bridal party rode in it to the country club. A tent lit by thousands of twinkling lights and candles sat on the golf course. Music billowed up the hillside from under the tent flaps, signaling the band was already in full swing when we arrived. Elegant tables set with fine china and crystal filled the tent, and at the far side was a wooden dance floor.

I craned my neck, searching for Maddie. I finally saw her sitting at table with her parents. For a moment, I was rooted to the floor. She seriously took my breath away with how beautiful she looked in her deep blue dress. It was pretty daring for her with its tiny straps, plunging neckline, and rather short hemline. Its sequins caught the candlelight and shimmered. Her dark hair was swept away from her face in a twist with little, curly pieces hanging down. I wanted nothing more than to jerk out the pins holding her hair up so I could run my fingers through the silky strands.

Trying to ignore the lovesick thoughts rolling through my head along with the ones steaming below my waist, I pushed myself forward and made my way over to her. "Hey," I said as I strolled up to the table.

She grinned. "Hi." Her gaze roamed over me, and she bobbed her head. "Wow, you look so nice."

I ran my hand down my tux lapel. "Thanks. I do clean up well, don't I?"

The Parkers and Maddie laughed as Gerard sashayed over to me. "Noah darling, it's time for you to sing."

For their first dance as man and wife, Mom wanted me to perform one of her favorite songs. It was cheesy as hell if you asked me—not me singing, but the song choice itself. It was from the movie *What a Girl Wants*, which my mom adored for some reason. Before Greg, I think she liked the fantasy of a long absent father coming back to his daughter and in turn reigniting the romance with the girl's mother. In the end, Mom loved the song *Long Time Coming,* and she always liked to tease me that I sounded just like Oliver James who sang the song in the movie. I wasn't too surprised when she asked me to sing it because when I really thought about it, the lyrics really did sound a lot like the shit she had been through and now the love she had found.

I nodded. "I'll be right there."

She arched her eyebrows teasingly at me about Gerard. "You better hurry, *Noah darling*."

I rolled my eyes. "Oh give me a break."

She giggled. "I might just have to start calling you that."

Leaning in closer to her, I challenged, "And I just might have to hurt you."

"We'll just see about that," she replied with a wicked grin.

"I'll come back when I'm done, okay?"

Maddie nodded. "Go and wow us."

I headed over to the stage. Behind one of the giant amps was my guitar—a Fender Stratocaster. I pulled it out of the case

254

and strummed a few chords to warm up. I plugged the amp in and then strode to the microphone. Tapping it a couple of times, I interrupted the buzz of conversation and clinking of silverware.

"Good evening. As the son of the bride, I'd like you all to join me in welcoming the happy couple, Greg and Maggie Anderson to the floor for their first dance."

The room erupted in applause. Greg took Mom by the hand and led her to the middle of the floor. As I started the first chords, he drew her into his arms, and she beamed.

It was a surreal experience having an entire band playing with me, especially back-up singers. Once I finished, the crowd demanded an encore, which made me grin so hard my face hurt. So I kept singing. From Granddaddy's instructions, I was able to play rockier versions of classics like Sinatra's *The Way You Look Tonight* along with Etta James's *At Last*. I kept it up while people finished their dinners, and then as Mom and Greg cut the wedding cake. They teasingly fed bites of sugary sweetness to each other before gleefully smashing each other's faces full of icing. As they laughed in each other's arms, I once again felt the familiar tightening in my chest. Focusing on the lyrics I sang, I pushed the unhappy thoughts from my mind. Instead, I was truly grateful that Mom had found love and happiness.

When I finally finished singing, everyone applauded and

whistled again. I grinned. "Thank you. Now I'm going to turn it back over to the real band."

After depositing my guitar, I hopped off the stage and weaved my way through the dancing couples. When I finally made it back over to Maddie's table, it was empty. I whirled around and frantically searched the crowd. My heart stopped with every second I didn't see her.

A hand tapped me on the shoulder. "Looking for me?"

When I spun around, Maddie grinned. I could barely disguise the whooshing breath of relief I exhaled at the sight of her. I licked my lips to wet where my mouth had gone dry. "Yeah, I was. I thought you'd bailed."

Quirking her eyebrows at me, she said, "That'd be pretty sad having your date bail on you at your mother's wedding."

I laughed. "Yeah, it would be pretty pathetic."

Maddie smiled. "Mom and Dad had to go to check on Josh. You'll give me a ride home, right?"

"Of course." I glanced out at the dance floor. "Hey, you wanna dance?"

"Um, I'm not that good at it," Maddie answered.

"That's true. I have seen you attempt it before."

She playfully swatted me on the arm. "Whatever."

"Come on then," I urged, taking her hand in mine.

We edged our way between the couples to find a place

under the sparkling lights. As I pulled her to me, she wrapped her arms around my neck while my arms crisscrossed her waist. Suddenly, conversation seemed to escape me. I couldn't help focusing on the way her ample curves fit so deliciously against me, making my dick twitch in my pants. Her Noa perfume made my head spin as well. To get my thoughts off how much I wanted her, I just blurted one of the first questions that popped into my head.

"So who did you go to prom with?"

Maddie peered up at me in surprise. "I didn't go."

"You didn't? Not even for senior prom?"

She shook her head. "I went to Homecoming with Percy from church."

I grimaced remembering that Percy was the glasses dude that Jake bummed homework from. He had struck gold that a girl as hot as Maddie went with him. "But why didn't you go to prom?" I pressed.

"Nobody asked me," she said, softly.

That was fucking mind-blowing. How someone as beautiful, kind, and cool as she was could be dateless was beyond me. Then thoughts of Jake's feelings for Maddie crept into my mind, and white hot anger coursed through me. Of course, he hadn't asked her. It would have been too embarrassing for him to explain why he was taking a choir girl priss. Instead, he'd gone to Prom with the most beneficial choice for his reputation and his dick—Presley. What an incredible douchebag! Any painful feelings of loss escaped me in that moment, and if Jake hadn't been dead, I would've wanted to kill him myself for being such a prick.

At the flush creeping on Maddie's cheeks, I realized I must've embarrassed her. "Maddie, I can't believe no one asked you. There's too many jerks out there who don't know what an awesome girl you are."

She stared in shock at me for a minute before she finally smiled shyly. "Thanks Noah."

"You're welcome."

We swayed in silence for a few minutes. When I glanced down at her, Maddie was biting her lip like she wanted to say something. Finally, she drew a ragged breath. "There was somebody I really wanted to go with, but he didn't ask me."

"Who?" I questioned, my heartbeat accelerating in my chest.

"No, it's silly."

"Tell me."

Her dark eyes stared into mine. "Jake," she whispered.

My heart shuddered to a stop before restarting. I fought to catch my breath as the voice of reason echoed through my mind. *Tell her, Noah. Tell her about the ring and the song lyrics.* But I couldn't—my mouth felt cemented together.

A nervous laugh escaped Maddie's lips. "Yeah, it's stupid, I know. I mean, we were just good friends and all. Plus, I wouldn't have been too much fun at the after prom parties."

*Dammit, you coward! Tell her!* the voice screamed in my mind. I drew in a ragged breath. There was no turning back now. I had to tell her the truth. "Maddie, there's something I need to tell you—"

"All right all you single ladies, move to the center of the floor. Maggie's gonna throw the bouquet!" the DJ's booming voice echoed over the sound system.

"Come on, Maddie. Let's go try for it!" my cousin, Isabella, shouted, grabbing Maddie by the elbow and dragging her away.

I rolled my eyes up toward the glittering lights. Dammit! Just when I was about to come clean, a freakin' bouquet toss stops me.

With all my mom's family and friends, there were quite a few single ladies itching to grab a symbolic nod towards matrimony. The band leader gave a drum roll as Mom turned around. Then on the count of three, she hoisted the large bouquet over her shoulder.

Total chaos ensued as there was a mad dash. Snatching and grabbing women even knocked two of my cousins to the floor. With them down, the bouquet sailed easily into Maddie's open arms.

Even though we weren't officially together, I couldn't help

259

muttering, "Oh shit!" under my breath.

Alex glanced over at me and laughed. "You're in for it now, cuz!" he joked. Although I hadn't said a word about how I felt about Maddie, I knew he could see right through me. But at the same time there was something else I wasn't telling him and that was about Jake and Maddie. He'd probably think I was a giant tool for not coming clean with her.

My thoughts were interrupted when a chair was brought to the center of the dance floor. Mom sat down as Greg knelt down before her. With a sly grin, he dipped his head halfway under her billowing dress and slipped her garter off with his teeth. All his friends, my uncles, and male cousins hooted and hollered. I, on the other hand, threw up a little in my mouth. Greg took it from his teeth and swung it triumphantly above his head before tossing it into the eager crowd.

Even though I was a single guy, I sure as hell wasn't going to mow out people to win my mother's garter. It was way too creepy. Thankfully, Greg's best man ended up getting it. He twirled it around his finger, winked at Greg, and then drunkenly leered at Maddie. I dragged her away before he could insist on dancing with her as was sometimes customary.

After the bouquet and garter toss, Mom and Greg left to get changed. Once they finished, they would be leaving on their honeymoon. While we waited on their grand exit, Maddie and I ate some cake. As the sugar rush danced over my body, I glanced across the table to find Maddie staring dreamily in the space. "Hey," I murmured.

"Hmm?" she asked.

"Are you okay?"

She nodded. "Oh, I was just thinking how romantic the wedding was and how wonderful it is your mom found such a great guy after being alone for so long."

"Yeah, it was nice."

"I sure hope I don't have to wait until I'm in my thirties to get married. I think twenty-five is a good age, don't you?"

Frankly, I'd never given it much thought. I'd certainly never considered a "perfect" marrying age or anything. "I guess."

Maddie raised her eyebrows. "Don't you want to get married?"

"Sure, I do. I just haven't given much thought to when."

I thought about Jake and the ring. Eighteen was a long shot away from her model twenty-five. I still couldn't fathom in my wildest thoughts the idea of Jake's settling down—least of all at eighteen or nineteen. Maybe he had intended a long engagement. Or maybe it was like Jason had suggested—Jake had just bought the ring with the hopes of bagging her and then bailing. But the more I'd learned about the real Jake, the less I thought his motives behind the ring were insincere.

Thinking of him proposing, I asked, "What if you weren't twenty-five? What if you were younger?"

Maddie shrugged. "As long as I was in love, it wouldn't matter how old I was. Sure, I'd like to finish college and all, but when the right guy comes along, it won't matter if I'm twenty or forty."

*Okay, dipshit, do it. It's the perfect time to tell her.* But once again, I was a selfish bastard and kept my mouth pinched shut. The prime moment once again passed me by. I was then interrupted with Mom and Greg saying their good-byes amidst a flurry of birdseed and bubbles. Mom hugged and kissed me bye. "I'll call and check in on you every day, sweetheart."

I laughed. "Mom, I'm seventeen. You don't have to do that." When she nibbled on her bottom lip, I said, "Don't worry about me. You just go have fun with Greg on your honeymoon." The moment those words left my lips I cringed.

"Okay, I will."

Greg and I gave each other one of those awkward man handshakes. "Have a good time," I said.

"Thanks." Greg patted my back. "And thanks again for coming around about me—it means so much to Maggie, but it means a hell of a lot to me too."

My mouth gaped open in surprise. I hadn't anticipated him saying something like that. "Sure man. I'm glad to," I finally replied.

262

After Greg and Mom left, the reception wound down, and it was time to go. My conscience weighed heavy on me that I hadn't come clean about Jake to Maddie. Even when I was alone with her on the way home, I still didn't tell her. I mean, hell, it should have been a fucking cake walk. I should've been able to turn to her and say, *"Maddie, Jake was in love with you. So much so he wanted to marry you, and here's a ring. Have a nice life."* I don't know what it was that made it impossible.

Maybe it was the sweet smell of her perfume that drove me wild with longing. Or maybe it was the way our hands brushed against each other sometimes when I shifted gears. Or maybe it was how much I enjoyed having her with me—just the two of us like we were meant to be together.

So I just couldn't find the words. And I began to wonder if I ever would.

# Chapter Eighteen

It was Thursday night, and Maddie and I were coming out of the movies. We'd spent every night together that week. Monday night we'd studied for our finals. I'd even been a good boy and gone to church with her on Wednesday night. It was getting serious. Way more serious than I'd ever bargained for. It wasn't about Jake anymore. It was about me truly being in love for the first time in my entire life.

Yeah, I was also a giant ass for scamming on my dead best friend's girl—or at least the girl he had feelings for. I tried defending myself by thinking about how Jake treated her— hiding her away, only acknowledging her as a friend. I tried not to think about the carat of commitment or the song lyrics. If I did, it just made me seem horrible.

I was lost in my thoughts as we walked down the sidewalk. "Earth to Noah!" Maddie said, waving her hand in front of my face.

"Huh?"

She grinned. "Didn't you hear me?"

"I'm sorry. I was thinking about something else."

She cocked her head at me, and her smile widened. "Yeah, I thought so." She stopped walking and motioned towards the coffee shop on the corner.

"Oh, you want to get something to eat?" I asked.

She rolled her eyes. "No silly. Look at the sign."

I stared past her to the window. "Thursday Open Mic Night." I looked back at her. "So?"

"Why don't you give it a try?"

I raised my eyebrows. "You want me to go in there and sing in front of a bunch of strangers without any preparation or my guitar?"

Maddie nodded. "Yeah."

"No, I don't think so," I replied and started walking on.

"Oh come on, Noah. You're too talented not to give it a shot," she called.

What Maddie didn't know is that I'd seen that sign before. I'd probably walked past it tons of times and thought about going in. But in the end, I was too much of a chicken shit to do it. It was one thing to play at Mom's reception when I'd practiced until the callouses on my hands gave testament to how I'd perfected the song. Just like I had no issues playing around my group of friends.

Strangers were another thing all together.

When I turned around, Maddie was smiling at me. "Come on, Noah."

"Fine," I huffed before I stalked back to her. "Don't say I told you so when you're embarrassed to be seen with me after my performance!"

"I seriously doubt that," she said, as she opened the coffee house door for me.

It was dark inside except for the tiny stage, which was bathed in glowing light. Great, I couldn't see the people heckling me, but at least they'd be able to see me.

Maddie jumped on the waitress the minute she came over to take our order. "How do you participate in the Open Mic night?"

The waitress glanced at her watch. "We're only doing a couple more numbers. It turns over to karaoke at ten."

Maddie nodded. "Well, my friend here is really talented, and he'd like to perform."

The waitress sized me up and down. I flashed a toothy grin and said, "What's up?"

She stared at me like I was a moron. "Looks like you're short a guitar," she mused.

"Yeah, I wasn't really expecting to do this tonight."

"All right, you can borrow Jimmy's. You're up in five minutes."

Maddie clapped her hands together. "Thank you so much!"

When the waitress left, I shot Maddie an exasperated look. "Seriously, you don't have to be so excited about me making a fool out of myself."

"I've never seen you act so unsure of yourself before." She shook her head. "Stop beating yourself up. You'll be awesome, and I know it." She then grinned slyly at me. "And deep down inside, you know it too!"

"Whatever," I grumbled.

The performer on stage finished to a round of applause. Jimmy, the manager, took the stage, and I fought my gag reflex. He motioned me forward, and I swallowed hard before rising out of my chair and making the pilgrimage across the stage. I stood at the edge of the stairs waiting on his cue.

"For our next performance, we'd like to welcome," Jimmy paused and put his hand over the Mic. "What's your name again, kid?"

"Noah. Noah Sullivan," I called.

Jimmy nodded. "We'd like to welcome Noah Sullivan to the stage."

The coffeehouse erupted in applause. It looked even more packed from the stage. I clung to Jimmy's guitar as I strode across the stage. I eased down on the stool and tried calming myself. I mean, I don't know what I was being such a pussy about. I'd sung at a funeral in front of hundreds of people. I'd be a total dipshit if I couldn't handle a measly crowd of fifty.

I adjusted the microphone. As I stared out into the crowd, I cleared my throat. "Um, I'd like to do a song by one of my favorite bands, Lifehouse." I caught Maddie's gaze. "I've had a lot going on in my life lately, and it kinda sums it up for me. So here's *Storm.*"

My fingers began strumming the familiar chords. *"How long have been in this storm? So overwhelmed by the ocean's shapeless form,"* I sang clearly. Closing my eyes, I then focused in on the lyrics. I couldn't help thinking how much the song meant to me because of Maddie. She had caught me when I'd fallen and saved me from the epic storm of grief just like the lyrics said. I wasn't drowning in sadness anymore. Instead I was drowning in her—her smile, her beauty, her giving heart and beautiful spirit.

But in the back of my mind was crippling fear. As soon as I told her about Jake, I was going to lose her. The thought alone was almost too hard to bear. I couldn't imagine what it would be like for that to actually happen. I already cared too much, and she wasn't even mine.

When I finished the last chords, I opened my eyes. I'd done it. I'd actually survived an Open Mic night. The clapping started slowly at first and then it exploded all around me. My head jerked up, and I stared in amazement out at the audience—some of them even got to their feet.

Jimmy met me on stage. "Hey man, that was awesome. What would you think about singing here sometimes?"

My heart thudded in my chest. "Really?"

He nodded. "Yeah, you've got some pipes for real, and I've never seen the audience connect with someone like they did with you."

"Yeah, sure," I said. My cheeks were starting to hurt from grinning.

Jimmy pulled the microphone to his lips. "Let's give one more round of applause for Noah Sullivan. Check back with us ladies and gentleman because you're gonna see Noah playing here regularly."

Before I could get back to the table, Maddie met me in the aisle. She practically lunged at me, throwing her arms around my neck and pressing against me. "Oh my gosh, you were so awesome!" she shrieked. As she pulled away, she kissed me on the cheek. "You're my hero!"

I laughed. "Whatever."

"No, you are."

"Because I sang on stage?"

"Yes, and because you faced your fear and did something you'd never do."

I rolled my eyes and grinned. "All right, come on, let's sit down and get something to drink."

"Okay." We ordered two coffees and eased back in the chair to watch the karaoke performances. As the waitress brought our order, a girl and guy were rocking a serious duet. Leaning forward on my elbows, I cocked my head at Maddie. "You know, you're kinda a hypocrite."

Maddie lowered her coffee cup and gazed wide-eyed at me. "What?"

"You pushed me into getting on stage when you know good and well you'd never do it."

"Why do you say that?"

I rolled my eyes. "Because I know you too well, Maddie." I motioned towards the stage where the guy and girl were goofing off. "You're just not the type of girl to do that."

A wounded expression came over Maddie's face as her shoulders drooped a little. I sighed. "Now don't be that way. There's nothing wrong with you."

"You really think I'm not brave or cool enough to do that?"

"Well…" I watched the girl shimming for a moment. "Nope."

She sat there for a minute, staring into her Caramel Macchiato. "So, basically all you see me as is this goody-two shoes virgin, right?"

"No, that's not how I see you," I protested.

Maddie shook her head. "That's all anyone sees! But I have

so much more depth than that—even Jake could see that."

"Yes, I'm sure he could." She pouted into her coffee. "Maddie, I'm sorry. I shouldn't have said that. You're so above caring what people think that you should just ignore me, okay?"

We sat in silence for a few seconds. Then she drew her shoulders back and smacked her hands on the table. "Fine, I'll prove myself to you!"

When she stood up, I choked on my coffee. "Maddie! Come back here!" I hissed.

She gave me one final death glare over her shoulder before flouncing over to the stage. She leaned over and whispered something in the DJ's ear. He nodded and handed her a notebook. She peered at the pages before pointing at one.

The song ended, and the couple bowed and started off the stage. "Well, ladies and gentlemen, we'd like to welcome a lovely lady to the microphone."

I would've imagined Maddie would have worn an expression like she was going to piss herself, but instead, she grabbed the microphone and stared confidently out into the crowd. A couple of guys whistled at her to which she had the balls to wink at. She nodded at the DJ, and he started the song.

An erotic bass thumped out of the speakers, and it took me just a second to realize what the song was.

*Don't Cha* by the Pussycat Dolls.

Maddie met my incredulous gaze and arched one eyebrow at me, showing me she had very deliberately and deviously picked a song to give me what for. Oh shit, this wasn't going to be good.

When the rest of the crowd recognized the song, they roared with pleasure. Next to the stage sat a table full of frat guys who'd stumbled in for coffee to sober up. Fuck, this had train wreck written all over it.

Maddie started off solid in her singing. Her movements were a little wooden—for a millisecond. Then it was like she was channeling her inner-Pussy Cat Doll. But that was nothing.

Slowly and deliberately, she started unbuttoning the shirt she wore over her tank top. I shook my head in disbelief. As she shimmied it off her shoulders, she didn't miss a beat. She eyed me before tossing it off stage. It smacked me in the face, and the frat guys cheered.

I had never seen anything so sexy in my entire life. Talk about lady in the streets and a freak in a bed kinda situation. By the second chorus, she started tiptoeing off the stage. Holy Hell. She was coming for me. When she pointed at me, the crowd roared. As she slid into my lap, I couldn't help but laugh. If she wasn't careful, she was going to ignite a different kind of response from me. I fought to jerk her closer to me and bring my lips to hers. I wanted to thrust my tongue in her mouth while running my fingers through her hair.

Luckily, Maddie began to laugh, and my horny thoughts momentarily passed. When the song ended, Maddie didn't leave my lap. Another eager singer took the microphone from her and hurried to the stage. A sheen of sweat had broken out over Maddie's face and body, and she had a sexy glow radiating off her. It was hard not to lean over and lick a sweaty trail up her neck.

"So what'd you think of that?" she asked breathlessly. Her erratic breathing caused her ample chest to rise and fall, thrusting her boobs closer and closer to my face. At any moment, my dick was gonna call me out, and there would be no hiding it from Maddie.

"I think I need to request prayer for you!" I called over the music. The truth was I needed a prayer request myself.

Maddie grinned. "I was that good, huh?"

I threw my head back and laughed. "Oh yeah, you were very good and very bad, too."

"So, you still think I'm the Pastor's Little Princess?"

"Nope, I think you're more of a very naughty virgin tease."

She cocked her head. "Hmm, maybe I like that."

"Now wait a minute," I began, giving her a look. "you have always worked not to conform to society's ideals—you're your own person, remember?"

"Yes, I remember. And one night singing a little karaoke to prove a point doesn't mean I'm abandoning everything I am,

273

Noah."

"Are you positive? Cause if you're not, I'm going to feel like I had some responsibility in all of this. The last thing I need is to feel like I've corrupted you."

Maddie smiled and leaned forward, sending her tits enticingly close to my mouth. "I'm positive. I'll be back to my boring self tomorrow." She made a sign across her chest. "Scout's Honor!"

I tried not letting my gaze hone in on where she'd touched her chest. We were interrupted by one of the frat boys stumbling over to our table. "Babe, that was seriously awesome. We've got a party coming up on Saturday night. Would you wanna come and you know…perform?"

Maddie flushed the color of her pink tank top. "Um, no thanks," she quickly replied.

"Whatever." He hesitated for a second. "Well, could I get your number?"

"No!" Maddie blurted.

"Okay," the guy replied before slinking back to his table in defeat.

I winked at her. "Charming college guys—my, my aren't we Miss Popular tonight?"

She giggled nervously. "You're never to tell anybody about this, you swear?"

"Oh, I don't know if I can do that. It might be too tempting."

"Noah," she protested, playfully swatting my arm. With my leg almost asleep, I shifted her weight over to my other leg. That caused her to lurch forward, and her lips were inches from mine. We both froze, staring into each other's eyes. When she licked her lips, I groaned. "Maddie…" I murmured as I started inching closer and closer to claim her delicious mouth.

Suddenly, she jerked her head back and scrambled out of my lap. She bolted so fast from the table I barely had time to call her name. I dug my wallet out of my pocket and threw some bills on the table as she scurried out the coffeehouse door.

Wait, what the hell did I do? Her eyes and body language told me she wanted the same thing I did. Just as I reached the door, I skidded to a stop. I knew why she'd bolted. Someone on the stage started singing The Pet Shop Boys version of *You Were Always on My Mind*, and I knew with absolute certainty.

Maddie was once and for all the one.

# Chapter Nineteen

The stifling May heat hit me when I got outside. I scanned the sidewalk for her. "Maddie!" I shouted. I hurried back in the direction of the movie theater where we'd parked. I found her slumped over on the hood of my Jeep. Her body rose and fell harshly with her sobs.

"Maddie," I said. Tentatively, I reached my hand out and touched her shoulder. Before I knew what was happening, she had wrapped her arms around me. "Shh, don't cry," I murmured into her hair. My arms tightened around her, pressing her against me. She felt like absolute and total heaven, and I never wanted to let her go. But in a way, I wanted to hold on as long as I could since things were about to change between us when I told her about the ring.

"It...was...our...song," she replied, in between sobs.

I fought the urge to say, "*Yeah, I kinda knew that.*" But if I did, then I'd reveal what a major ass I was for not telling her about the ring.

"It was?"

"Um hmm," she whimpered.

"Whose song was it?" I questioned, wanting to hear her at least vocalize it.

"Mine and Jake's," she replied in a whisper. I closed my eyes as my emotions rocketed through me, causing me to shudder.

Maddie pulled away from me and wiped her eyes. "Jake sent it to me one day after we'd been working on poets who wrote about Courtly Love. You know, how they couldn't have the person, so they had to tell them how they felt in words, rather than actions."

I fought an exasperated snort. Jesus, Jake was even deeper than I'd ever fathomed. Here I was thinking he'd just heard a jam, liked the song, and decided to charm her by making it theirs. Oh no, he'd searched out a song and related it to literature—an even more surefire way to melt Maddie.

God, what a player!

But then the more I thought about it, it almost seemed like a way of keeping her guessing. He could keep her at arm's length, but at the same time appear as a hopeless romantic. It caused the blood to boil in my head, and if the asshole hadn't been dead, I would've killed him myself for doing that to her. Once again, it was like my best friend was a total stranger to me.

As if she were reading my thoughts, Maddie shook her

head. "Yeah, but what's a song right? It's about being with the person totally and completely, not just being on their mind."

"Yeah, I guess so."

She smiled ruefully at me. "I mean, I don't think he ever really thought of me in that way. Sometimes the way he would talk to me or look at me made me think it, and then sometimes late at night when we'd be talking, he'd say things like how much he cared about me—oh and he did kiss me once."

I felt like I was in a club and the music had screeched to a halt. "He what?"

She nodded as a red flush entered her cheeks. "Yeah, it was right before he left on Spring Break. He came by my house. I told him to be careful and have fun—just not too much fun," Maddie said with a smile. "Then when he got ready to go, he turned back to me and he—he kissed me. I didn't question him about it—he didn't mention it the entire time he was gone until that last day."

"What did he say?" I questioned, softly.

"First, he said he'd bought me something that he wanted to give me. He said he'd had it for a month or so, but the right time hadn't ever come up. Then he said he'd been thinking about our kiss. And that there were things he wanted to tell me. But he got another call and had to go." She looked up at me with tears brimming in her eyes. "And then he was gone."

*Tell her now, you asshat!* I drew in a deep breath, but

278

Maddie brought her hand to my chest. "It's okay, Noah. I don't want to talk about it anymore. I mean, whatever it was that I felt for Jake or what we had together—it's in the past. So, let's talk about something else, okay?"

What could I say? *No, wait a minute, I need to tell you that Jake didn't wanna just kiss you again, but he wanted to marry you.* But I didn't. The words just wouldn't come, so I merely nodded my head and opened the door of the Jeep for her.

I drove home feeling like an absolute tool.

The next week flew by in a whirlwind of graduation activities. We didn't have school—we were officially finished. GPA's and class standings were tallied, and I wasn't too surprised to find that Maddie was going to be the Valedictorian. Mom was thrilled that I'd managed to graduate with honors, but I was thrilled I was graduating period.

We spent the mornings marching in and out of the 'God dome', the mega-church in town where all the county high schools held their graduation ceremonies. We'd nicknamed it 'the God dome' because it was roughly the size of the Georgia Dome. The Senior Advisors, Mrs. Clarke and Mr. Duncan, religiously timed us and made sure everything was going to come under an hour.

When it came down to it, Maddie effortlessly gave her speech. And for one so shy, her voice echoed throughout the

'God dome' flawlessly. Of course, there was one part she did falter on. That was when she mentioned Jake. Several of us had gotten permission to wear black armbands in memory of him. His parents planned on attending, and his mom was going to accept his diploma during a special part of the service.

In the end, the whole ceremony was a blur, and before I knew it, I was tossing up my cap with the rest of my classmates.

I waded through the crowd towards my family. Showing a unified front, my mother and father were sitting together. My family took up about three rows considering both Alex and I and one of my other cousins, Brittany, were graduating.

"Congratulations, Noah!" Mom shouted over the roar of the crowd. She hugged me to her and kissed me on the cheek.

My dad was grinning behind her. "Way to go, son," he said, sounding like the proud—rather than prodigal—father.

"Thanks," I said.

Across the aisle, I saw Josh. He beamed and waved at me. I waved back.

"Ready to go eat?" Mom asked.

"Sure," I replied.

At first, Mom had wanted to rent out a room at the country club to celebrate my graduation and my cousins. But Grammy wouldn't hear of it. She'd been up since four a.m. cooking, and we were all going to pile into her house like we did at

Thanksgiving and Christmas.

We partied long into the afternoon. My uncles had even allowed my dad to come, and I was glad to see him and my Uncle Mark talking like old times over steaming plates of fried chicken, green beans, corn, and okra. It was a surreal feeling seeing him sitting there. He was still working overtime to make things right between us. Although I knew he wanted to desperately, he hadn't pushed me about bringing my step-mother or introducing me to my half-sisters who were seven and five. That was just going to have to wait. I wasn't quite ready to go there yet.

At four, Alex found me through the crowd. "It's about time we left."

I nodded as that familiar feeling of grief-fueled dread entered the pit of my stomach. "Hey Mom, we're going to the cemetery now."

"Okay, sweetie."

Mrs. Nelson had asked for all of Jake's friends to meet at Rolling Gardens around four. She was going to have Jake's cap and gown along with his diploma sealed into the mausoleum, and she wanted his friends to be there for it.

So Alex and I climbed into my Jeep and headed down the road. I couldn't help shaking my head at how it wasn't supposed to be like this. It should've been Alex and me riding along the highway with an inebriated post-graduation Jake. The corners of my lips curved up as I thought about how stoked he would've been to be finished with school. I could almost picture him standing up in the back, hanging precariously out the side of the Jeep and screaming at passing traffic like an idiot. But instead, the backseat was ominously quiet.

FUCK! It shouldn't have to be this way. We should have had the radio blaring, been singing along at the top of our lungs, with our futures burning bright ahead of us. Instead, only Alex and I had futures left. Once again, the burning ache raged its way through my chest, causing me to rub my heart over my shirt. "I think I'd rather be shot than have to go do this," I admitted.

"Yeah man, I know what you mean. I don't know why there has to be so much shit in life you have to do when you don't want to," he mused.

"I guess the closer we get to being adults, the more we'll have to do it," I said.

"Maybe you're right. It sure is a pisser though. I mean, your whole life you want to be older. Old enough to drive, to smoke, to drink, to graduate, and to go to college. Then when you finally make it, you find out it all kinda sucks!"

I laughed. "You got that right."

There were already several cars at the cemetery. I wasn't surprised to see Maddie and Pastor Dan. We'd talked about going, and I knew Pastor Dan was going to say a prayer.

282

Mrs. Nelson smiled as she saw Alex and me walking up. Jason and Jonathan stood behind her, but Mr. Nelson wasn't with her. Figured, that the Asshole wouldn't come. He'd probably thought it was stupid idea.

Once we were all gathered around the vault, Mrs. Nelson cleared her throat. "I just want to thank you guys for taking time out of your parties and celebrations to come be with us. I won't have this opportunity again—I will imagine Jake graduating from college and how his life would have turned out, but it won't be tangible. This diploma and robe are real. I especially want to thank Maddie for all the time she spent tutoring Jake. I don't know if he would have made it without her. I want to thank all of you for being such wonderful friends to Jake. He loved you all, and we love you too." As she began to choke up, she nodded to Pastor Dan.

He smiled sadly and stepped forward. "If you'll all bow your heads please," he said. We obediently lowered our heads and waited for his voice to echo through the cemetery. After he finished, a chorus of "Amen's" rang through the cemetery. Several of the girls including Maddie wiped the tears from their eyes. Jason and Jonathan took the cap and gown along with the diploma and gently eased them in beside Jake's urn. Then a cemetery worker in a blue jumpsuit stepped forward. His nametag read 'Earl'. He wiped his face on a red bandana and then started sealing the vault back up.

We all stood around in reverent silence for a few minutes. Mrs. Nelson nodded and turned to us. "Thank you all again for coming. We love you." She motioned for Jason and Jonathan. They both took one of her arms and led her down the hillside to the car. I exhaled noisily with relief.

"Tough day, huh?" Maddie questioned behind me.

When I whirled around, she once again took my breath away. Her long dark hair cascaded in waves over her shoulders almost to her waist. I had to hold back from reaching over and running my fingers through it. Her dark eyes held a sadness that only I could fully understand. "Yeah, it's been a rollercoaster for sure. You hanging in there?"

She nodded.

I smiled. "By the way, you did a great job on your speech today."

"Thanks. I was afraid I would choke up," Maddie said, with a grin.

"Nah, I knew you'd do great."

We were interrupted by Blaine. "Hey, Noah. Hi, Maddie," he said.

"Hi," we both echoed.

Blaine turned to me. "Listen man, I'm having a bon voyage party tonight. I'd really like to see you there."

I eyed Maddie before I said, "I don't know. I mean, we're

leaving for Rio on Sunday morning. I have a lot to do…"

Blaine snorted. "Yeah, I know, but that's why you really have to come." He glanced over at Maddie. "Duh, where are my manners? You should come, too, Maddie."

She raised her eyebrows in surprise. "Really?"

Blaine grinned. "Yeah, why not? You can make up for lost time." When Maddie gave him a blank look, he said, "You know for all the times Jake invited you to our parties and you never came."

Maddie nodded. "Thanks, Blaine."

"So I'll see you two at my house?" he asked.

"Um, yeah, maybe," I replied.

"Good deal, man." He snaked his arm around Maddie's shoulder, and I stiffened. "Listen pretty lady. Noah doesn't sound too convinced, so I'm trusting you'll work your sweet magic on him and get his boring ass to the party."

Maddie laughed. "Okay, I'll try."

"Awesome! See you guys later!"

When Blaine was out of earshot, I threw a wary glance at Maddie. "You aren't serious about wanting to go, are you?"

"Yeah, I think I am."

I sighed. "Do you even know what goes on at Blaine's parties? It isn't Bible Study and worship music."

Maddie shot me a death glare. "I didn't think it was, Noah."

"I just don't think you'd like it, that's all."

"Well, I think I would," she countered. She stood before me with her arms folded across her chest, a determined look etched on her face.

"But why now after all these years?"

"Because I want to have a little fun, okay? Today is graduation day. Four years of working my tail off to earn the coveted Valedictorian spot. Doesn't that earn me the right to party a little?"

I scratched the back of my neck. "Well, maybe."

Maddie barreled on. "Plus, I'm leaving for a month of missionary work on Sunday, and in case you didn't notice, I'm standing in the cemetery where we just interred Jake's cap and gown. I think I could use some down time."

"We could go for ice cream," I suggested.

She gave me a truly heinous look. "All I'm asking for is one time, Noah. One time to say I actually attended a high school party."

I groaned. "If you seriously want to go, I'll take you."

She grinned. "Good. I'll tell my dad."

"Whoa, whoa, wait a minute! You can't tell your dad you're going to a party at Blaine's. He'll never let you out of his sight."

"Duh, I realize that. I'm going to tell him you're taking me to the movies, and then I'm going to spend the night with Mandy."

My eyes widened in horror. "You're going to *lie* to Pastor Dan about where you're going?"

"Yeah."

"What about that speech you gave me awhile back about them trusting you and all?" I shook my head in disbelief. "I think I've corrupted you or something." Although a large portion of me was doing a fist pump of pride at Maddie's new rebellious behavior, the other part felt horrible that it was because of me that she wanted to do some naughty things. I mean, she'd definitely been making an impact on me for the better, but I shouldn't be leading her astray.

Maddie laughed at my expression. "Noah, I don't think one little white lie isn't going to kill me!"

"It's not just a white lie. What about the other night at karaoke?"

Her eyes widened in horror. "You promised not to ever mention that!"

"I'm not mentioning it…I'm just reminding you," I replied, lamely.

Maddie shook her head. "I don't need reminding." She glanced over to where her father stood. "I'll meet you back here in just a minute, okay?"

With a sickening feeling in the pit of my stomach, I

watched her practically skip away—the virginal good girl off to lie to her holy father. Oh, shit, this couldn't be good.

# Chapter Twenty

The party started just after dark and conveniently after Mr. and Mrs. Johnson left for the airport. When I parked the Jeep, I glanced over at Maddie. "I just want to prepare you for some of the things you're gonna see tonight."

"I'm not a baby, Noah," she snapped.

"Okay, okay," I muttered as I hopped out of the Jeep. She may have been putting on a brave front, but she would see. I'd just wait to see her reaction when a couple started going at it in front of her and naked people were running around. Then she'd be singing a different tune.

We'd barely made it to the bonfire by the pond before Callie, the girl who I dated most of 10<sup>th</sup> grade, thrust two beers in our hands. "It's so good to see you, Noah," she slurred.

"Um, yeah, good seeing you too."

Although she was standing with her latest flame, Callie inched closer to me. "Man, we had some good times together, didn't we?"

I shifted nervously on my feet—scared of what direction

the conversation might be headed in. "Yeah, we did."

Running her finger down my chest, Callie shopped at the waistband of my shorts. "Do you remember that camping trip when we went skinny dipping, and we got all those splinters from screwing on Old Man Bradford's dock?"

Maddie squeaked beside me, and I knew it was time to get the hell out of there. "Yeah, good seeing you," I muttered before taking Maddie's arm and leading her away. Once we put enough distance between Callie and the ghosts of my sexual past, I turned to Maddie. "Sorry about that."

"It's okay," she murmured. She was eying the plastic cup in her hand suspiciously.

"You don't have to drink anything tonight."

She eyed me before downing half the cup. "Refreshing," she replied, her body shuddering as the alcohol hit her stomach.

I rolled my eyes. "Come on," I said. Even in their drunken stupor, kids were shocked to see Maddie at the party. One guy stopped us. "Hey, I know you," he slurred. "You're that smart girl. What the hell are you doing here?"

Before I could say anything, Maddie stepped forward. "I was invited."

The guy raised his eyebrows. "Cool. Wanna another beer?"

"Sure," Maddie replied.

"Awesome!" he said. He glanced at me before giving

Maddie a seductive grin. "If you're not with him, maybe we could go somewhere and talk?"

Maddie shook her head furiously from side to side. "No, no, we're definitely together." At her declaration, my brows shot up in surprise. She smiled sweetly at the drunken asshat before replying, "Thanks for the beer." She quickly pulled me away.

"So we're together huh?" I questioned.

Tilting her head, she replied, "It's the truth, isn't it? I mean, I did come here with you."

I bobbed my head while fighting not to say, *Yeah, but that's not exactly what I hoped your statement meant.*

After she took two long, lingering sips, I sighed. "Uh, don't you think you need to take it a little slow—you know considering you've never had alcohol before?"

"I'll be fine," she snapped, shooting me an exasperated expression.

When I saw Presley cutting through the crowd towards me, I cringed. I'd avoided her at all costs since that night at her house, but it looked like I wasn't going to be able to get away this time.

She smiled hesitantly at me. "Noah, can I talk to you?"

The usual plastic cup was missing from her hand, and there was an unusual sincerity in her voice. I glanced over at Maddie. "Um, I guess so. But only for a minute." As I started into the brush with Presley, I turned back to Maddie. "Stay right here, okay?"

"Fine."

I followed Presley further into the woods. When she deemed we were far enough from prying eyes, she stopped. She glanced up at me through her eyelashes, and I swallowed hard. "Presley, I came out here to talk and nothing else. Do you understand?"

She snorted. "Believe me, I don't want to do anything with you but talk!"

"Fine, then start talking."

Presley bit her lip momentarily before blurting, "I'm pregnant."

The world titled around me before spinning wildly in a crazy mosaic of colors like Willy Wonka on crack. I knew I wasn't panicking because there was a possibility I was the father. It was the realization of who the father most likely was.

"Say what?"

Presley rolled her eyes. "You heard me the first time before you spazzed!"

"Yeah, yeah, I just wanted to hear it again to make sure I wasn't hallucinating or something."

"Fine. I'm pregnant, dickweed. Can you comprehend that now?"

"Loud and clear."

Presley's expression softened. "So…"

"Is it….?"

She nodded.

I'll admit that there was a small part of me that was pretty skeptical. I mean, we're talking about the school mattress here. "Um, are you absolutely sure?"

At my question, I expected her to be outraged and haul off and knock the shit out of me. But she seemed to anticipate it. "Yes, I'm absolutely sure. We were exclusively together the entire month of March, which is when I got pregnant."

I held up my hands in surrender. "Okay, excuse me for sounding like a giant douchebag here, but considering your reputation, do you really expect me to believe without a doubt that Jake is your baby's father?"

Presley narrowed her eyes at me, and I took a step back in case she hauled off and knocked the hell out of me. "I will be happy to do a DNA test for you and any other assholes who want to doubt me, but there's no way in hell that it is anyone else's but Jake's."

"Holy shit," I murmured as I staggered back on my feet. Jake was going to be a father. The thought made me feel lightheaded. "So what do you want to do? I mean, do you wanna have it or have an abortion?"

"No, I want to keep it," she replied.

That was pretty shocking considering Presley wasn't

exactly the maternal type. It was kinda like Paris Hilton, minus the Chihuahua, standing before me telling me she was dropping off the social scene to raise a kid.

"Are you sure?" I asked.

"Yes, I'm positive."

"Wow…" I murmured.

"Noah, I might have had a funny way of showing it, but I did love Jake. He's the only guy I've truly loved with my heart—not just my body." She slowly rested her right hand on her stomach and smiled. "Don't you see how amazing this is? I've got a little piece of immortality growing within me—a part of Jake will live on through this baby."

My jaw dropped open, and I stared at her in disbelief. Seriously, had the world gone freaking crazy? The ultimate good girl, Maddie, had just begged me to come to a keg party and was now slightly inebriated. The ultimate man-whore and horse's ass, Jake, had actually had a soft side. Now the reigning school slut had turned into a motherhood worshipper like Angelina Jolie.

And me? I didn't even want to begin on the wacked out rollercoaster of realizations I'd been through. Hell, I'd even become a hopeless romantic in love with "love" and the good girl. Jesus, it was too much.

"Have you told Jake's parents yet?" I asked.

She shook her head. "No, I wanted to wait until I was out of the first trimester. You know, in case something happened. I didn't think they could bear losing Jake and his baby too."

"That was thoughtful of you," I mused.

"Besides I thought Jake might have told them first." As soon as the words left her lips, she widened her eyes like she'd revealed a great secret.

"Wait, are you telling me that Jake knew about the baby?"

Presley slowly nodded her head.

The world became tripped out Willy Wonka again. I steadied myself by leaning against a tree trunk. "Are you shitting me?"

"No."

"When? When did you tell him?"

Presley refused to meet my intense glare. "The day before the accident," she said in a whisper.

"You're kidding me, right? You've known for five weeks that you're carrying Jake's kid, and you didn't tell anybody? What the fuck, Presley!"

She continued staring at the intricate floral design on her toenails.

"Didn't you think that was something I needed to know?" I demanded.

"You wouldn't understand."

"Try me."

She jerked her head up to glare at me. "I was afraid if I told people Jake knew I was pregnant, they'd think that—you know he killed himself or something instead of it being an accident."

Oh geez, I felt like an ass. "But Presley, people wouldn't have thought that," I protested.

"Get serious, Noah. Of course they would have. A guy like Jake finds out he's gonna be a father, and then he mysteriously blows up on a tractor? Wouldn't you have thought that?"

I shook my head. "No, I wouldn't."

"Yeah right."

"I'm serious. Jake was never the kind of guy to kill himself—no matter what kinda shit had gone down in his life."

Presley seemed to appreciate my answer. "Whatever," she mumbled.

I took a tentative step towards her. "Um, what did he say? You know…about the baby."

"He was pretty shocked. I told him I was sorry I had to tell him over the phone, but I'd just gotten back from the doctor, and I was scared. He was really cool and calmed me down. He asked me what I wanted to do, and I told him I wanted to have it. I also told him I didn't expect anything out of him—least of all marriage. He said we'd just have to see how it went, but that no matter what he would support our baby."

"Oh," I said.

"And—" she began as tears welled in her eyes. "And he told me he really cared about me, and that he always had."

"That's pretty wild."

She smiled. "Yeah it was." She reached out and touched my arm. "Noah, I'd really appreciate it if you wouldn't tell anybody about Jake knowing."

At the pleading look in her eyes, I realized it would only cause more trouble and heartache if people knew the truth. I didn't want to do that to Presley in her condition, and I didn't want to do it to Jake either.

"Yeah, I promise."

"Thanks," she said, and kissed me on the cheek.

"So how are you going to play this off?"

She drew in a deep breath. "Well, everybody saw us together the day of the Pre Break Binge—I thought I'd just let them assume it happened then."

"I guess that makes sense," I said. "So are you like what two months or something?"

"Ten weeks actually."

Suddenly, it hit me like a searing bolt of lightning. "Whoa, wait a minute! You knew you were pregnant when—when you....when we...." I couldn't even finish the sentence. *Oh Holy Hell!* Not only was I crushing on my dead best bud's girl, but now I'd been in a partial hookup with the chick who carried his child. Seriously, I felt like I was on a warped version of the *Young and the Restless* or some lameass reality show.

For once, Presley actually blushed. She shifted on her feet. "Yes," she said.

"Dammit, how could you!" I shouted. Like a raving maniac, I ran my fingers through my hair and then turned on her. "Don't you know how sick and twisted that is for me? I defiled the girl having my dead best friend's baby!"

Presley rolled her eyes. "You didn't defile me, Noah. It was just a make-out session," she protested.

"Oh, no, don't cop out on me. You had your hand on my-my..."

I couldn't even finish my sentence. I glanced up at the sky. Oh yeah, I was going to hell for this one. I frantically thought about maybe going by Pastor Dan's house and confessing my sins or something. Of course, I'd never be able to see Maddie after that. They'd probably ship her off to a convent or something—anything to get her out of my sinful presence.

"Look Noah, I'm sorry. I really, really am. Yes, I came in the room that night with the intentions of doing stuff to get information out of you."

"But why not just ask me directly in the first place instead of talking to *this*," I said, as I touched my crotch.

Presley rolled her eyes. "Would you calm down?"

"I'm sorry. I'm not the manwhore, remember?"

"Look, I just needed to know whether Jake had told you about the baby or if he'd told his parents. I had to do it in a way that you wouldn't suspect, and for me, that was making out with you." She cocked her eyebrows at me. "It wasn't like we hadn't before."

I wagged my finger at her. "That was 9th grade for Christ sake, and I barely touched your boobs then!"

"I'm sorry, Noah, but I was desperate."

I heaved a defeated breath. "Okay, whatever."

"You can't imagine how surprised I was when out of nowhere you said something about a ring, and then I knew he hadn't said anything. In the end, Jake would understand."

In a really warped way, I knew she was right. I started to open my mouth to protest when I heard cheering and yelling through the trees.

"TAKE IT OFF!"

"Yeah, Maddie's got game!" someone else replied.

Oh shit, I'd forgotten all about Maddie. "Presley, I've gotta go," I said, before I turned on my heels.

I started sprinting back through the woods. When I broke through the clearing, I skidded to a stop. Everyone was stripped down to their underwear and was swimming in the pond. I scanned the half-naked bodies for Maddie. My heart skipped a beat when I saw her.

Casey McKenzie had her pressed to him, and his hand was inches from the curve of her ass.

I didn't bother taking off my shirt or short. I ran full force into the water, knocking people out of the way. When I reached them, I pulled Casey off Maddie. He threw me a pissed look. Man-handling wasn't on my top ten list of favorite things to do, but I grabbed Maddie by the arm and began dragging her out of the pond.

"Way to be a cock blocker, Sullivan. We were just trying to have some fun!" Casey called.

"Yeah, it'll be real fun when I punch the shit out of you," I mumbled.

I pulled Maddie into a thicket of trees away from the others. She stood before me in the moonlight in a pretty daring white thong and a thin, white camisole that clung to her frame like a second skin and left very little to the imagination of what was beneath. Before I could stop myself, the horny male in me did a perverted rove over her body.

It took only a nanosecond for that traitorous part to rear his head. I shifted on my feet. *Quit being a perv, asswipe and think of something else!!!* Then the most horrific images flashed in my mind. Presley and me together in her room, my mom and Greg hitting it on the couch, and finally, a furious looking Pastor Dan punching me in the face for thinking about his daughter in that way. The last one was the one that did the trick.

I cleared my throat. "What the hell are you doing?" I demanded.

She cocked her eyebrows at me. As she brought one of her hands to her hip, she swayed back and forth. "What does it look like I'm doing?" she slurred.

"*Well,* it looks like you're half naked and drunk off your ass!"

"Maybe I am. What's it to you?" Maddie questioned.

"Jesus Christ, I leave you for less than thirty minutes and you're drunk?"

I knew in her defense she was a lightweight who had never tasted alcohol before. Hell, it probably only took one to get her in the condition she was in.

"I was just trying to have a little fun," she protested.

"Yeah and so was Casey," I countered.

At the thoughts of Casey feeling her up, the blood rushed to my head, which thankfully caused the other part of me to fully simmer down.

Maddie's lips curled into a smile. "Noah, will you do something for me?"

Oh, shit. I didn't like the sinfully sing-song tone of her voice. "What?" I croaked.

"Would you stop acting like a gentleman for five minutes

and kiss me?"

I swear to God her lips were already pursed, and she was purring. No lie, she was freakin' purring like a cat in heat. Before I could protest, she wrapped her arms around me. Her full breasts pressed into my chest, and I groaned. She stared up into my eyes, and I couldn't help myself. I brought my lips to hers. They were everything I'd imagined they'd be. Warm. Soft. Inviting. Sexy.

One seemingly innocent kiss sent my hormones up and raging again. Almost on autopilot, I thrust my tongue into her mouth to dance against hers. My arms snaked around her waist, jerking her flush against me. I groaned against her lips as I thrust my hard-on against her. Instead of pulling away, Maddie rocked her hips back into mine. Holy hell! How was this chick a virgin? She was so fucking responsive to everything I did.

Maddie released my lips and dipped her head, kissing along my neck. When she ran her hands teasingly down my chest, I moaned. She glanced up at me through hooded eyes. "I've wanted to touch you here for so long." Raising my shirt up, her warm palms rubbed against my chest, and she giggled. "That day when Josh puked on you, and you had to take your shirt off—I wanted to touch you so bad."

I laughed. "I think I got that impression from the way you were ogling me."

"Noah," she whispered, her breath was like fire scorching

against my neck. "Will you be my first?"

*Motherfuckingshitdamnhell!* My eyes snapped open as the world around me screeched to a halt. I shrugged away from her. "Maddie, you're drunk. You don't know what you're saying," I protested.

She slowly shook her head at me. "No, I know what I'm saying, and I know what I want."

"Well, *I* know you, and I know the sober you would never be standing here in your underwear propositioning me to sleep with you."

Her face fell. "Don't you want to sleep me? I mean, don't you find me...sexy?"

At her words, my lower half caught on fire, causing me to shift on my feet. I cursed under my breath. "Oh come on Maddie. Don't ask me things like that."

She pressed herself closer against me. "Please Noah," she begged.

So let me recap here. I was out in the middle of Eastbumblefuck. The girl I thought I was in love with was standing before me, soaked to the bone, in nothing but a *white* camisole and her underwear. Oh, and she was begging me to sleep with her. What do you think I did?

Like some testosterone raging Incredible Hulk, the horny asshole in me broke free, and I seized the moment. I crushed my mouth against hers. Her lips opened momentarily, and I took the opportunity to plunge my tongue in her mouth, thrusting hard and fast against her.

Panting, we rammed against the trunk of an oak tree. Then I became an eight armed octopus, raking my hands over her body. I cupped her breasts, teasing her nipples to hardened points. "Noah," Maddie moaned.

All the while, I moved my hips against her, mimicking what I wanted to do once we weren't clothed. I slid my palm along her thigh and then between her legs. When I began stroking her gently, she cried out and rocked against my hand.

But as I dared myself to slide one finger in her heat, an overwhelming feeling of disgust and regret washed over me. That was all it took for the Horny Hulk to deflate. I jerked away from her. I tried catching my breath while I raked my hand through my hair. "I can't," I murmured.

Tears sprung in her eyes. "Why?"

"Because I care about you too much to do this. You'd hate yourself in the morning, and you'd hate me even more. It's your gift, remember? It's yours to give, and I'm not your husband to take it."

"It's me, isn't it?"

I rolled my eyes. "Jesus, are you even listening to me? More than that, are you incapable of *feeling* how much I wanted you?" I gestured wildly towards my crotch. "Damn, I'll probably either have to go take a dip in the pond or take a cold

304

shower tonight because of you."

My little pep talk didn't help. She started sobbing. "I just want someone to love me."

*Man, you're so fucking blind. Jake loved you...hell, I love you.* I tentatively put my hand on her shoulder. "You have lots of people who love you, Maddie."

She shook her head. "Not like that. I mean a guy—a guy like you who wants me as more than a friend. I'm almost eighteen years old, and I've never had that!"

There had been so many times that I should've told her about the ring, and here was another example. Most of all, I needed to tell her how I truly felt about her. I opened my mouth to say something, and then it happened. She turned around and puked all over a bush. I grabbed up her hair as she heaved over and over again. She wiped her hand on the back of her mouth.

When she finally glanced up at me, there was such hurt in her eyes. I stepped forward just in time for her to tip forward and pass out. I stared up at the sky and rolled my eyes. "Fuck my life!" I grumbled as I gathered her up in my arms and started towards the Jeep.

# Chapter Twenty-One

Holding Maddie, I couldn't unlock the door, so I had to ring the doorbell. Thankfully Mom, rather than Greg, answered the door. At the sight of me carrying an unconscious Maddie in my arms like some hunk off the cover of a trashy romance novel, her eyes widened. "What in the world?" she demanded.

"She got drunk at Blaine's party and passed out," I grunted as I stepped through the foyer.

Mom slapped my arm. "Noah! How could you let her get drunk?"

I rolled my eyes. "Jesus Mom, I didn't force her to drink it."

"Don't say, 'Jesus'," she admonished.

"Whatever."

"Well, you should've been watching her better."

"Presley needed to talk to me," I replied.

Mom arched a dark eyebrow skeptically at me.

"*Yes*, she really needed to talk to me," I said.

Mom sighed. "Get her settled on the couch and then you

and I are going to have a long talk about this party," she ordered, in a no-nonsense tone.

I didn't argue. Instead, I gently laid Maddie down on the couch. I pulled the mauve throw off the back and draped it over her before rubbing her cheek tenderly. When I turned around, Mom's expression had completely changed. Instead of being in a pissed Rambo mode, she was gaping at me.

"What?" I asked.

"You love her," she murmured.

My eyes bulged. "No, I, uh…shit!"

Mom smiled knowingly at me. "Yes, you do. I can't believe I didn't see it until just now."

Maddie stirred on the couch, and I stiffened. "Can we please discuss this somewhere else?"

Mom nodded and motioned for the sun room. I followed her out there and shut the door behind me.

"There's nothing wrong with you loving her, honey," Mom said, softly.

"I know that."

"Then why are you fighting it so much?"

Grimacing, I jerked a hand through my hair. "Because….of Jake."

Mom's brows furrowed in confusion. "What does Jake have to do with Maddie?"

"Everything," I muttered before I plopped down in a wicker chair across from Mom. "You know that night that Mr. Nelson and I were in Jake's room?"

She nodded.

"Well, we found something that was pretty shocking." From the look on her face, I could tell my mom was preparing herself for anything considering it was Jake. "It was an engagement ring."

Well, maybe she hadn't prepared herself for that. "What?" she questioned in a high, pitched shriek.

I nodded. "Yeah. He had the box wrapped up in the song lyrics to *You Were Always on My Mind*".

"But who in the world was Jake in love with?"

I drew in a painful, ragged breath. "Maddie."

Mom widened her eyes. "You can't be serious! Jake Nelson, who was never faithful to a girl for over five minutes, was in love with a preacher's daughter?"

"Yes."

"How?"

I rolled my eyes. "I don't know *how*. Why do any two people fall in love? It just happens."

"You're right, sweetie. That was a silly question." Mom cocked her head in thought. "And I suppose Jake did have his good points."

"And he changed," I admitted.

"He did?"

"Yeah, in the last few months of his life. Then he'd also told me he'd fallen in love, but he wouldn't tell me who because he hadn't told the girl yet. I just never imagined it was Maddie."

She leaned forward and took my hand in hers. "But did Maddie love Jake?"

Even though I knew the answer, I didn't want the words to leave my lips. "Yes, she did," I murmured.

"And does Maddie love you?"

My gaze snapped to meet Mom's. "What?"

Mom smiled. "You heard me."

I got up from the chair and started pacing around. "I don't know if she does or not. I mean, I know she loved Jake—she probably still does. Jesus, what kind a friend am I to hit on my dead best friend's girl?"

"But she wasn't his girl, Noah," Mom protested.

"Yeah, she was. He may not have openly acknowledged it as well as he should, but he loved her. I thought he was incapable of loving anyone but himself, but I was wrong."

"Have you talked to Maddie about any of this?"

"No."

"You haven't told her about the ring?"

I couldn't help squirming under Mom's intense glare. "No."

"Why not?"

"Because I was waiting. I wanted to be sure it was her before I said anything."

Mom raised her eyebrows. "Waiting for what? For Maddie to realize she liked you instead of Jake?"

I stared her before blinking a few times in disbelief. How in the hell could she see through me so well? "Maybe," I muttered.

Crossing her arms over her chest, Mom said, "I'm guessing you've known the ring belonged to Maddie for a long time, but you didn't want to tell her."

"Yeah," I muttered.

"But why?"

"Cause I'm a selfish prick!" I exclaimed rising out of my chair.

Mom didn't bother chastising my language. She knew I was too upset. "Honey, you have to tell her about Jake. But most of all, you have to tell her how you feel about her."

I raised my eyebrows. "And just what am I supposed to say? 'Oh by the way, Maddie, deep down, Jake was in love with you. How do I know? Oh, because he bought you a fat diamond engagement ring. But I guess it's a good thing he's dead because guess what? I'm in love with you'!"

Mom gave me an exasperated look. "No, I think you can do it better than that."

I sunk back down in the chair. "I've never...felt this way about anybody like I do Maddie. I'm...afraid."

"Of being shot down?"

"Of losing her," I murmured.

Mom sat down beside me. Her eyes welled with tears. "Oh sweetie, I've always wanted you to be in love with someone. I was so afraid I'd caused you to be jaded and bitter towards love. I'm so happy you've found it. But more than anything in the world, I don't want you to get hurt."

"Thanks, Mom," I said. Then I shook my head. "But you're right. I have to tell Maddie the truth. It isn't fair keeping all this from her. She deserves better than that." I glanced back at the living room. "As soon as she wakes up, I'll tell her."

Mom smiled. "Good. You'll feel better when you do." We stood up to start inside, but Mom doubled over. "Ouch!"

"Are you okay?"

She nodded. "Yeah, your little sister gets temperamental this time of night. She must be hungry."

I stared at her belly. "Want to feel her?" Mom questioned.

*Not just no, but HELL NO!* screeched in my mind, but I bit my tongue. "Um, uh..." I finally muttered.

Mom laughed. "Only if you want to, Noah. I'm not going to

make you do it."

I forced a smile to my lips as I prepared to conquer the unknown. "Sorry. It's just kinda weird thinking about it, but yeah, why not. I'll do it."

She took my hand in hers and placed in on a particular spot. I felt a tiny bump, bump under the surface. I glanced up at Mom. "She's pretty strong."

"Yes, she is."

"By those kicks, I guess she's going to be the one to inherit the Sullivan sports gene that I obviously missed out on," I mused.

"You didn't miss out on the sports gene. You simply chose not to do it."

"Huh?"

"Don't you remember playing T-Ball?"

"Yeah. I sucked."

Mom shook her head. "No, you didn't. You were one of the best players on the team."

"I was?"

"Yes, you were."

"Then why did I quit?"

"I don't know. Maybe you were afraid of not measuring up to your father, or maybe you were afraid of hurting me. Who knows. Sometimes we just have two sides to us, Noah. One

312

that we're willing to let the world see, and then the other that we hide deep within ourselves."

Mom's words cut me to my soul. Maybe Jake and I weren't so different. He had hid a side of himself from everyone—except for Maddie and Pastor Dan. So why would it be so crazy to think I'd done the same thing with the part of me that was like my dad?

Mom smiled. "As for your sister, she's not hiding her ability to be an accomplished dancer—I'm getting a tap dancer vibe."

"Maybe."

"Do you know I can remember the first time I felt you kick?"

I raised my eyebrows. "You do?"

Mom nodded. "It was right after your father told me he didn't love me, and he wasn't going to marry me."

"Seriously?"

"He'd strung me along for a few months after I told him I was pregnant. Then he finally leveled with me. I was crying so hard and all the sudden I felt you." Tears welled in Mom's eyes, and she smiled. "It was like you were telling me in your own little way that you'd always be here for me—no matter what happened."

Wow, I was kinda overwhelmed. "Mom…"

She waved me away with her hand. "I'm sorry, sweetie. I'm on hormone overload right now."

"Well, that's true, but I wanted to say—" I drew in a deep breath. "I wanted to say thanks."

Mom's eyebrows furrowed together. "For what?"

"You know—for having me and for always loving me, no matter what."

My declaration sent Mom's hormones skyrocketing. She was laughing and crying at the same time as she pulled me into her arms. "How did I get such a wonderful son?"

I fought the urge to argue with her that deep down I was a real shit. A real screwed up mess and a half-assed version of a man. But I kept my mouth shut.

Mom patted my back. "All right, I think that's enough on the shows of affection. We need to get to bed."

After we walked back into the living room, Mom eyed Maddie's damp cami and underwear. "Let me get something to put on her. She'd die of mortification to wake up in the morning half-naked." She turned and headed down the hall to her bedroom.

I sat down on the couch next to Maddie, watching her sleep. Her hair was still wet from swimming. As I pushed a stray strand away from her face, my heart thudded in my chest.

Mom came back with a gown. She gave me a look. "Even though you've practically seen everything, you can have the decency to turn your back."

"Well, I haven't gotten to see everything," I countered, shooting Mom a sly smile.

She rolled her eyes. "God, what a typical man thing to say." She motioned to Maddie. "You can pull her up for me before you turn around."

"If you insist," I replied. I peeled back the blanket and gently grabbed Maddie's shoulder's pulling her forward. Once Mom held Maddie's shoulders, I turned my head, so I wouldn't get a glimpse at her bare breasts after Mom pulled off the cami. At the sound of the fabric smacking to the floor, I jumped. I waited until I knew Mom had pulled the pale blue gown over Maddie's head. Once she was clothed, I eased Maddie back down on the couch and covered her up. She didn't stir once.

Mom started for the stairs but then stopped. "Coming?"

I shook my head. "I want to stay downstairs with her in case she wakes up in a strange place and freaks out."

She gave me a skeptical look, and I rolled my eyes. "Oh come on, Mom! Give me a little credit that I'm not going to molest a passed out girl!"

Mom nodded. "All right. Goodnight then. Come and get me if you need anything."

"Okay."

I sat listening to Maddie's small snores for what felt like an eternity. Each time I would almost doze off, my mind would begin whirling again, and I would wake up. I'd probably been asleep maybe an hour when I snapped wide awake. There was something I needed to do, so I grabbed my keys and headed for the door.

It was after four am when I pulled into Rolling Gardens. I'd never been to a cemetery at night before. I guess I had this freaky image of skeletons or zombies busting out of graves doing highly choreographed dance moves like in Michael Jackson's *Thriller*. I was relieved when I found everything quiet as the dead, no pun intended. I grabbed my flashlight out of the dashboard and started the walk towards mausoleum.

Once I reached the bronze plaque baring Jake's name, I cleared my throat. "Hey, man," I said, my voice echoing a little off the marble walls. "Yeah, I realize you're probably wondering what's gotten my ass out at this time of night, least of all what I'm doing here in the cemetery talking to your ashes."

Kicking at a blade of grass with my toe, I added, "I'm kinda wondering the same thing myself. But let me tell you something buddy, things have been pretty fucked up since you died. I mean, there's all this drama shit going on. Yeah, I know—when is there not drama, but seriously, you left one more freakin' mess when you blew out of here." I glanced up at the bronze plaque as a chill went over me. I shuddered and shook my head. "Sorry dude about that last line."

I sat down on the bench bearing his name. "Listen, man, I just wanna say I'm sorry about the whole Presley thing. I would've never made out with her and almost gotten off had I known she was…pregnant." Another shudder ricocheted through my body. "And what's up with that? You found out that weekend, and you couldn't even call me and tell me what was going on? That was some epic news man—shit that your best friend deserved to know! Best friends are supposed to talk to each other—tell each other about things. Not leave freakin' cryptic text messages and shit!"

With my blood pumping, I hopped off the bench. "And there's one more thing, and that's Maddie!" I cried, my voice rising a little. "I mean, what the hell was that all about? You loved her, you dickhead, didn't you?"

I threw my hands up in exasperation. "And you thought you couldn't tell me? I was your best friend, you douchebag! I had a right to know who you were in love with—not get some bullshit answer like, 'I'll tell you when I tell her'. I had a right to know you had some semblance of a heart. But what do you do? You hide her away like you were ashamed of her or something. What a dumbass!" The ache in my chest tightened, and I rubbed the place over my heart, trying to get rid of it.

I stepped forward. "Maddie is—amazing. She's beautiful and sweet and kind and way too good for you! If you loved her, how could you not tell her every single day? Seriously dude, she deserved better!"

I started to stalk away, but then I stopped. I turned back as tears welled in my eyes. "Hey man, I gotta be honest. *I* deserved better, too." Wiping my eyes, I added, "All those years through all your bullshit, I was by your side. Even though most of the time you treated me like crap, I was still there. When your dad was an ass, when you needed homework help, or a DD, I WAS THERE! But what about you, huh? Living some double life, going on mission trips, and volunteering and then lying about the whole damn thing! What the hell? Yeah, you were really acting like a Christian, man! WWJD, right? Well, I guarantee you Jesus wouldn't be panty chasing and getting drunk every other night!"

I dried my eyes. "Yeah, I know what you'd say right now. What about me, huh? Yeah, I'll admit I haven't actually been playing fair. I've scammed on your girl, right? Well, it's over. I'm telling her the truth about the ring just as soon as she wakes up. And if she wants you, I'll walk away, man. You can have her in life and in death. But I am going to tell her how I feel. If there's one thing I've learned from your death, it's to be honest with the people you love."

Turning on my heels, I headed down the hill to my Jeep. When I got there, I stood with my hand hovering over the door handle. I mean, what the hell was I doing here? What had possessed me to come out to the cemetery in the middle of the night to yell at Jake? Did I think he was going to talk back? I thought by confronting him in some way, I'd feel better. But I didn't.

I shook my head and climbed inside the Jeep. Making a right out of the cemetery, I started the drive over to Jake's house. It was almost five when I pulled into the driveway, but I didn't care. I marched right up the steps and rang the doorbell.

The Asshole answered the door in his robe. He raised his eyebrows. "Good morning, Noah. Nice to see you up so early on a Saturday morning," he muttered, sarcastically.

"Yeah, I know it's early, but I need the ring."

"Why?"

"Because I know who it belongs to."

His expression softened. "You do?"

"Yeah, I do."

He held open the door for me, and I stepped inside the foyer.

Mrs. Nelson appeared on the landing of the stairs. "Martin, who was it at the door?"

"It's Noah, Ev," he replied.

She hurried down the stairs. "Is something wrong, Noah?"

"No, Mrs. Nelson. I'm sorry to wake you guys up so early, but I came by for the ring."

"So you know who it belongs to?"

"Yes, I do."

"Who is it?" the Asshole pressed.

I drew in a breath. I realized once I spoke the name, I couldn't deny it or take it back. "It's Maddie Parker," I finally replied.

The Asshole literally gasped. "Pastor Dan's daughter? The one who was tutoring Jake?"

"Yes."

"That's unbelievable."

With a shrug, I replied, "That's what I thought, but the more I've been with her, the more I see what he saw in her. The fact that he hid her away kinda goes along with the song lyrics too."

Mrs. Nelson didn't say anything. She appeared deep in thought. Finally, she glanced up at me. "Thank you so much, Noah. I know this wasn't an easy undertaking."

I wheezed out a frustrated breath. "No, it wasn't. In fact it was pure hell."

She gave a bark of a laugh before motioning me with her hand. "Come on up, and I'll get it for you."

I followed her up the stairs and then turned down the familiar hallway to Jake's room. It was just the way it had been the last time I'd been in there. When she saw the look on my face, Mrs. Nelson smiled. "Martin wants me to pack up everything, but I just can't. Not now."

I merely nodded. She opened Jake's top dresser drawer and took out the ring box. She handed it to me along with the song lyrics. It weighed much heavier in my palm than it should have.

"There's something else I want you to take, Noah," she said. She went over to Jake's closet and took out a bag. "This is what he had with him at his grandparents when he was killed." She dug among some possessions until she pulled out an ordinary notebook and handed it to me. "I think you'll find some of the reading interesting."

I raised my eyebrows at her. "I will?"

She nodded. "Jake was always a complicated little boy. A lot more than Jonathan or Jason. I shouldn't be surprised that his teenage life was complicated too."

I didn't know what to say. She was trying to tell me something, but I was too physically tired and emotionally spent to understand. I merely bobbed my head and started toward the door.

"Noah?" she called.

I whirled around. "Yes, Mrs. Nelson?"

She stared down at her hands. "Tell Presley we'd very much like to see her, and we certainly want to be a part of our grandchild's life."

The wind left my body, and I collapsed back against the door frame. "Excuse me?"

Mrs. Nelson jerked her head up to give me a genuine smile. "You know what I'm talking about."

The hairs on the back of my neck prickled, and I just wanted to be out of there. "Okay, I will," I replied. Then I bolted from the room. I sprinted down the stairs, not even calling a goodbye to the Asshole who was standing in the foyer.

I don't think I took a breath until I was safely inside my Jeep. Instead of heading home, I drove down to the cul-de-sac below Jake's house. I grabbed the notebook and flipped it open. The first couple of pages were notes and homework from school. Some of it was in Jake's handwriting and others were in Maddie's. I was half-way through the notebook and wondering why the hell Mrs. Nelson wanted me to have it when I came across the note.

*Dear Maddie,*

*I know you're probably wondering why I'm writing you a letter. I'm surprised myself that this dumb jock is actually putting thoughts down on paper. But you shouldn't be surprised though. It's your influence, I know.*

*I don't know how to tell you this, but I've screwed up. I know you hate that word—but trust me, it's the only one that can fully describe what a mess I've made of my life. The bad thing is what I've done affects us. I got some news today that pretty much floored me. I'm going to be a father, Maddie. Presley is pregnant, and it's mine. I know that for sure.*

*I don't know if you know how much I love you, Maddie. You probably don't since I've been such an asshole and kept it all inside. I've always hoped that deep down you knew—that you felt it when we were together. If you didn't, I'm so sorry. I can blame anything and everything, but in the end, it's all my fault. I should have told you. I wish I would have said all the things that were inside me. I wish I'd made you mine, but I didn't. And I'm still being a coward because instead of doing it to your face, I'm giving you a letter instead.*

*I can never thank you enough for what you've meant in my life. You didn't make me a better person. Instead, you dragged the real me out—even if it was only for short periods of time. I wish I had your courage, Maddie. Don't ever let people make you doubt yourself, and don't ever forget what an awesome girl you are.*

*I don't want you to ever think any of this was your fault. To question if we had allowed ourselves to go to the next level, would this have happened? Don't ever do that, Maddie. I love you too much for you to blame yourself for my stupid and irresponsible actions. I also loved you too much to take the gift that wasn't mine to take. The truth is you're too good for me, and you deserve someone better—someone like my buddy, Noah, who would worship you each and every day you were together—"*

I stopped reading and gasped. My breathing came in erratic

pants. Tears burned and blurred my vision, and it was several long minutes before I could start reading again.

*I know this sounds like good-bye, and it is in a way. I know you'll never have me after this—after I've cheated on you in the way I have. Yeah, we weren't an official couple, but I should have told you months ago that I had feelings for you. But it's okay; I understand. For once in my life, I'm going to do the right thing. I'm going to support Presley, and I'm going to be a father to our child.*

*No matter what happens, I'll always love you—you'll always be on my mind.*

*Love Jake*

I must've stared at the letter for twenty minutes after I read it. I read it and reread it—trying desperately to let each and every word sink in. I couldn't believe he'd mentioned me—that he'd suggested I'd be somebody who would love Maddie. How in the world could he have known that?

Most of all, he was stepping aside. For the first time in his life, Jake was really being a man. He was taking responsibility for his actions. More than that, he was actually making sacrifices for somebody—two people in fact. "Dammit!" I cried, banging my fist against the steering wheel. It wasn't right he was gone. Just when he had gotten his shit together, he'd been taken away, and it wasn't fucking fair. There was a baby who would never know his or her father, and Presley

324

would have to truly be a single mother.

It hit me like a train charging through my chest that Mrs. Nelson had known. She'd read the notebook, and she'd known. More than that, she hadn't told the Asshole. I started to wonder why in the hell she hadn't told me. Then I imagined she felt there was some purpose in this quest—something more for me to discover than just *her*. It was then I realized how wise Mrs. Nelson had been. I'd discovered so much about Jake, but I'd discovered a lot more about myself. And she'd wanted that for me. Just as Jake was an adopted member of my family, I was of hers—well, to everyone but the Asshole.

As the first streaks of amber and orange made their way across the morning sky, I knew I needed to head home. I was exhausted—mentally and physically. The house was still and quiet when I walked through the door. Maddie was still sleeping.

I eased down in the floor beside her. I didn't know what I was going to do. Should I give her the ring and leave things the way they were? Should I give her the ring and the letter and tell her how much I loved her? Dammit, why was my life so complicated!

My head started to dip as I nodded off. At the sound of a soft moan, my eyes snapped open to see Maddie waking up. Her eyelids fluttered as her head slowly moved from side to side. When she opened her eyes, she frantically scanned the room.

"It's okay. You're at my house," I whispered.

At the sound of my voice, she bolted up on the couch—causing the blanket to fall away. The perv in me couldn't help but noticing how sexy she looked with her hair all wild and the way the satiny, spaghetti straps of the gown hung loose on her shoulders. Then I remembered it was my mother's gown. Damn, a psychiatrist would have a field day with me.

"Noah, what am I doing here?"

"You got drunk at the party, and you passed out. I knew I couldn't take you home, so I brought you here."

Her eyebrows shot up in surprise. "I-I got d-drunk?" she stammered.

"Yes, you did."

"Oh no," she moaned, her face flushing.

"It's okay, Maddie. It happens sometimes."

"Not to me it doesn't!"

"Well, it did last night."

Raking her hand through her unkempt hair, Maddie moaned, "But your mom—she must think I'm terrible!"

"Actually, she was more pissed at me."

She stared down at her hands. That was when she noticed the gown, and she gasped. "M-My clothes?"

I sighed. "The truth?"

"Yes!" she screeched.

"You took them off at the party."

Mortification filled her face as Maddie covered her mouth with her hand. "I did?"

"Everybody went swimming in Blaine's pond. When we got here, my mom put the gown on you."

Maddie nodded. She absentmindedly traced the outline of the design on the blanket. "Um, did I...did we...?"

I held my hands up defensively. "No, of course not."

Surprise flashed in her eyes. "We didn't?"

My lips formed a crooked grin. "I'd like to think if you'd been with me, you'd remember it," I teased.

"Noah," Maddie pleaded.

I knew I didn't have to tell her anything about what went on the night before because she would never remember any of it, but I'd been lying to her for so long that I wanted to level with her. "We kissed."

"Oh we did?"

"Yes," I answered dutifully. "In case you're wondering, it was pretty amazing."

"It was?" Maddie questioned in a whisper.

"Yeah."

She stared up into my eyes and then smiled slightly. "I wish I could remember."

I returned her smile. "I wish you could. Maybe we'll give it another try."

Her face flushed again, but she did nod her head. "Did anything else happen?"

Oh fuck. She would have to ask that. Playing with a thread on my shirt, I finally replied, "A little." When her eyebrows shot up, I quickly replied, "Just a little second base action." I decided to pace myself and not totally freak her out by admitting I'd gotten to third.

"Did I enjoy it too?"

I snapped my gaze to hers. "I think you did," I murmured.

"Good."

We sat staring at each other for a moment before I cleared my throat. "Maddie, I really need to talk to you about something. But first, why don't you get a shower, and I'll fix us some breakfast?"

"Okay."

I took her upstairs. I quickly detoured past my bathroom— afraid for her to see what a slob I was—and got her set up in the guest bathroom. "I'll leave your clothes outside the door for you."

"Thanks, Noah."

When I heard the water turn on, I went back downstairs and out to the Jeep. I quickly fluffed her wrinkled clothes in the dryer along with her underwear, which I tried not to ogle for too long, and then I took them back upstairs.

I met Mom in the hallway. "Morning, honey."

"Morning."

"I'll go start on breakfast, okay?"

I nodded and followed her back downstairs. Mom whipped up a quick batch of bacon, eggs, and toast. She had just finished when Maddie walked shyly into the kitchen. "Good morning, Maddie," Mom said.

Maddie smiled weakly. "Good morning, Mrs. Anderson." Toying with the hem on her shirt, she stared down at the kitchen floor. "I want to apologize for my behavior last night," she began.

Mom shook her head. "No need to apologize. We all have our moments. It doesn't change who we really are."

Maddie jerked her head up in surprise at Mom's answer. A pleased expression formed on her face as she eased into a seat at the kitchen table. Mom made small talk with us through breakfast, but I could tell both Maddie and I were anxious to be alone. As soon as she put her napkin on her plate, I stood up. "Wanna go for a walk before I take you home?"

Maddie nodded. "Thank you for the delicious breakfast and letting me stay last night," she said politely.

Mom smiled. "You're welcome."

I led Maddie outside through the glass door. We walked out in the backyard, and I steered her over to the swing. It was shady there under a canopy of trees.

"So what is it you want to talk to me about?"

I stared into her eyes. "I've not been honest with you."

"About what?"

"Jake."

Maddie's brows rose in surprise. "What do you mean?"

I sighed. "Remember that night you and I took Jake's things down to the funeral home?"

She nodded.

"Well, earlier that night, Mr. Nelson and I found something in Jake's room. Something he was meaning to give to the girl he truly loved." I reached into my pocket and pulled out the ring box. I leaned over and gently put it in her hands. "It was wrapped in the lyrics to *You Were Always on My Mind*."

Maddie gasped as she cracked open the box and stared down at the diamond. "I don't believe it."

"You should because it was meant for you." My heart constricted in my chest as I added, "And you were meant for him." Maddie snapped her gaze from the ring to me, and I nodded. "He loved you, Maddie."

"How can you be sure?"

I slowly took the rolled up notebook out of my back pocket.

I flipped it to his letter and handed it to her. Without another word, I got up off the swing. Leaning back against a tree trunk, I watched her devour the words on the page. Tears welled in her eyes. When she finished, she gazed up at me.

"Are you okay?" I asked.

Nodding, she wiped her eyes. "It's just hard to believe, that's all. I mean, he hinted at things along the way, but there was nothing definite. But now, actually reading his words—actually knowing but not being able to do anything about it..."

She started sobbing. I eased back on the swing and took her into my arms. I knew this wasn't going to be easy, but frankly, it was a real bitch. Her tears wet through my shirt, and as I held her, my mind was clear. There were no impure thoughts that would send me into overdrive. All I cared about was comforting her.

After a while, she pulled away from me. "Presley's really pregnant?"

"Yes, she is."

Maddie moaned. "I loved him and he loved me, but *she's* having his baby. How much more screwed up could this get!"

"So you really loved him, huh?" I asked.

She stared at me in surprise. "I cared for him very much, and I loved him as a friend. But yes, I think I did love him. Why?"

I shook my head. "Never mind," I mumbled as I got up

from the swing.

"Noah, wait!" she cried, grabbing me by the sleeve. "What did you mean when you said you hadn't been honest with me?"

Shit. I was hoping she'd be so overwhelmed with grief she'd forgotten I mentioned that. I ran my hand through my hair. "Mrs. Nelson asked me to find the girl for Jake. For a long time, I thought it was you—then after that night in the coffeehouse, I knew it was you. But I—I didn't want to tell you."

"Why not?"

"Because I didn't want you to belong to him!"

"You didn't?"

The blood boiled in my veins as I thought of losing her, and it turned over to white hot anger. "No, I didn't. He was a jerk, Maddie. Can't you see that? Hiding you away, dating other girls, *screwing* other girls. You deserved better!"

"He might have been a jerk sometimes, but he was trying to change. And at the end, he'd stopped partying and sleeping around," she protested.

"Oh big deal!"

"For him it was a big deal. And just because he couldn't tell me how he felt, doesn't make his feelings any different."

"How can you say that? If it had been me, I would have told you every day how much I loved you. There wouldn't have been a day that passed by without me admitting how many times I thought about you, missed you, or wanted to feel you in my arms!"

Maddie stared at me in shock.

"Love isn't just about words in freakin' song lyrics. It's about actions, too."

"You aren't any different!" she cried, before turning on her heels and starting to stalk away.

I stared at her retreating form for a minute. "Excuse me?" I called.

She whirled around and shook her head at me. "You say if it was you that you would have told me all those things, but you wouldn't."

"Why not?"

"Because you haven't!"

My heart jolted in my chest.

Maddie stepped toe to toe with me. She jerked her chin up. "So tell me. Stand before me right now and tell me all those things you would if I was yours."

Suddenly, I felt like an old black and white movie I'd seen. This dude morphed into a totally different person. When I spoke the next time, it was like a stranger was speaking. It weirded me out. "Why? So you can go back to your memories of Jake? So you can accept me because I'm alive when all along you'll wish I was him!"

"No, I would never do that," Maddie protested.

"Don't be so sure."

Maddie thrust the notebook at me. "So are you calling Jake a liar? It's all right here. He said you were the one for me—the one who would adore me."

I stared at the notebook, refusing to answer.

"Yeah, maybe Jake was a jerk for treating me the way he did, but at least he realized what he'd done wrong and was trying to make it right. And in case you missed it, this was good-bye. If Jake had lived, there would have been never been an us—no matter how he truly felt about me."

Maddie's expression softened as she touched my arm. "Just admit to me that you've changed—for the better. I mean since we've been friends, look at all you've done. You've connected with your father, you've accepted your mom's remarriage and a baby on the way, and Josh—" her voice broke. "You were able to connect with him on a level that surprises me."

My emotions were churning. I knew what I wanted to do, but something inside wouldn't let me. Some part of myself that I'd overcome was slowly weaning its way back. Suddenly, I understood Jake completely. I understood how he couldn't truly be himself. There was always that asshole part that played out. I did the only thing I knew how to do and that was to shut down and turn on her.

334

"What is this shit, huh? What is this desire of yours to "fix" everyone?"

"I don't know what you're talking about."

"Oh come off it, Maddie. It's a plain as day. What is your prerequisite for a guy? Does he have to be some screwed up, emotional jackass before you'll give him the time of day?"

"No! That's not true!" she argued.

"It looks that way to me. You found Jake and fixed him up. Seems like you've fixed me too. But I'll tell you something, Maddie. I don't like being your project!"

"Stop it, Noah. Don't do this."

"Do what? Tell the truth? That's what it looks like to me. You seem to have a funny way of falling for fixer-uppers. But what happens when I'm completely whole? Would you walk away?"

"I'd never leave you."

"And what about you, huh? Who's gonna save you from yourself?"

Tears welled in her eyes. "Please."

I shook my head. "Oh, I see. You don't play fair. You can dish it, but you don't want to take it. You're the good little girl who tries to save everybody—Jake, me, your brother, your parents. But what about you?"

"I thought this was about us," Maddie whimpered.

"It's never been about us, don't you see that? It's always been about Jake, my dad, Josh and Will, and all the rest of the shitty baggage between us. It's never about the players, remember? It's about the damn game that makes us act and react the way we do!"

"Please don't do this, Noah," she whispered.

"Do what? Be honest? I'm just trying to do what you've taught me, Maddie. To be the person you want me to be!"

Maddie shook her head. "But can't you see?" she cried. "I love you! I love you more than I ever imagined I could love a guy. And it scares me, okay? It scares the hell out of me!"

I stared at her in disbelief. She really loved me. God, I'd wanted to hear her say that for so long, but it had the opposite effect I thought it would. It stunned me where I was speechless. I wanted to cry out how much I loved her to, but it was like something was binding me, and I couldn't speak.

When I didn't respond, she shook her head. Then she glanced down at the ring in her hand. "Give this to Presley."

"What?"

"She needs it more than I do."

"But Jake meant for you to have it," I protested.

"It doesn't matter. She and her baby will need it."

"What, to keep the Jake myth alive and kicking?" I asked.

"No, to validate the truth. The truth that's in this notebook.

Jake was going to stand by Presley, and he was going to be a father to his child. This way, it'll give all the gossips the hard evidence they need to believe the unfathomable—that Jake Nelson wasn't a selfish jerk, and he was a man of his word."

Maddie took my hand and placed the box into in. She closed my fingers around it. "Two good-byes in one day. And I owe money to the cuss can," she mused.

I didn't know what else to say. I felt jumbled—bound and gagged by my own foolish pride and stupidity. After everything that had happened and everything I had felt was I honestly going to stand here and let her walk away? I was screaming on the inside, but nothing would come out.

"Good-bye, Noah," Maddie said, softly. Then she turned and walked out of the back yard. I didn't know how she was going to get home, but clearly, she didn't need or want me to take her.

I must've stood frozen in the middle of the yard for at least an hour. How in the hell had I gotten here? I'd gone from being desperate to keep her to driving her away. I'd let her stand in front of me and tell me she loved me, and I didn't say a damn word.

I was a total fucked-up mess.

# Chapter Twenty-Two

I stayed in my room most of the day. Mom wasn't on call, so she checked on me throughout the afternoon. Each time she cracked my door, she found me sprawled across the bed, staring up at the ceiling. She never pressed me to open up or questioned me about what was wrong—I guess she just wanted to make sure I hadn't slit my writs with my razor or something emo like that. I don't know how she knew what had happened with Maddie—I guess it was just the Sixth Sense she seemed to have whenever I was upset. Probably the fact that Maddie stormed away earlier also helped her reach her conclusion.

Closed off in my bedroom, I didn't watch TV or listen to music or even text anyone. All I did was think. I thought about Jake until my chest constricted so hard I thought I would suffocate. I thought about Maddie until my already weak heart felt like it would explode in agony. And finally, I thought about what an incredible idiot I was.

There were a million things I should've been doing. After all, I was leaving in the morning for Brazil. I assumed a couple of streets over, Maddie was packing for her Costa Rican mission trip. God, it was so typical—me leaving for the sin city of South America, and Maddie off to do the Lord's work.

Of course, with both of us leaving the country, it also meant there'd be no way to make things right between us. I would be gone for two weeks, and she was going to be gone for a month. After that, who knew what would happen. Then when the end of August rolled around, we'd be going to separate colleges, and our ties would be completely severed.

The very thought of never seeing her smile again or being with her sent a slow ache raging through my chest. This time I didn't fight the tears that burned and scorched my throat. Instead, I gave into them and actually fucking cried. I sobbed like a pansy until I wore my ass out and finally went to sleep.

Wonderful aromas wafting up the stairs woke me up at a little after six. No surprise that Mom had cooked my favorite meal, one of Grammy's recipes for chicken casserole. I went downstairs of my own volition before she could come back and beg me to come down. Greg and Mom didn't press me to talk at dinner. They rattled on about work and about the wedding pictures that had just come back. It was only when they started talking baby names that my head jerked up from my plate. Mom was still desperately hoping to name the baby Emma, but so far, Greg, a *Friends* fanatic, thought that was copying Ross and Rachel's baby.

Tonight, however, he'd come up with a compromise. "What

if we named her Emma Madelyn—you know, Madelyn after my mother? We could even do Madelyn Emma and call her Maddy Em or something cutesy like that."

An uncomfortable silence hung over the table. Mom's fork clattered on her plate as she shot Greg a look. When he realized he'd hit a sore subject with the name, he hung his head. "I'm sorry, Noah. I completely forgot about Maddie's name."

I thought about what the old me would have done. I would've probably yelled at Greg for being an unthinking bastard and stormed off from the table. But as much as I hated to admit it, I was changed. So, I scooted my chair out from the table and stood up. "I think Madelyn is a really pretty name," I said sincerely.

Then I took my plate to the sink. I walked calmly out of the kitchen—no huffing or exasperated eye rolls—leaving Mom and Greg in shock at the table.

A few minutes later, Mom rapped on my door. "Noah?" she questioned.

"Hmm," I murmured.

She cracked open the door and peered tentatively inside. "Sweetie, Greg and I were going to make ice cream sundaes. Would you like one?"

Poor Mom, still trying to feed my heartache with sweets just like she had when I was a child. I remembered the day that Jake duct taped me to the chair, we went for ice cream for a

340

week. Of course, it also made me think about Maddie and the night we went to Baskin Robbins, and my stomach cramped.

I smiled. "No thanks, Mom."

"Okay, well, we're gonna be downstairs watching a movie if you change your mind."

"Sure."

Mom closed the door, and I heard her padding down the hall. My chest ached. I missed Maddie, and I missed Jake. More than anything, I wished I could talk to him. He would understand me. Hell, he might even have a few words of wisdom for me in the situation I found myself in. But I couldn't talk to Jake. So I tried to think of the next best thing.

I pulled out my cell phone and scrolled through the numbers. I selected one and then listened to it dialing. He answered on the third ring.

"Hey Dad, it's me. Can we talk?"

It was after nine when I hung up with my dad. We talked about so much that by the time I got off the phone, my head hurt. It wasn't all good stuff either. I came clean about a lot of things as did he. But it was nice being able to reach out to him. With my head pounding, I went downstairs to get some pain medicine out of Mom's goody-bag.

Mom and Greg were on the infamous couch in the living

room. Fortunately, this time they weren't in a compromising position. Mom was leaned back against Greg with a bowl full of popcorn balanced on her belly. The romantic sap in me thought the scene was kinda sweet.

When they noticed me, they both smiled. "Hi, sweetie," Mom said.

"Hey. I've kinda got a headache, and I wanted to get some medicine out of your bag."

"Here, I'll get it for you," Mom insisted.

"No, that's okay."

Mom wouldn't hear any of it. She was off the couch in an instant—well as fast as she could with her growing belly. Back in the kitchen, she fixed me some water and then handed me two pills.

"Thanks," I said.

When I started to go back upstairs, she grabbed by arm. "Come watch a movie with us, Noah," she pleaded. I don't know who was more upset—me or Mom.

"Okay," I reluctantly agreed.

Her eyes lit up, and she practically dragged me into the living room. I eased down in the chair and propped my feet up on the ottoman. "What are we watching?"

"*Say Anything*. A classic from the 80's," Greg answered.

"Well, the 80's were more Greg's generation than mine

since he's older than me," Mom joked with a wink.

Greg laughed as he wrapped his arms around Mom. "Yeah, by a measly three years!"

She smiled while snuggling closer to him. "That's true."

"Hey Noah, want some popcorn?" Greg asked.

"Yeah, sure," I said, as he passed the bowl over to me.

We settled down as the opening credits appeared. It didn't take me long to both like and hate the movie. For one, it was about a kinda slacker guy who fell in love with the goody Valedictorian—ring any bells?

I was practically in tears when the girl broke up with the guy—much in the same way Maddie had said good-bye earlier today. When the guy, Lloyd, did his epic feat to win her back, I was on the edge of my seat. He stood outside her window all night playing Peter Gabriel's *In Your Eyes*—a song that meant something to both of them. Not only was I impressed that he was able to hoist that massive boom box over his head most of the night, but I also felt empowered.

Mom interrupted my moment. "Oh, pause it a second, honey. I've got to pee, again," she groaned as she hopped off the couch.

Once he heard the bathroom door close, Greg whistled at me. "Hey Noah, Maggie told me what happened with Maddie."

"Yeah," I said tentatively, silently praying he wasn't trying to get all fatherly on me.

343

"Well, I, uh…" He glanced down at his hands. "I just wanted you to know there's a six pack of beer hidden behind my golf clubs in the garage—you know in case you were thirsty later."

I couldn't help laughing at his suggestion and the fact he was whipped enough to be hiding booze from Mom. Giving him a genuine grin, I replied, "Thanks, Greg. I appreciate that."

He nodded. "No problem."

When Mom came back from the bathroom, I winked at Greg. "Yeah, I think I'll go outside for a while—you know, get a little fresh air."

Before Mom could argue that the movie wasn't over, Greg piped up. "That sounds like a good idea, Noah. You take as much time as you need."

I nodded as I headed into the kitchen. As I flipped the light on in the garage, I had to admit Greg was pretty cool. It was almost laughable he feared Mom enough that he was hiding his beer. Despite the fact Mom was half-Irish, she hated alcohol in the house. Her Southern Baptist roots from Grammy's side must have won out on that one.

I found the beer just as he said it would be. I grabbed up three bottles and headed for the swing in the back yard. I downed the first one in three long gulps. The second one I sipped slowly—as I gathered my thoughts and tried to figure out what the hell had gone wrong. Finally, on the third one, the scene from the movie flashed before my eyes, and I knew what I had to do.

I had to get Maddie back.

But more than that, I had to do something—something epic if I was going to win her love and trust again. I tossed the beer bottles over the fence and raced inside the house for the phone.

# Chapter Twenty-Three

Mom remained quiet the entire ride to the airport the next morning. I knew she wasn't thrilled about my trip, even though she'd known about it forever.

"Sweetie, are you sure you're up for this?" she finally asked.

"Yeah, I'm looking forward to it."

She nodded. "I just wish you weren't going to be gone so long."

I rolled my eyes. "It's really not that long, Mom."

"I know, I know."

But she still didn't look convinced. Greg eyed me in the rear view mirror before turning to my mom. "He'll be fine, Maggie. Noah's a responsible young man, and he's not going to go to a foreign country and go wild. You've done an amazing job raising him."

When he glanced back at me again, I grinned. Yeah, Greg was turning out not to be a tool at all. I was glad Mom had him, and I was pretty sure he was going to make a great dad for my little sister.

We headed off the interstate and towards the South Terminal of Hartsfield-Jackson Airport. After we inched up to a spot, Greg hopped out and helped upload my suitcases.

Mom eyed them. "You sure are taking a lot with you for just two weeks."

I glanced at Greg. He nodded and then got back into the car. I drew in a deep breath. "I'm not going to Rio anymore, Mom."

"What?"

"I'm going to Costa Rica," I admitted.

"But what's in Costa Rica?"

"Mission work…and Maddie."

Mom gasped. "You're going after her, aren't you?"

"Yeah, after the movie last night and what an ass I'd been, I figured I needed a grand gesture, so I called her dad and got all her flight information. He really helped me out."

Tears sprung in Mom's eyes, but she smiled. "I think that's wonderful, sweetie."

"Even though it means I'm going to be gone a month?"

She nodded. "Even if you were going to be gone six months." She reached out and touched my cheek. "I want you to be happy, and I know she makes you happy."

Wow, I hadn't expected that. It must've been the pregnancy hormones, and I decided I needed to thank my sister someday for saving me a lot of airport grief.

I smiled. "Thanks, Mom."

She pulled me into her arms, squeezing me so tightly to her that I felt her baby bump. "Mom, I can't breathe," I joked.

As she released me, she kissed me on the cheek. "Call me every day, okay?"

"I will."

"I don't care how expensive it is. I'll pay." She wagged her finger at me. "I'll want to hear all about the work you're doing and how you're getting along."

"Okay." I ducked my head to keep Mom from ruffling my hair. I didn't even dare to glance around for fear of who all had seen me being an utter and complete Mama's Boy.

She kissed me one last time, and then she turned and got into the car. Greg gave me a thumbs-up sigh. I smiled. Then I waved and watched their taillights fade in the distance.

With a determined step, I walked into the airport. I made it through check-in and security fine. It was only when I started to the concourse that my heart started racing uncontrollably. By the time I reached the gate, I had broken out in a nervous sweat. I scanned the crowd for Maddie. They were already boarding, so she must have already gotten on the plane. As I waited in line, I tapped my foot anxiously. What if Maddie still hated me for what I'd done and said? What if she refused to even hear me out? I mean, this whole plan was batshit crazy, but part of it hinged on her forgiveness and acceptance. It would blow being stuck in a foreign land with my tail firmly between my legs.

Pushing those thoughts from my mind, I took a deep breath and started towards the plane. Once I boarded, I walked down the aisle, searching for my seat. My heart skidded to a stop and restarted when I got to it.

There was Maddie.

I would've loved to have said it was fate, but in truth, Pastor Dan had given me her flight details the night before along with promising not to say a word.

Maddie glanced up from her iPad. Our eyes met, and she gasped so loud her entire body shuddered. With a wide-eyed expression, she jerked the buds from her ears and shot up from her seat, narrowly missing hitting her head. "Noah? What are you doing here?"

"I'm going to Costa Rica to do missionary work. What does it look like," I replied, hoisting my carry-on into the compartment above us.

Maddie's dark brows furrowed with confusion. "But I thought you were going to Rio with Alex and the other guys."

"Can't a guy change his mind?"

"But I don't understand," she murmured.

I sighed. It was now or never time to explain my feelings. "Well, I'm not going to be as eloquent as you, Miss

349

Valedictorian, but to put it bluntly and to quote Kelly Clarkson, my life would suck without you!"

A hesitant smile crept on her lips. "Did you seriously just say that?"

I laughed. "Sadly, I think I did. Don't you know you bring out the hopeless romantic in me—give me a chance and I might be quoting from bad 80's songs in a few minutes."

She rolled her eyes. "Cut to the chase, Noah. What are you really trying to say?"

I brushed an errant strand of dark hair out of her face. "Maddie, there aren't words that can fully express how sorry I am for the absolute ass I was yesterday. I don't know what kind of ridiculousness came over me, but I'm very, very sorry. I know Jake loved you and you loved him, and I'm okay with that. I'm okay with the fact you're a natural born caregiver, and you're always going to have this annoyingly, sweet need to take care of others." When she started to protest, I put my finger over her lips. "But babe, I just need you to let go sometimes and give others a chance to take care of you. Most of all, I need you to let *me* take care of you."

"Um, okay," she murmured.

"I'm not finished."

"You aren't?"

I grinned. "No, I'm not."

"All right."

"There's something else I need to say—something I should have said to you yesterday and even weeks before that." Gently, I traced my thumb over her cheekbone. "Madeline Elizabeth Parker, I am truly, madly, and deeply in love with you."

Tears sparkled in Maddie's dark eyes. "Noah—"

I held up a hand to silence her. "Let me finish. I've been in love with you since the day I saw you after Jake died. You appeared to me like an angel, and in a way, you have been my angel. You are so beautiful sometimes that it stuns me, and it leaves me speechless. When you smile that smile that spreads across your face and brings out your dimples, it makes my heart melt." I leaned in closer to where my breath brushed against her cheek. "You've been my beacon of light in my storm of grief, and I don't know if I could live without you."

Maddie blinked a few times in disbelief. "Oh Noah, did you really just say all that?"

"Yep."

"And you really mean it?"

"Every single word."

Closing her eyes, she rubbed her cheek against my hand. "Do you know what it means to me to hear you say that? I've hoped and dreamed that you would, but to actually hear it off your lips…" She popped open her eyes and stared up at me. "It's amazing."

"I'm glad to hear you say that, too, because I want everything with you. But if you can't forgive me for being such a monumental asshole, I'll accept that, and we can just be friends. All I care about is being with you."

Before I could say anything else, her mouth was on mine. The warmth of her tongue slid my lips open, and neither one of us could enough of each other. The sound of someone clearing his throat broke our moment. Maddie pulled away and blushed.

A balding man gave us an impatient look. "Now that you two have had your moment, do you think I might get by?"

Maddie's face flushed crimson all the way down her neck and onto her shoulders. "I'm so sorry, sir," she said as apologetically as she could. She then flopped down in her seat and buried her face in her hands.

"Hey," I murmured, nudging her leg with mine. When she didn't look up, I eased down beside her. "Come on, Mads. Don't be embarrassed by a little PDA."

She tentatively raised her head and gave me a weak smile. "Sorry. Getting embarrassed is just one of my little quirks."

I laughed. "And I love all your quirks."

She took my hand in hers. "I love you so much, Noah."

"I love you, too."

Shaking her head, she said, "No, I need you to understand that regardless of whatever feelings or infatuation I thought I had for Jake, it's the real thing with you."

Her words caused my heartbeat to accelerate to a full gallop in my chest. The way she was looking at me also told me how much she meant her words, and I couldn't stop myself. As the seatbelt sign came on, I leaned over and kissed her. It was quite a different experience from earlier, but it was wonderful all the same. She pulled away just as the plane started taxing down the runway and gave me a disapproving look.

"What's that look for?" I asked.

She nibbled on her bottom lip for a moment, which did nothing for my raging hormones. "While we're being honest, I feel I need to tell you that just because I love you nothing else has really changed yet."

"It hasn't?"

"I mean, what I believe is still the same. Just because I love you doesn't mean I'm going to automatically…"

I shifted in my seat as my sex drive went down in flames. "Yeah, yeah, I know. You're virginity is safe, I swear," I said, making a Scout's Honor pledge across my chest.

"That and other things too." She glanced around the cabin before lowering her voice. "It might be a while before I'm ready to…you know, polish your knob or things like that."

I snorted and rolled my eyes. "We've seriously got to work on your sexual lingo!"

"Is that not what it's called?"

"Yeah, it is, but it just sounds so ridiculous coming out of

353

your mouth. In fact, I think you might owe a quarter to the cuss can."

Her finger drew lazy lines along the back of my hand. "So you're really going to be able to wait until I'm ready?"

"Yep."

"Even when I'm so beautiful it leaves you speechless?" she teased.

"Don't worry, I know I'm strong enough to refuse you. I did the other night."

Her eyes widened. "When I was drunk?"

"Yes, ma'am." I leaned over and whispered into her ear, "You were so incredibly sexy when you propositioned me in your sexy white cami and blue panties."

Maddie's hand flew to cover her mouth in horror. "I did?"

I shot her a wicked grin. "Oh yeah. But I was a true gentleman and said no to your advances."

Once again, a red flush crept over her cheeks. When she finally met my gaze, she gave me a hesitant smile. "Well, just don't look for it happening again anytime soon!"

I shook my head. "One can only dream."

Maddie giggled before smacking my arm playfully. "So you're really willing to wait until I'm ready?"

I stared into her dark eyes. "Although it probably means I'm completely and totally whipped, I'll do anything you ask me to as long as it means I get to be close to you."

"Oh Noah," Maddie murmured. She cupped my cheeks in her hands and bestowed a long, lingering kiss on me.

I knew in that moment I'd found the perfect love, acceptance and happiness I'd been searching for. And I had Jake to thank for it.

One Year Later

"Mom, we're gonna be late!" I called, as I smoothed down my hair.

"Give me a minute!" came her muffled reply from down the hallway.

Glancing in the mirror, I surveyed my appearance. Outfitted in a blue polo shirt and khaki pants, I guess I looked appropriate enough for Jake's Life Celebration. I mean, I don't know what the hell you're supposed to wear to these kinda things. I'd never even heard of one until Mrs. Nelson had called me two weeks ago to invite me. It was hard to believe a whole year had passed since Jake had died. I still thought of him each and every day, and I still missed him like crazy.

Mom swept into my room. "Would you mind getting Emma Grace downstairs for me while I finish packing her diaper bag?"

I bobbed my head. "No problem. Happy to help."

"Thanks sweetheart," she murmured.

"Mom?"

She whipped around to glance questioningly at me. "Take a deep breath, okay?" I instructed with a grin.

With a laugh, she rose up on her tiptoes to kiss my cheek. "Being a mom in your mid 30's is so different than in your teens. I don't know whether I'm coming or going."

"You're doing great," I reassured her.

She blew an errant strand of dark hair out of her eyes. "Even with Greg, it's not as easy as it was with you."

"That's because I was a super special baby."

Mom laughed. "True. Very true." She then hurried out of my room, and I heard her pounding down the stairs. I crossed the hall into the nursery and once again was bombarded by a pink overload. In response to Mom's choice for the nursery, Greg often mused the line from *Steel Magnolias* that the room looked like it had been hosed down with Pepto Bismol.

My sister played happily in her Pack N Play. "Hey Baby Girl," I said. She jerked her head up to peer at me. As always, Mom had her decked out to the nines with a frilly dress, tights, and a headband with a giant flower on it. Why she needed a headband since she barely had any hair was beyond me.

Emma Grace grunted and held her arms out to me. "Okay, okay, don't be so pushy, Miss Spoiled," I teased.

When she rewarded me with one of her beaming smiles, my heart instantly melted. "Emma Grace, give your favorite brother a kiss." She leaned over to bestow a slobbery smooch on my cheek. "That's my pretty girl."

It was hard to believe she was almost seven months old. Time had flown since her birth at the beginning of October. I'd managed to leave my dorm at Georgia Tech to head over to Wellstar-Kennestone to be there for her arrival. Mom had offered to let me stay in and watch, but I'd said, "Oh hell no!" without hesitation.

In the end, I sat in the waiting room with Grammy and my aunts and uncles while Greg stayed in with Mom. Once Emma Grace made her grand entrance, I went in to see Mom. Emma Grace was barely half an hour old when I held her in my arms as tears streaked down Mom's cheeks, and Greg boohooed like a total pansy. Well, I guess I shouldn't make too much fun of him—someday I guess I'll know what it's like to have a kid of my own.

Hoisting her onto my shoulder, I headed down the hall to the stairs. When the doorbell rang, I got a little more bounce in my step. Throwing it open, a smile stretched across my face. In a way too sexy sundress for her own good, Maddie stood on the front step.

"Hey beautiful," I said.

She grinned. "Hey yourself. And thanks."

Emma Grace squealed happily and waved her tiny hand at Maddie. With a giggle, Maddie said in a sing-song voice, "Aw,

358

does my precious angel think I'm ignoring her?" She then took Emma Grace from me. As Maddie smothered her in kisses, I cleared my throat. "Um, hello? Where's my compliments and lovin'?"

Maddie's dark eyes took on an amused glint. With a slightly sexier lilt to her voice, she said, "Aw, does my precious, but jealous, boyfriend think he's getting slighted for his beautiful baby sister?"

I poked my bottom lip out teasingly. "Yes, I do."

"Then let me remedy that." Leaning over, Maddie brought her lips to mine. I shivered with need when she thrust her tongue into my mouth. She'd come a long way in the almost year we'd been dating. We'd been an official couple since that day on the airplane. Although it was a grueling, eye-opening experience, I wouldn't have taken anything for our time in Costa Rica. Thankfully, when it came time to leave for college, things weren't too hard considering I was in downtown Atlanta at Georgia Tech, and she was at Georgia State.

Just as we were getting hot and heavy, another squeal of protest from Emma Grace caused us to pull away. "You are such an attention whore," I teased.

"Noah, don't say that word in front of Emma Grace!" Maddie admonished.

I grinned at her outrage. "She doesn't know the difference."

"It's still not right."

With a smirk, I questioned, "Don't tell me I'm going to owe the Cuss Can?"

Maddie giggled. "You just might."

I groaned as Mom's heels clicked down the hall. "I'm finally ready," she said with a smile.

Mom leaned over and kissed Maddie's cheek. I was happy that two of my most favorite women in the world got along so well. Well, I guess I should say my three most favorite women since Emma Grace adored Maddie as well. Maddie loved spending at least one night of our weekends home baby-sitting for Mom and Greg to give them a date night. With Emma Grace in bed by seven, we had the evenings to ourselves to watch movies and make-out a little.

Of course, we hadn't gone there yet. Third base was as far as Maddie would let me, and it was seriously killing me. I mean, yeah, she was keeping me satisfied with that, but I wanted to really be with her. But I loved her too much to pressure her, and I knew when the time was right, we would go there.

Once we got Emma Grace loaded into the SUV, we headed over to Jake's. At first I thought the Life Celebration might include all his old buddies, but Mrs. Nelson told me she wanted to keep it very small—just the immediate family, which included me and Maddie. As we neared his house, the familiar pangs of grief tightened in my chest. It was true that time healed all wounds, but it didn't quite mend a broken heart.

When we arrived at Jake's house, Jason greeted us at the door. "Hey guys!" he said with a beaming smile. As Mom and Maddie stood talking with Jason and the Asshole, I headed on down the hall to the kitchen.

Mrs. Nelson bustled around, putting the final touches on the food. I couldn't help smiling when I saw who she was balancing in her arms.

Two months after Emma Grace was born, Presley gave birth to a beautiful, healthy baby girl—Evelyn Hope Nelson. Evie, pronounced Ev-e, was Mrs. Nelson's namesake, and I had to give Presley props for doing something so thoughtful. Of course, Presley was practically a member of the Nelson family now—Jake's old room had been given to her and Evie so she could divide her time between her house and Jake's. Even the Asshole had warmed to her, and as for his granddaughter, Evie had him wrapped around her tiny finger. It was good for Presley having the support considering she was in college and working part-time. Of course, the Nelson's took care of most of the financial obligations for Evie. And I had to hand it to Presley. She'd really done a 180 and was a good, caring mother.

It was hard imaging Jake with a baby period, but the thoughts of him with a daughter was too surreal. Deep down, I knew he would have been fiercely protective of Evie and would have loved her with all his heart and soul. I would have given anything if he had been able to be there to hold her and rock her to sleep—especially to change her dirty diapers, which he would have loathed.

"Hi Mrs. Nelson," I said.

She whirled around and gave me a genuine smile—one I hadn't seen on her face for such a long time. "Well hello." She reached over to give me a hug. As I pulled away, I stared down at Evie. Her blue eyes—Jake's deep shade of blue—peered up at me.

"How's my goddaughter doing?" I asked, tenderly touching Evie's dark head. Like Emma Grace, she was outfitted in a fluffy and frilly dress along with a hair bow.

Mrs. Nelson beamed. "Absolutely wonderful. Wanna hold her?"

I smiled. "Sure." As Evie was passed over to me, I kissed her cheek. If anyone had doubts about her being Jake's baby, all they had to do was look at her. It wasn't just her eyes—she was an exact replica of Jake from her nose to the shape of her mouth. It was like Presley hadn't even had a part in the baby— Evie and Jake's baby pictures were identical as well. It was bittersweet looking into her tiny face and seeing him staring out at you.

"Where's Presley?" I asked.

"She and Jonathan went to get some ice." A knowing smile

played on her lips before she turned back to stir the green beans.

"They've been spending a lot of time together lately," I mused. Jonathan and I had ended up rooming together at Tech, rather than Jake. It hadn't escaped me that he was often talking to Presley on the phone or going places with her. He tried to play it off that he enjoyed spending time with Evie, but I knew better. They were falling for each other, but neither one of them knew how to do it because of Jake. And I knew all too well what having the specter of Jake hanging over you felt like.

Maddie entered the kitchen then. At the sight of Evie in my arms, she grinned. "How's Miss Mini-Me?" she asked.

I laughed at her reference to Evie being a perfect Jake clone. "She's good." Glancing past her, I saw Jason holding Emma Grace while Mom and the Asshole talked.

Presley and Jonathan breezed in the backdoor then, loaded down with shopping bags. At the sight of me, Presley gave a beaming smile. "Hey Noah. Glad you could make it."

"I wouldn't miss it for the world."

When Presley opened her mouth to say something else, Evie gave a loud cry and began squirming in my arms. With Presley's hands full, Jonathan quickly deposited his bags on the counter and took Evie from me. She immediately stopped crying.

I quirked my brows at him. "I never knew you were such a

363

natural with babies," I teased.

An amusing flush entered his cheeks. "It's not that. She just knows me better than you," he replied, cradling Evie to his chest.

"Okay everyone, let's sit down to eat," Mrs. Nelson instructed.

As we crowded around the dining room table, I still couldn't help but feel Jake's absence. I wanted to hear his laughter and his voice echoing through the room. With a resigned sigh, I eased down in my chair next to Maddie. Sensing my emotions, she reached over and squeezed my hand.

Before we started eating, the Asshole stood up in his chair. "I just wanted to thank you all for coming out today to honor the one year anniversary of Jake's death." Surprisingly his voice wavered for a moment. "It means so much that Jake's memory is still being kept alive by those who loved him, and that he will live on not just in his beautiful daughter, but through all of his family and friends."

I tried not to let my mouth fall open in shock at the Asshole's sincere comments. "So raise your glass, even though it's only tea and coke, to Jake."

I grabbed my glass and hoisted it in the air. "To Jake," Mr. Nelson said.

"To Jake," we all replied in unison.

Later Maddie and I lay tangled in each other's arms on the couch watching a movie. Mom and Greg were at work, and Emma Grace was fast asleep. "You know our one year anniversary is coming up soon," I mused.

"It is." She kissed my cheek. "I'm so proud you remembered without me having to remind you," she said with a teasing grin.

I laughed. "How could I ever forget?" Playing with a strand of her long, dark hair, I said, "I was just wondering what you wanted to do to celebrate. Go to a fancy dinner or stay in? I'm down for whatever you want to do."

Maddie's fingers drew circles over my hand. "Well, I was thinking I wanted to do something big."

"Like what?"

She glanced up to give me a smile that lit me on fire from head to toe. "Make love for the first time."

I shot up on the couch and stared at her in shock. "Are you serious?"

"Yes."

"But I thought—"

Maddie brought her finger to my lips. "If I've learned anything in the last year, it's to say what you feel and experience as much life as you can. You've held up to your end of the bargain, Noah. You show me each and every day how much you love me, and you've been so very patient and

365

understanding with me. I know I should wait until I get married, but I know that I love you."

"And I love you too." I brought my lips to hers, kissing her with a mixture of hunger and love. When I pulled away, I smiled at her. "I'm not going anywhere, Maddie. You mean everything to me—you saved me from the darkness and brought me to the light. And I can't imagine a future without you in it. I intend on spending the rest of my life with you."

Maddie kissed me tenderly. "I love you, Noah."

"I love you too."

While that traitorous horndog male in me did a happy dance that I was going to get laid in a few weeks, the emotional side of me realized the enormity of the situation. Yeah, I was nineteen, and I'd found my soul mate. And like Maddie had said, Jake's death had taught me to live in the moment while also looking to the future.

And with my family and friends and Maddie at my side, my future was very, very bright.

# A message from Katie Ashley

Please do me a tremendous favor by leaving a review on Amazon, Barnes and Noble or Goodreads. If you're not comfortable with leaving a review, find one that you think expresses your feelings and like that review. You don't know how much it means to Independent Authors.

### Find Katie online at:

http://www.katieashleybooks.com

http://katieashleybooks.blogspot.com/

### Facebook:

https://www.facebook.com/katieashleybooks

https://www.facebook.com/katie.ashleyromance

### Twitter:

www.twitter.com/katieashleyluv

# About the Author

Katie Ashley is the New York Times, USA Today, and Amazon Best-Selling author of The Proposition. She lives outside of Atlanta, Georgia with her two very spoiled dogs and one outnumbered cat. She has a slight obsession with Pinterest, The Golden Girls, Harry Potter, Shakespeare, Supernatural, Designing Women, and Scooby-Doo.

She spent 11 1/2 years educating the Youth of America aka teaching MS and HS English until she left to write full time in December 2012.

# Acknowledgements

Thanks always to God for his immense blessings in both my professional and personal life. Thanks to my family, friends, and church family for supporting me along this crazy journey.

Thanks to my former Young Adult Literary agent, Fonda Snyder. You were a pleasure to work with during my rocky path to traditional publication. You never ceased believing in me, Noah, and my other novels. Your input was integral and valuable to Don't Hate the Player. It was a pleasure working with you for eighteen months, and I will always be grateful for your dedication to me and my career.

Thanks to Marion Archer, my sister from Down Under! I can't tell you how much you mean to me as a friend and as a critique partner. Honestly, you helped to make DHtP so much stronger, so much deeper, and so much more amazing than I could ever imagine. Between our zoom chats and comment bubbles, I was able to dig even deeper into the story after so many years.

To Hannah Wiley: Thank you for everything you brought to

Don't Hate the Player from your multiple critiques to you being a cheerleader and commiserating during the submission process. Most of all, I thank you for your friendship all these years and for believing in me and my writing.

To Letitia Hasser for a kickass cover. Thanks for all your hard work and dedication on my covers. And thanks for not strangling me when I couldn't make up my mind!

To JB McGee for your awesome formatting and always letting me procrastinate aka proofread until the last minute. You rock professionally and personally.

Thanks to Cris Hardarly for being the sweetest and most amazing friend and support. Thanks also to Shannon Furhman, Emilie Grey, and Tamara Debbaut for your amazing fan art, pimpage, and support of my writing. To all my supporters in my street team, Ashley's Angels, and to my street Team Captains Michelle Eck and Cris Hardarly.

To some of the original readers back in the day Debra Driza, Jennifer Wood, Rachele Mielke, and Rebecca Rogers.

To every reader who has ever picked up one of my books and every blogger who has reviewed it I give you my eternal gratitude and love!!!

Printed in Great Britain
by Amazon.co.uk, Ltd.,
Marston Gate.